Hope

Book Two

∞

Harvester of Light Trilogy

By

S.J. West

Hope

List of Watcher Books in the Watcher Series

The Watchers Trilogy

Cursed

Blessed

Forgiven

The Watcher Chronicles

Broken

Kindred

Oblivion

Ascension

Caylin's Story

Timeless

Devoted

The Redemption Series

Malcolm

Anna

Lucifer (Coming Summer 2014)

S.J. West

Other Books by S.J. West

The Harvest of Light Trilogy

Harvester

Hope

Dawn

The Vankara Saga

Vankara

Dragon Alliance (Coming Fall/Winter 2014)

Hope

S.J. West

CHAPTER ONE

"Are you sure, Skye?"

I looked at Kirk's horrified reflection in the mirror of my vanity. Teegan stood beside him with both her eyebrows arched, a sure indication she thought I had completely lost my mind and was about to make a monumental mistake.

"You're not her," Zoe said from her spot on my bed hugging a blue flower shaped pillow to her chest.

I still wasn't used to seeing Zoe at her true age. To my mind she should still look like the seven year old girl I found underneath Simon's protective shield, but in the two weeks we'd been in the Southern Kingdom, her growth had increased exponentially. Her body had finally caught up with her true age of eighteen. I just prayed that was the extent of her odd accelerated aging.

"Seriously Skye, you haven't even asked your father if what she told you is true," Zoe reminded me. "At least wait until you do that before cutting off all your hair."

"It's not just because of that. I need a change," I said to my friends. "I might not be able to control much else, but I can control this one thing in my life." I looked at Kirk. "Cut it."

Kirk gathered a section of my hair with one hand and held a pair of styling scissors in the other poised to cut my hair to a point just above my shoulders. A good six inches needed to be lopped off for the new me I envisioned for myself to make her first appearance. Kirk met my eyes in the mirror once more almost begging for a last reprieve. I nodded my head urging him to do what I wanted. The metallic song of metal sliding against metal was suddenly deadened as the sharp edges of the scissors met the strands of my hair slowly making the first cut.

For over half an hour Kirk clipped and shaped my hair into the style we had been discussing for days: an asymmetrical layered bob which fell somewhere in the style spectrum between punk rocker and sophisticated lady. The new layers framing my face gave the illusion of a different girl staring back at me in the mirror.

After he was done, Kirk stood back and admired his own handy work.

"Not bad," he said in surprise. "I think I like it."

Teegan gave me a wink and thumbs up.

Zoe stood from my bed and walked up behind me.

"I like it too. How do you think I would look with a cut like that?"

"No!" Kirk and I said simultaneously with equal vehemence.

Zoe stuck her tongue out at us. "Spoil sports. You guys never let me have any fun."

Her body might have caught up to her real age, but Zoe still acted like a seven year old most of the time.

"Do you honestly think I would willingly cut those natural golden curls?" Kirk said in exasperation. "I never thought I would cut Skye's hair. At least let me get over one trauma at a time before you throw a new one at me."

I smiled. "You act like it was your hair being cut. You know it's just hair. It'll grow back."

Kirk pressed a flared hand to his chest. "Honestly, it might as well have been mine as much as it hurt me to do it."

Kirk quickly packed his scissors in his backpack lying on my bed.

"Come on, Teegan. We better leave before Mr. Lande wonders where we are."

"How are our dresses coming along anyway?" Zoe asked. "You know the dance is tonight."

"They'll be done," Kirk promised with a wave of his hand. "We've had so many new orders we've been working almost around the clock at the shop. I'm surprised he let us come here this morning, but I guess it doesn't hurt to do a favor for the daughter of a council man."

"That's true," Zoe agreed. "People do seem to give Skye's father whatever he wants."

It didn't take me long to figure out my father was an important man in the Southern Kingdom. Usually all I had to do was ask for something, and it was given to me on a silver platter. There were a total of five people on the council, including the man who used to be President of the United States, and they were all treated like royalty. When I asked my father if Zoe could live with us, he had no trouble in obtaining a new apartment with three bedrooms.

"Teegan and I will be back tonight to help you guys get ready for the dance," Kirk told us, tossing his backpack over one shoulder.

After Kirk and Teegan left, Zoe and I got ready to leave for our own jobs.

No one in the Southern Kingdom got a completely free ride. Just because my father was on the council didn't mean I could loaf off and do whatever I wanted. To make the community work, we all had to contribute our fair share. Zoe and I chose to work in the greenhouses Doc Riley was in charge of supervising.

As we were walking out of our apartment, the door to the apartment adjacent to us opened. Ash smiled with genuine happiness when he saw us.

"Good morning, ladies. Ready to go to work?"

"Honestly? I think I might have to change jobs," Zoe said, looking at her nails in dismay. "I can't seem to keep the manicures Kirk gives us clean for more than a day. All that dirt," Zoe shivered.

"It's a small price to pay for fresh food," I admonished. "And you've certainly eaten your fair share of it since coming here."

"Quit picking on my girl," Kale said, coming out of the apartment he and Ash shared.

"Seriously, Kale?" Zoe placed her hands on her hips. "I am not your girl. Teegan is. Well, she would be if you could say more than a lame 'hi' to her every time you come within a five foot radius. Man up and ask the girl out already."

If there was ever a perfect guy for Teegan it was Kale. She definitely wouldn't have to worry about not being able to speak because Kale could carry on a conversation with himself if he had to. With his naturally tanned skin and corkscrew curly brown hair, they were physically a perfect match too, each looking like they should be frolicking on a beach somewhere. Kale was from Hawaii which was why he professed to love wearing Hawaiian shirts, cargo shorts and ultra-white sneakers all the time. He claimed it kept him in touch with his heritage.

"Then who would take you to the dance tonight?" Kale asked.

"I'm sure Skye would share Ash with me," Zoe said.

Ash looked taken aback by Zoe's suggestion.

"What?" Zoe asked seeing the sudden look of alarm on Ash's face. "You wouldn't be interested in taking two hotties to the dance?"

"No, it's not that," Ash said. "I was just hoping to have some time alone with Skye to talk about something important."

This was news to me. Ash hadn't mentioned needing to speak with me, though in the past two weeks we hadn't been able to talk much.

After we arrived in the Southern Kingdom, Doc Riley made us stay in the hospital for a couple of days to make sure we didn't experience any adverse side effects from being exposed to the barrier. Then we were all questioned separately about the events leading up to the time we became trapped in the radiation field. Even though my father was on the council, I was still subjected to the same questions my other friends had to answer. None of us mentioned the claim Lucena Day made about being my real mother. I didn't ask my friends why they omitted that small fact from their statements, but I had to assume it was close to the same reason I didn't. What would the people of the Southern Kingdom do to Lucena Day's child? Plus, I couldn't exactly make myself say the words. Not yet. Not until I talked to my father about it.

Ian had it worse than any of us. He was placed in a high security jail cell for over a week before Doc Riley was able to have him remanded into her custody. She argued with the council that his blood could hold the key to defeating the Harvesters. Before we came, no one on this side of the barrier had ever even heard of the Cain virus. Doc Riley convinced the council that if she could study Ian she might be able to find a way to distribute the virus to every Harvester in the Eastern Kingdom, finally giving humans a fighting chance to regain control over the world. Ian was soon fitted with a security bracelet which emitted an alarm if he stepped out of the boundaries the council set for him. Ian didn't seem to mind the restricted access. I think he was just glad to be out of Alliance and out from under Freddy's control.

I was surprised Ash hadn't told me before now that he needed to speak with me about something important. Since being reunited, we'd only had time to have one serious conversation, and

I had monopolized most if by telling him everything which happened after Rose snatched him away from me. Ash let me do what I always did with him: bare my heart and soul then help me pick up the pieces afterward. When I needed to cry, he held me in his arms and let me unburden my heart without trying to make me believe everything was going to be all right. We had both grown up in a world where happily ever after didn't exist, if it ever had, and he wasn't about to start lying to me now.

"Do we need to talk about it before then?" I asked, wondering how serious whatever he wanted to say was.

Ash shook his head. "It can wait until tonight." I saw Ash's eyes travel to my hair. "Like your hair by the way. Looks good on you."

"Yeah, looks pretty cool," Kale agreed with a nod. "Though I'm a sucker for women with long brown hair," he said wistfully.

It wasn't hard to guess who he was seeing in his mind.

"Oh shut up," Zoe said with a roll of her eyes while tugging on a sleeve of Kale's shirt to make him start walking down the hallway. "Until you get the guts to tell Teegan how you feel, you don't get to day dream about her around me."

Zoe and Kale continued to banter back and forth like brother and sister as they began their descent down the central stairwell of our apartment building. Ash walked by my side as we gave the other two a wide birth in front of us.

"Listen," I said to Ash, "I know we haven't had a lot of time to talk, but I'll make time if it's important to you."

Ash grinned as we descended the steps behind our friends. "I know, Skye. But it can wait until tonight."

"Why can't we talk about it now?" I asked, more than a little curious what he considered to be so important to talk about but not urgent enough to discuss immediately.

"Because it's something I would rather talk about when we're all dressed up and don't have anything to worry about except having a good time. Heading to work isn't the most romantic time to have a talk."

The word 'romantic' sent up a red flag in my mind. It was the first time Ash had ever used the word when referring to me. I thought back to that moment in the library after we disposed of the Harvester bodies and before he fell unconscious from the injuries he sustained in the fight with them. I felt sure then Ash was about to tell me how he truly felt for me. If he was waiting for a 'romantic time' to have a talk with me now, was he about to declare his true feelings for me?

Ash seemed to assume I understood his intentions because he casually took hold of my hand as we walked out the double glass doors of the apartment complex we lived in. In all the time I had known him, only once had Ash held my hand: the night we escaped the breeding camp. Back then it was to make sure I kept up with him. Now, it seemed to convey a completely different meaning, and I honestly wasn't sure how I felt about it. There was a time I would have been head over heels in rapturous joy, but that was before Jace became a part of my life. Now, my heart felt torn in half between the two men who held it. I couldn't prevent feeling like I was betraying Jace by letting Ash to do something as innocent as hold my hand.

As we walked onto the street outside our complex, I had to marvel once again at the ingenuity of those who built the Southern Kingdom. Basically, it was a circular indoor city with twenty story buildings forming a double circle. A monorail system was sandwiched in between the buildings and a green pastoral oasis sat in the middle of it all, Central Park. My father said it was given the title to bring back memories of its name sake.

Ash held my hand while we rode the monorail and didn't let go as we got off at our stop in front of the greenhouses. He was assigned to work in the corn farming units next to the orchard unit Zoe and I worked in.

"You're having lunch with your dad today right?" Ash asked.

"Yeah. I'm planning to ask him about Lucena and get that whole nightmare over with once and for all. I need to know the truth one way or the other."

"Just remember," he said, squeezing the hand he held tightly, "no matter what the answer is you're still you and nothing can change that. You're the best person I know, Skye."

"That's probably because you don't know many people," I said, trying to shrug off his praise.

Ash smiled. "I know enough." He leaned down and gave me a kiss on the cheek. "See you tonight."

"Ok, see you."

I let go of his hand and watched him enter his greenhouse before I stepped into mine.

Once inside, I saw Doc Riley was already giving everyone their instructions for the day. Zoe, Ian, and a few other volunteers stood around her in a semi-circle. When Ian saw me, he arched an imperious eyebrow and turned to pointedly look at the digital clock on the wall which showed me I was five minutes late.

"I know," I mouthed silently coming to stand with everyone else.

"Well, nice of you to decide to join us, Skye," Doc Riley said. From anyone else it would have sounded like a condescending remark, but I knew Doc Riley was just picking on me for being late. She was a hard-as-nails woman to most people, but for some reason she held a soft spot in her heart for me.

After giving everyone their instructions, Doc Riley pulled me to the side out of earshot of everyone else.

"So is today the day?" She asked in a hushed conspiratorial voice.

Other than Ash, Doc Riley was the only other person in the Southern Kingdom I had told about Lucena Day's claim to being my mother. She urged me to speak with my father about it as soon as I told her, but I just couldn't bring myself to do it. Something inside me already knew the answer. I worried having my father confirm it would push me past the point of no return.

"Yes, I plan to ask him at lunch today."

Doc Riley nodded. "Good. You need to get to the truth. If what she said is true, then it will unburden your father from a lie. I'm sure keeping such a secret from you hasn't been easy to do all these years, especially something so monumental. But, anyway, I digress. I have something for you to take on your picnic."

Doc Riley walked to one of the large stainless steel refrigeration units on the far wall and took out a small Tupperware bowl. When she walked back to me, she handed me the bowl.

"Try these out," she said excitedly. "They're a hybrid I made of a strawberry and grape. Simply delicious!"

The combination seemed odd to me, but I thanked her for her generosity and tucked it inside my backpack to share with my father later.

The wait for lunch time was made easier with work. In the orchard unit, we took care of a cornucopia of apple, orange, and pear trees. We were in the middle of harvest time for the apple trees which took a lot of man power since we weren't allowed to squander gas or electricity on machines to help harvest food. Everything which could be done by hand in the Southern Kingdom was.

"So, I hear you have a hot date tonight," Ian said coming to stand beside the ladder I was perched on to collect apples.

I looked down at him and saw he had already collected his first bushel. Ian may have had the Cain virus, but he still maintained some of his Harvester abilities like super strength and agility. He could collect more fruit in an hour than I could in a whole day of working.

"It's not a hot date," I told him, continuing to pluck apples hoping he would get the non-verbal hint I didn't want to talk about it with him.

"Out of sight, out of mind?" He asked.

I looked back down at him. "What is that supposed to mean?"

Ian shrugged and put his container of apples on the ground. "Seems like only, what two weeks ago, you told Jace you loved him while he sacrificed himself to the Queen for us. Or did you just do that to make sure he didn't change his mind and try to run off before we could make our escape?"

A red, blurry haze clouded my vision. I quickly descended my ladder and promptly slapped Ian's face, drawing the unwanted attention of a few of my co-workers. My hand throbbed from the force of the blow and a patch of red flamed against Ian's cheek before slowly disappearing.

"How dare you! Don't assume to know how I feel about Jace or Ash for that matter. You have no idea what I'm going through."

"What I know is that Jace gave up his freedom so you could have yours. And how do you repay him? You jump into the arms of another man without giving him a second thought. Do you even think about him anymore? Don't you wonder what the Queen has him doing for her? If you thought the people of Alliance were bad, you don't know what bad is. That woman is pure evil. I sure as hell wouldn't want someone I claimed to love to be under her thumb."

Ian's words brought my fears for Jace's safety bubbling to the surface. I couldn't prevent the tears which racked my body next any more than I could have stopped the flow of a river. I put my hands over my face to shield my display of grief from Ian. For the past two weeks, I tried to put on a brave face for my friends. They all seemed so happy to be in the Southern Kingdom. I didn't want to dampen their joy with my feelings of loss and worry.

I felt Ian try to put his arms around me but pushed him back.

"Don't," I told him. "Don't touch me."

"I'm sorry," he said.

I believed him, but that didn't matter.

"I just wanted to make sure you hadn't forgotten about Jace," he continued, the hostility in his voice gone. "He's not here to fight for you so I thought I should at least try to make sure you remembered he was out there."

"Do you think there's been a day that's gone by I haven't thought about him? Do you think it's easy for me to walk around this place and try to pretend I like it here? I don't want to be here, Ian! I want to be out there looking for him!"

"Then why aren't you? You're father's a big wig around this joint. Can't he help you?"

I shook my head. "I've asked but he says he can't do anything. I think he just doesn't want me to leave. He just got me back." I wiped the tears from my face. "But don't you dare think I've forgotten about Jace. He's in my thoughts all the time. I just haven't figured out a way to get him back yet."

"You know I'll help you if I can," Ian said. "I just don't want to see you make a mistake with this Ash guy. I know you've been friends for a long time, but if you ask me, he had his chance while you guys were running around the Eastern Kingdom alone together for the past five years. Jace has always been upfront with you about his feelings. He never tried to pretend he wasn't in love with you, and I knew you were in love with him even before you said it. Everybody in that van saw it but you, until it was too late."

I closed my eyes, lifting a hand to my temples to ease the sudden headache which was squeezing my temples like a vise. "Leave it to a reformed Harvester to be the champion of romance."

Ian shrugged. "Just looking out for Jace's girl." He held his hands out palm up. "Forgive me?"

"I'll forgive you this one time," I said, pointing my index finger at him. "But just remember, I haven't forgotten about Jace. I couldn't forget about him even if I tried."

As Ian picked up his bucket of apples, he winked at me. "Like the hair by the way."

"Thanks. Needed a change."

"Suits you. Kinda shows your spunk but keeps you looking like a lady at the same time."

The sound of a whistle marked lunch time. I suddenly realized I was just leaving one emotionally charged conversation for another.

CHAPTER TWO

My father was waiting for me outside the orchard unit when I stepped out. He had aged since I last saw him as a child, but time had only made him more handsome. The gray in his brown hair accentuated the sharp angles of his classically handsome face and gave him an air of wisdom. He leaned down to me and kissed my forehead before taking my arm as we walked to the artificial pond built in the center of Central Park. The nuclear powered sun slowly made its way across the blue sky above us mimicking what the real sun had done in the days before the war. The gentle breeze blowing across the greener than green grass almost made me forget things around me were man made.

"What to try one?" I asked my father, handing him the Tupperware bowl filled with the fruit Doc Riley had given me. It truly did look like the misbegotten child of a grape and strawberry with its thin purple shell dimpled with small seeds.

My father's left eyebrow arch involuntarily. "You're sure it's safe to eat? It looks like it might eat me instead."

I laughed causing my father to laugh as well. The rich rumble of the sound coming from his chest made me smile. Before the war, laughter filled our home around every corner. Now, it seemed to be a rare commodity.

"Doc Riley is always trying out new hybrids in the greenhouses. I haven't tried it either so we'll both be her guinea pigs."

Before I lost my nerve I picked up a piece of the fruit and popped it into my mouth. The juices spilled out of the thin purple skin and pooled against my tongue. The sweetness was on the verge of being overwhelming until a slight tartness revealed itself.

I swallowed the juices and nodded. "It's good."

Since being reunited, my father had done what seemed like a million little things to make me feel comfortable in our new home. He didn't push me to tell him about the last five years of my life, and I wasn't in a rush to know how he survived what happened after Ash and I escaped from the breeding camp. I knew that knowledge would most likely lead to a retelling of how my mother died. Or at least the death of the woman I always believed to be my mother. I needed to know if what Lucena Day said was true. Was the most reviled woman in history responsible for giving birth to me? And if she was, what did that mean for me?

"Dad, I need to ask you something. I've been putting it off, but I just can't anymore. I have to know the truth."

"You know you can ask me anything, Skye."

I looked my father straight in the eyes because I needed to see his initial reaction. I feared he might try to lie to protect me, but protection wasn't what I wanted. I wanted the truth.

"Is Lucena Day my real mother?"

He didn't seem surprised by the question. He actually looked like he was expecting it.

"In a way," he answered, suddenly finding something interesting on the red and black checkered blanket we sat on to pick at.

"What do you mean 'in a way'? She either is or isn't."

My father took in a deep breath as if preparing himself before looking back up at me.

"Lucena *is* your biological mother, but she is *not* the woman who gave birth to you, raised you, and loved you."

"How can she be my biological mother and not my birth mother?"

"Your mother and I tried to have children for a long time. When we finally learned she was sterile, we went to Lucena for help. Back then your mother's sister was a fertility specialist, among other things. There wasn't anything medically Lucena could do to help your mother, but she offered to donate her own eggs, fertilize them with my sperm, and implant them inside your mother's womb."

"Why would Mom go through all that?"

"Because Emma and I were desperate to have you. You should have seen your mom when she found out it worked and you were on the way. It was like she swallowed sunshine she glowed so much."

"Why don't I remember Lucena? If she was Mom's sister why wasn't she ever in our lives?"

"She and your mother had a falling out right after you were born. Your mother pretty much told her she was never allowed to see you again."

"What happened to make her do something like that?"

"I'm not sure. I didn't push her for an explanation because she seemed so distraught by whatever it was. Lucena was never in our lives that much anyway. She was always busy with her work. I just assumed your mother was frightened she might try to take you away from us one day because even then Lucena was rich and powerful. Plus, I don't think your mother wanted you to know her sister was your biological mother. The possibility of you finding out the truth seemed to scare her more than anything."

"So if Mom was Lucena's sister, and I'm her biological daughter, why did she keep us in a breeding camp?"

"I suppose Lucena thought keeping us in a camp was better than having us run around in the wilderness with you. In her way, she loved you and wanted to make sure you were looked after."

It finally put into place pieces of my past I could never quite figure out. My family was the only one not required to have children for the Harvesters. Now I understood why. My mother was incapable of having children on her own. Ash's family wasn't as fortunate. While in the camp I saw Ash's mom give birth to two boys and two girls. As soon as they were born, they were each taken away to be raised by the Harvesters for spare parts.

"She told me I was supposed to go live with her the night Ash and I escaped. Is that true?"

"Yes."

"I try not to think about that night," I confessed. "But, I dream about it a lot. I remember Mom hugging me so tight I couldn't breathe. She kept saying over and over how much she loved me, and that she was sorry she couldn't have brought me up in a better world."

"She always blamed herself for how Lucena turned out."

"Why?"

"Because she was Lucena's big sister. She felt like she should have seen the person Lucena really was and stopped her before things got so out of control."

I closed my eyes and let my mind replay that night.

"I remember all the houses being lit on fire and people screaming before Ash and I made it out. I tried to go back, but he wouldn't let me. Right before we crawled through the hole you told us to look for in the fence, we heard machine gun fire."

"Things didn't turn out quite like we planned. A lot of people ended up dying that night instead of escaping."

"How did you survive?"

My father snorted. "Lucena's people shot me in the back, but it didn't kill me. Up until a couple of weeks ago I wished they had finished the job."

I wanted to ask him what happened to Mom but couldn't bring myself to voice the question. Did it really matter? She was dead. I didn't need to know the gruesome details.

"How did you end up here in the Southern Kingdom?"

"Lucena sent me here."

I felt like I couldn't breathe.

"You work for her?" I whispered.

"It's not like that Skye. She just used me to bring a message to them."

"What message?"

"That she would leave them alone as long as they didn't try to invade the Eastern Kingdom."

"But what about the nukes the south sends over to destroy the breeding camps?"

"They're just nuisances to her. It's not enough to cause her any real hardship."

"Then why do it?"

"The Council thinks it's a morale booster for the people here. Most southerners want to help those in the east, but they're not desperate enough to do anything substantial. The leaders believe sending the nukes to destroy some of the breeding camps makes everyone here feel like they're doing their part to help."

"So it's just a publicity stunt to them?"

"Yes. It appeases the masses enough to let them still feel good about living in paradise while everyone else in the world is scrounging around just trying to find a way to survive each day."

My father hung his head and looked away from me, like he couldn't meet my eyes anymore.

"You don't know how often I thought about leaving here and going back across the barrier to find you."

"You never would have found me," I told him with certainty. "Ash and I kept on the move every day. It would have been worse than trying to find a needle in a haystack because the needle would have kept moving."

"But at least I would have been doing something instead of living here safe and sound while the two of you were out there fighting for your lives. A father shouldn't abandon his child."

I reached out and touched my father's arm, forcing him to look at me.

"You didn't abandon me. It wasn't your choice. Besides, you gave me Ash. He protected me more times than I can count."

"When Ash first got here, I thought you were dead. I knew he would never leave you on his own. And then when he woke up and told me what happened the last time he saw you, I was sure you were dead."

I squeezed my father's arm. "Don't think about that. I'm not dead."

"I wanted to bash that Rose woman's face in when she told me she left you in that library."

"You and me both," I admitted.

My father smiled over our shared dislike of Rose and placed his free hand over the one I had on his arm.

"If she hadn't told me I would be seeing you soon, I'm not sure what I would have done to her I was so mad."

"How did you know you could trust what she said?"

"Doc Riley seemed to trust her, and I've always trusted Doc Riley."

I wanted to tell him what Rose proved to me the last time I saw her. I hadn't shared her ability to time travel with anyone but Doc Riley because I suspected Doc Riley already knew the truth. To think my future self was responsible for sending Rose and Simon back to particular points in my life seemed ludicrous. But the facts were irrefutable. They helped when they were needed and only then. I couldn't fault them for doing what my future self was telling them to do. And now I understood why Rose left me in that library and made me spend time with Jace. But, I didn't know why it was so important for me to fall in love with him. Or maybe that wasn't the real reason. Maybe we were just supposed to make sure Ian made it to the Southern Kingdom to help us win the war against the Harvesters. There were so many possibilities for why Rose left me. Plus, there were more than likely things which hadn't even happened yet that might be the real reason. I just didn't know.

CHAPTER THREE

Because of the dance that night, we were given the rest of the afternoon off from work. Apparently, the dance was an annual event for the younger crowd living in the Southern Kingdom. I couldn't imagine living beneath a mountain for all my life like most of the people my age here. Every time I thought about it too much, I suddenly became claustrophobic and yearned to feel the great expanse of the outside world again. The surface was a far cry from perfect, but at least it didn't feel like a prison.

As soon as I arrived back home, Zoe practically ordered me to go take a shower before Kirk and Teegan were to arrive. I was just drying my hair with a towel when the duo entered my room.

"You'll be the belles of the ball," Kirk declared, a dreamy look on his face while he and Teegan set out their hair and make-up paraphernalia on the vanity.

"Did you bring the dresses we ordered?" Zoe asked, practically bubbling over with excitement.

Kirk pointed to my bed and Zoe pounced, picking up her dress and twirling around with it against her body.

The royal blue color of Zoe's dress accentuated the bright blue of her eyes. It had wide strips of chiffon hanging from the waist, spaghetti straps at the shoulders and an ornate beaded top I assumed Teegan must have slaved over. I knew it would look perfect on her as she twirled around on the dance floor. I, on the other hand, chose something a bit more conservative. It was a short and simple cap-sleeve black lace dress over ivory silk.

Just like when I was in Alliance, Kirk styled our hair and Teegan applied our make-up.

"Are you coming to the party?" I asked Teegan as she dabbed a little foundation across my cheekbones.

She nodded with a big grin.

"You don't think I would let my girl be the only one not going to the biggest shindig on this side of the barrier, do you?" Kirk asked.

"Kale really does want to take you instead of me," Zoe told Teegan.

"Pfft," Kirk rolled his eyes and continued using a large barreled curling iron on Zoe's hair. "That boy can't seem to put two words together around Teegan much less form a complete sentence to ever ask her out."

Teegan threw the make-up brush in her hand at Kirk and hit him on the shoulder.

"Well it's true!" Kirk defended.

Zoe let out a small giggle.

"I'm sorry Teegan," Zoe apologized. "Kale told me he can't even think straight when he's around you, much less get a coherent word out. But at least with me you don't have to worry about him being pawed all night by another girl. I'll keep him safe for you."

Teegan winked at Zoe sealing their pact to keep Kale safely out of the arms of the other girls in the kingdom.

There was a soft tap, tap, tap against my bedroom door. I immediately knew who it was and asked Teegan to excuse me while I went to answer it.

Blue stood on the other side of the door wagging his tail eagerly, looking up at me with his one good eye waiting to be let in.

"Come on boy," I told him, reaching down and scratching him behind the ears. I knew my father must be back home since Blue was here. He had taken Blue out for a walk knowing how loud the four of us could get when we were together.

Blue walked in and jumped on my bed to find his regular spot. Even though we didn't have to sleep close together anymore to keep warm, Blue still slept against my back each night. It was all he knew, and I wasn't about to change things between us now.

Once Kirk and Teegan were through with their magic touches, Zoe and I surveyed ourselves in the full length mirror attached to the back of my bedroom door.

Zoe looked like an angel with her svelte figure and golden curls cascading down her back. Next to her I felt like a piece of raw meat while she was a surf and turf meal for the eyes.

I didn't look at myself much, just a glance to make sure things were in their proper place. I was scared I might see the girl I once saw in the mirror in Alliance. That girl wasn't someone I ever wanted to see again.

"All right ladies, we'll see you at the party," Kirk said, gathering up his hair styling supplies while Teegan put away the make-up.

As Zoe and I walked them out of the apartment, I heard my father open the door of his study. When we turned to face him, the book he had in his hands slipped from his fingers onto the floor.

Zoe giggled. I think I must have just looked puzzled.

"Sorry," my dad said, leaning down to pick the book back up. Blue walked into the living room and went to my dad as if he were making sure he was all right.

"You ok, Dad?"

"Yes," he said, clearing his throat. "You just look so much like your mother. I thought you were her for a split second."

I didn't know what to say so I mumbled, "Thanks, Dad,"

"Anyway," he said, casting the ghost of my mother aside. "When are Ash and Kale arriving?"

"Any minute," Zoe answered.

Just then a knock came to the apartment door.

"Speak of the devils," Zoe eagerly opened the door before I had a chance to compose myself.

"Hey guys," Zoe chirped.

Ash was dressed in a black tuxedo with a matching bow tie. The suit made him look dapper which was a word I had never associated with Ash before. His face was clean shaven bringing out the strong angular features of his chin and cheekbones. I had to wonder if Kirk snuck into the boy's apartment considering the neat style of Ash's slicked back hair.

Kale looked like Kale, just washed up. He wore his usual Hawaiian shirt, except this one looked like it had actually met an iron and ironing board. He was wearing blue jeans instead of cargo shorts, but he still had on his signature pristine white tennis shoes. His curly brown shoulder length hair looked freshly washed and an attempt to slick it back was made but natural curls will not be denied.

"Really, Kale?" Zoe whined, crossing her arms. "You couldn't dress up just this once?"

Kale shook his head. "Women," he nudged Ash with his elbow, "can't even appreciate it when you make an effort. Am I right?"

But Ash wasn't paying attention to Zoe and Kale's tiff. He was staring straight at me like I was the only person within a million miles.

Kale waved his fingers in front of Ash's face. "Dude, snap out of it."

Ash seemed to remember where he was and looked over at Kale.

"What?" Ash asked.

"You were just staring at Skye like some psycho," Kale said in a low voice. "Thought I'd help a brother out and snap you out of it before you started giving off a stalker vibe, man."

Ash looked back at me with a troubled frown. "Sorry," he mumbled.

My father suddenly appeared at my side.

"So, I expect you both to have my girls back home by midnight."

"Yes, sir," Ash and Kale said in unison.

"All right, then." My father turned to me and kissed me on the cheek. "Have a good time, sweetie. I'll be waiting up."

I had a feeling the last statement was more for Kale's benefit than Ash's. After all, my father had given Ash the responsibility of keeping me alive at one time. I felt pretty confident he trusted him enough to keep me safe at a dance for a few hours.

Zoe and Kale walked ahead of us cracking jokes and having a good time with one another. I could understand Kale's behavior since he basically grew up in the Southern Kingdom, but Zoe's acceptance of everything around her troubled me. I felt at least twenty years older than the two walking in front of us and wished I could be what I was supposed to be: a carefree eighteen year old girl. But, my life hadn't been lived within a protective shield or inside a fortress which let you imagine life as being normal when it was anything but.

"What are you thinking about?" Ash asked me.

I looked up and saw the concern in his eyes before I let my attention wander back to Zoe and Kale. "Sometimes, I wish I could be more like her."

"Zoe? Why?"

"She's so…comfortable with it all. It's like being here doesn't faze her one bit. She wants to be here. She can enjoy everything they have to offer and not seem to care what's happening outside."

"You don't like it here?"

I sighed. "It's not that I don't like it, but I can't just forget what's going on in the real world. Eventually the people here are going to have to wake up and face the truth. The outside world is dying, and they're not even trying to do anything about it. They're acting like nothing exists outside of this place."

"I guess they've just been here for so long they figure the rest of the world doesn't matter to them anymore. Why face a nightmare if you don't have to? It's easier to ignore a problem than find a way to solve it."

"I can't do that, Ash. I can't turn my back and pretend everything is all right because it isn't."

Ash stopped walking which made me stop and turn back to face him.

"Are you thinking about saving the world or just one person in it?" He asked.

"I don't forget about the people who mean something to me," I replied, hoping he would leave it at that.

Ash stared at me for what seemed like an hour but in reality was only a few fleeting seconds.

He walked up to me and laced our fingers together, sliding his skin against mine intimately.

"I know what I'm about to ask might be impossible for you to do, but for tonight, can we pretend we're like everyone else down here and forget about what's outside of this place? We can figure out a way to save the world tomorrow. All I want is one night with you where I don't have to think about anything or anyone except you. Can you give me that, Skye?"

The look of heartbreaking longing in Ash's eyes made me suddenly feel guilty for being so caught up in my own worries. I wanted to give Ash what he asked for, but I wasn't sure how long I would be able to pretend the outside world and all its horrors didn't exist. He was one of only a few people who truly understood me and knew how hard it was for me to let things go. All I could do in response was nod my head, letting him know I would try my best to give him one night where I didn't worry about anything but being with him.

The dance was held near an elaborate dolphin inspired water fountain in the center of Central Park. White lights twinkled in the trees around us giving the illusion of a million fireflies lighting the festivities. A band was set up on a stage playing songs which had been popular before the war. Everything looked perfect. Everything looked normal.

Zoe turned out to be a natural dancer. It didn't seem to matter what song played she knew exactly how to move her body to the beats. I felt like a fish out of water flailing around on hot concrete desperately trying to not make myself look like a complete fool. Ash was about as bad at dancing as I was, but I couldn't quite tell if he was doing it on purpose just to match my own poorly timed steps or if it was real. I hoped for his sake he was just trying to not make me feel bad.

"Hey guys!"

Kirk and Teegan bounced over to us. I saw Kale's mouth open slightly as his eyes went all googly at the site of Teegan and wondered if he even realized he was doing it.

Kirk had worked his magic once again with Teegan. Her hair was perfectly straight falling down to her waist. She had the barest hint of make up on her face, but Teegan was someone who didn't need the assistance of make up to accentuate her natural beauty. She wore a white chiffon dress with a heart shaped bodice which set off the rich cinnamon brown color of her skin.

"Hi," Kale said, staring at Teegan like she was the fifth wonder of the world.

"Oh my god," Zoe said, grabbing Kale's hand and Teegan's hand and firmly placing them one on top of the other. "Go dance with the girl, you goof."

Kale's eyes widened like a trapped animal.

"But…" he started to say before being cut off by Zoe.

"Listen, you like her and she likes you. I'm tired of being your go between. Now shoo," Zoe waved her hands like she was chasing away two children. "Go have fun. You can thank me later."

Kale turned to Teegan. A slow grin spread his lips before he tugged Teegan onto the dance floor and twirled her into his arms.

"I guess you're my date now," Zoe said, lacing an arm around one of Kirk's.

"That was very impressive, Ms. Zoe," Kirk complimented. "You may have the makings of a match maker."

Zoe shrugged like it was no big deal. "Come on let's dance!"

Before I knew it, Ash and I were alone again, just in time for the first slow song of the night.

Ash pulled me in tight against him. I wrapped my arms around his waist and laid my head on his chest as we swayed to the music. The warmth emanating from his body lulled mine to relax for the first time that night. The gentle play of his hands trailing down my back to rest on my hips felt so natural I didn't feel the need to move his hands to a less intimate site.

"Skye…"

Reluctantly, I lifted my head from Ash's warmth to meet his pained gaze.

"What's wrong?" I asked.

"Come with me," he said in a hoarse voice, taking one of my hands to lead me away from the others around us.

Underneath one of the twinkling trees in the park, Ash ducked behind it and leaned his back against its trunk using it as a brace before pulling me in close to his body. In the secluded oasis,

I felt his hands travel up and down my back as he looked into my eyes with so much tenderness I wondered what he would say next.

"I know I never showed how much I cared about you when we were in the Eastern Kingdom, but I never felt like it was the right time to tell you," he began. "That's why I kept bringing us back to the barrier. I kept praying we would find a way to make it through. I knew if I could only take you somewhere we didn't have to struggle so hard to survive I could show you how I really felt about you and maybe we could start a real life together. That's all I've ever wanted, Skye. I want for us to have a chance at a real life without having to worry about the Harvesters taking our children away. And now we have that. We have a chance to be happy if you'll just let go of the outside world and give me a chance to make that happen. I love you more than anything or anyone. I just couldn't allow myself to admit it to you before now. I don't want to lose you to someone else without you knowing how I feel."

My heart yearned to accept Ash's offer of happily ever after. How many cold, sleepless nights in the Eastern Kingdom had I wanted him to offer me his love? For more than five years I silently pined for Ash. My heart aching for him to love me the way I loved him. It was a love I thought could never be broken. Then I met Jace and everything changed for me. Maybe it wasn't supposed to be possible to love two people at the same time, but I couldn't deny my love for Jace anymore than I could deny I loved Ash. And I couldn't lie to Ash. He deserved to know the whole truth.

"Ash, I…"

A loud boom from the direction of the dance cut my words
off. Ash and I looked around the tree back towards the dance floor.
A fire now blazed in the middle of the stage where the band had
been playing. People were screaming and trying to get as far away
from the blaze as possible. A man with long messy hair, dressed in
a ratty looking green coat was silhouetted by the flames behind
him. He grabbed the microphone off the floor where the singer
must have dropped it and spoke.

"You should all be ashamed of yourselves," he yelled,
crazed with anger. "Prancing around here like you ain't got a care
in the world! Well, let me tell you good citizens of the south, y'all
are just as bad if not worse than the Harvesters! At least they ain't
pretending to be your friends by offerin' food and clothes. At least
you know where you stand with those bastards. No, it's the ones
offerin' you help you can't turn your backs on!"

A group of ten guards made a mad dash towards the stage
from every direction.

"Do you know what your government is doin'?" He
demanded, realizing he didn't have much time left before he would
be taken away.

"They're rounding up those of us left on the surface on this
side of the barrier and tradin' us in to the Queen just so you people
can have your cushy little lives down in this hole. I hope y'all go to
hell like you deserve for lettin' it happen right under your damn
noses!"

The man didn't get a chance to say anything else. He was tackled by two guards causing the mic to fly out of his hands into the flames behind him. For a moment, I thought the guards were going to push him into the fire too, but instead they tasered him, quickly rendering him unconscious.

The dance was quickly dispersed by the guards. We were ordered to return home immediately and not venture out onto the streets anymore until further notice. Ash and I went back to the dance floor and found our friends before we left.

"Did you see that?" Kirk said excitedly. "Do you think he was telling the truth?"

"Dude looked off his rocker to me," Kale said with a shrug, almost non-plussed by the accusations made by the man.

"We should get the girls home before something else happens." Ash took my hand into his and quickly led the way back to our apartment complex.

When we reached the door to our apartment, Zoe said, "I'll go let your Dad know what happened."

After Zoe was gone, Ash brought me in close to his body to plant a chaste kiss on my lips.

"Promise me you'll think about what I said tonight," he whispered.

"I will," I replied, instantly feeling like a coward for not saying anything about my feelings for Jace.

"I'm not in any rush, Skye. I'll wait as long as I need to have all of you. Half of your heart isn't enough for me."

But what if that was all I was able to give him? I thought to myself. Before I could voice the question, Ash turned from me and went into his apartment.

CHAPTER FOUR

The apartment was quiet when I walked in. Zoe was nowhere to be seen. I presumed she was in her room changing into her favorite pair of pink sweats to sleep in. Blue was lying in front of my father's study door. He raised his head and padded his way to me as I entered.

"Dad in his office, Blue?" I asked, not really expecting a response back from my Weimaraner but people who love their pets tend to do that. We talk to them like they actually understand everything we're saying.

I knocked softly on the study door. I didn't get an answer so I pushed the door open to double check and found the room empty of my father's presence. I was just about to close the door when I heard muffled voices. Stepping further inside, I went to stand in the center of the room until I heard the voices again. They were faint but definitely coming from the right of me. Against that wall was a tall bookshelf. I walked over to the shelf and could hear the voices more clearly. My father's voice was unmistakable and from his tone he was extremely angry about something.

I stood frozen not sure what to do. If I looked for the way into what I had to presume was a secret room, would he be angry with me for finding it and invading his privacy? But, why did he have a secret room in the first place? Who was he arguing with so vehemently on the other side of the wall? Before I had a chance to decide my next move, the bookshelf swung inward and my father walked out.

He looked startled when he saw me and stood completely still, like he had been caught doing something he shouldn't have.

He didn't say a word to me just continued to walk behind his desk.

"What's in there?" I asked, sure he wouldn't volunteer any information without being asked directly.

"Every person on the council has one," he said, like that should be answer enough.

I stared at him waiting for him to say more, but he didn't.

"Who were you arguing with in there?"

I half expected someone else to come walking out of my father's secret lair but they never did.

"I don't have to explain everything I do to you. You're my daughter, not my keeper." My father's sharp words cut me to the quick. It was the first time he'd ever used such a dismissive tone with me.

"Dad, what's wrong? Does it have to do with the man at the dance?"

My father's eyes narrowed on me. "Drop it, Skye. There are things happening which you simply don't need to worry about. They don't concern you."

He may have been my father but that didn't stop my temper from flaring up.

"The council is trading humans on this side of the barrier to Lucena so the people living down here don't have to worry about being invaded by the Harvesters. How can you stand there and tell me we shouldn't discuss what's happening?"

"You don't know what you're talking about," my father's temper was quickly matching my own, now I knew where I got it from. "Let the matter drop."

"No," I said, not wanting to go against my dad but feeling the need to make him admit the truth of what he knew to me.

"I am your father. And what I say goes underneath this roof, young lady."

Under any other circumstances I would have laughed at such a clichéd statement, but my father sounded completely serious. I had never seen him look so mad before. Why was he so scared to tell me the truth?

"When Lucena sent you here, was that part of the message you were made to give to the council? Was that part of the bargain to keep her from coming through the barrier?"

My father turned away from me and looked out the window behind his desk. I could see his reflection in the glass against the dark cityscape outside.

"Things aren't always so cut and dry, Skye. Sometimes you have to dance with the devil to keep him, or her in this case, away."

A low pitched whine of a blaring siren broke through our conversation. It was a civil defense siren which was a common sound to be heard during the war between the Harvesters and humans. It usually meant wherever you were living was either being invaded or a nuclear bomb was on the way.

A pre-recorded woman's voice resounded over the blare of the siren.

"You have… fifteen minutes… to evacuate before detonation of self- destruct."

My father whirled around to face me.

"What's going on?" I asked, as waves of bad memories almost overwhelmed me with the familiar rise and fall of the siren.

"I don't know." My father reached for the phone on his desk and punched a red button located on the key pad.

"Jon Blackwell," he said to whoever came on the other line. He paused listening to the person on the phone. My father nodded his head, "All right." He hung up the receiver and looked up at me. "There are trip wires around the perimeter of the city in case of an invasion. All fifteen of them have been activated which automatically sets off the self-destruct. Go to your room and grab whatever you can carry in a small bag. We have to leave *now*."

He walked from behind the desk and dashed back into his secret room.

Zoe was stepping out of her bedroom when I walked back into the living room.

"What's going on?" She asked.

"Hurry up and grab a bag of stuff from your room," I told her. "We have to leave the city."

"You have…fourteen minutes…to evacuate before detonation of self-destruct."

Zoe and I spent two minutes, at least according to the automated voice's rather annoyingly calm countdown, changing into warm clothing and packing up what we could grab quickly. I searched under my pillow and pulled out the one thing I was not going to leave the city without-- the small heart shaped rock Jace gave me. I slipped it in the front pocket of my jeans for safe keeping. When Zoe and I met my father in the living room, I noticed he was only carrying a small black bag, not big enough for anything substantial.

My father banged on the door of Ash and Kale's apartment when we left ours.

They both came to the door with backpacks over their shoulders.

"Come on boys," my father said. "We don't have much time."

By the time we all walked out of the apartment building, there was a mad crash of people in the street running for escape. Gun fire could be heard in the distance, but I couldn't see who was firing at whom.

"Where are we going?" I yelled to my father over the noise of the crowd and siren.

My father grabbed one of my hands.

"Don't let go," he ordered. "Doc Riley should be waiting for us in the park with a transporter."

I grabbed Zoe's hand and she tugged on Blue's leash to pull him in closer to us to make sure he didn't get trampled by the throng surrounding us. Ash and Kale followed close behind.

The scared crowd of people around us made walking difficult. The sound of gun fire seemed to get closer and closer the further down the street we went.

"Damn fools," my father said only loud enough for me to hear.

"Are the guards shooting people?" I asked, having only seen the guards of the Southern Kingdom be allowed to carry guns.

My father looked down at me. "No."

But he didn't have time to elaborate.

"You have… seven minutes…to evacuate before detonation of self-destruct."

Finally, we broke through the crush of people and entered Central Park. The park area was almost deserted, only a scattering of people were running through it.

"Where are we going?" I asked my father, running along beside him doing my best to keep up.

"The pond."

I didn't have enough breath to ask why Doc Riley was meeting us at the pond. Two minutes later I had my answer.

Doc Riley and Ian were standing on the end of the pier which reached out to the middle of the pond. Behind them floating along the side of the dock was a black armored vehicle I had never seen before. It looked like the spurious child of a tank and a boat.

"You have...five minutes...to evacuate before detonation of self-destruct."

"Glad to see you made it," Doc Riley said, giving me a brief hug. "Climb in children and buckle up."

The interior of the vehicle was larger than I expected. There were ten bucket seats built into each side wall and a driver seat and passenger seat up front near the glowing blue control panel. Ash helped me buckle Blue into one of the seats while everyone else grabbed a seat of their own. Doc Riley took the drivers chair and my father sat up front with her.

"You have...four minutes...to evacuate before detonation of self-destruct."

Ash made to help me into my chair, but I pushed him towards the empty seat across from me.

"I can take care of myself, Ash, just get in your seat."

I felt Ash put his hands on my shoulders. Before I knew it I was turned around and facing him.

In a blur of motion, he put his hands behind my head and pulled me towards him. His lips crushed mine in a desperate kiss. His mouth opened to deepen the kiss causing my already racing heart to pump even harder inside my chest. The warm feel of his lips and tongue almost made me forget we were on the verge of being blown up.

"You have...three minutes...to evacuate before detonation of self-destruct."

"Dude!" Kale said, breaking the moment. "There's time for that later!"

Ash reluctantly pulled his lips away from mine. When I looked into his eyes, they seemed almost glazed over like he was intoxicated.

"Just in case," he said to me.

He didn't have to finish the sentence. I knew what he meant-- just in case we didn't make it.

CHAPTER FIVE

I dropped into my seat and quickly buckled the safety harness. When I looked over at Ash, he was staring at me like he might not ever see me again.

"You have…two minutes…to evacuate before detonation of self-destruct."

"Hold on, children," Doc Riley yelled from the front. "The first drop is a doozy!"

Doc Riley was never one for over exaggeration. Whatever she did up front instantly caused an almost free fall effect. I involuntarily grabbed the harness crisscrossing my chest as the light from the Southern Kingdom was lost, plunging us into a darkness so thick I thought it might suffocate me. The force of the fall made me feel like my stomach had suddenly been lodged inside my throat. Our landing must have been cushioned by water, but it was still jarring.

"Everyone all right?" My father yelled through the pitch black.

Everyone acknowledge they were fine in mumbled *yeahs* and *yeses*

"Dude, where's the light?" Kale asked.

"This is only the first step of our journey," Doc Riley called back. "We're in an aqueduct underneath the mountain. It will take us to a neighboring lake. I have to use night vision goggles to see where I'm going so we can't have any lights on. Sorry for any bumps along the way, children, but it can be a bit tricky driving through a hole as narrow as this one. Just make sure your harnesses are secure."

I tugged on my belt to make sure it was still buckled. As Doc Riley weaved us back and forth through the tunnel, the motion of the vehicle made me feel like a bobble head doll. I could only presume she was doing her best not to run us into the rock walls of the tunnel but still get us as far away from the blast zone as quickly as she could.

Suddenly, we all felt the vehicle vibrate and zoom forward by an unseen force. It had to be an aftershock from the bomb going off in the Southern Kingdom. I prayed Kirk and Teegan made it out in time. I couldn't afford to lose any of my friends. They kept me sane in a world which was anything but.

I felt Zoe grope in the darkness trying to find my hand but finding a leg instead. I placed my hand on top of hers and squeezed it reassuringly. To say I felt protective of Zoe was an understatement. Since she had entered my life, I felt like she was my responsibility to keep safe and out of harm's way. She may have looked older, but I knew the frightened seven-year-old I first met was still inside her. We held hands in the dark allowing our human contact to reassure us everything would turn out all right even if it was an illusion.

I'm not sure how long we were in the tunnel, but my guess would have been at least half an hour. Finally, it felt like we were angling upward. The vehicle lurched forward to break the surface of the water allowing murky rays of moonlight to enter through the front glass. After being in total darkness for so long, the light felt like the sun glaring into my eyes forcing me to let go of Zoe's hand to shield them.

"Over there," my father said from the front. I peaked between my fingers to see him pointing to a spot to our left.

"Hold on, children," Doc Riley said. "Almost there."

The gentle sway of the vehicle on water was soon disrupted as we emerged onto dry land. We rolled on an incline then came to a flat spot before coming to a complete stop.

I heard my father and Doc Riley unlatch their harnesses and took that as my queue to do the same. Everyone else in the back followed my lead.

Doc Riley emerged from the cockpit first with my father standing slightly behind her securing the black briefcase he brought with him firmly behind his seat.

"Time to see who else made it out alive," she said, walking to the hatch and unhooking the latch to open the door.

Ash took my hand when we stood giving me a quick, reassuring wink. Whenever things seemed their bleakest during our travels through the Eastern Kingdom, Ash would sometimes wink at me, squeeze my hand and say, "Come on." It was his way of giving me hope.

By the time we all made it out, a dozen other vehicles like ours were in different stages of making it to the same spot. As people emerged, Doc Riley took on her role as physician and made sure the others were physically unharmed. My father delegated jobs for the rest of us. He asked Ash, Zoe, and me to gather up as much dry wood as we could to make a fire against the cold.

"We'll be staying here for the rest of the night to take inventory and make a list of everyone who made it out. Tomorrow we'll travel to the alternate settlement site," my father told us.

"Alternate settlement?" I asked.

"There's another underground facility further south of here," he explained. "But we need to wait for the others so we can all travel there together."

"So there are two Southern Kingdoms?" Zoe asked.

"The alternate site isn't as nice as the one we just lost," my father told us. "But it has everything we need to survive."

Two Southern Kingdoms...

I wanted to ask why the leaders of the old world didn't use the alternate site to save more of those left behind in the Eastern Kingdom, but I didn't really need to ask when the answer was so obvious. They wanted to save the alternate site for the scenario we found ourselves in now. They wanted to make sure that if they lost their first nirvana, there was a second one ready for them to use as a backup. The selfishness of such a plan wasn't lost on me.

Ash, Zoe, and I walked toward the woods to do as we were asked. We were all silent as we gathered up fallen branches to take back to camp. Zoe was a few feet to the left of me when I felt Ash rest a hand on my shoulder and turn me to face him.

"Are you ok?" he asked.

"Probably better than I should be considering things," I admitted. "This might sound stupid, but I'm more comfortable here on the outside than I was down in paradise."

Ash's lips spread into a grin. "Were you feeling a bit too pampered down there?"

"You think I'm silly to feel more at home in a wasteland, don't you?" I sighed and didn't wait for his answer before I continued. "It's just that everything down there was an illusion. They tried to remake the old world but nothing ever felt real to me. Things were just too perfect."

"It may have been fake but at least it felt safe," he said.

"Even that turned out to be an illusion," I reminded him.

"Stand still."

The click of a gun made both Ash and I freeze where we stood.

"Put the wood down and turn back towards the lake," the man ordered.

We did what he said. As I turned, I saw Zoe facing the same situation we were with another armed gun man. In that instant, I wished I had mental telepathy instead of the power to heal. I wanted to scream to Zoe to not use her power. I knew if she erected a shield around herself our captors might not ever let her go. They could have all our food and transportation for all I cared. Things could be replaced. Zoe couldn't. If these were the same people who invaded the Southern Kingdom and ultimately destroyed it, I feared what they might do to us if they knew we had supernatural powers.

With our hands on top of our heads, we walked back to the lake. Lit torches made a circular jail for the survivors from the Southern Kingdom. My father was anxiously waiting for us within its perimeter.

"What's going on?" I asked him as we walked inside the circle of torches.

"Outsiders," he whispered. "They're the ones who invaded the Southern Kingdom and set off the self-destruct."

"Why would they want it blown up?" Zoe asked.

"My guess is to force us to do what we had to do to survive: come outside."

"But why?" I questioned.

"Why do you think?" I heard the man who brought Ash and I back ask from behind me.

I turned around and saw that he was in his mid-fifties with white hair balding at the temples and a shaggy white beard and mustache covering over half of his face. His dark brown eyes felt like they were boring holes into my skull. He was shaking slightly, but I couldn't tell if it was because he hated us that much or if it was a medical condition.

"I don't know," I said, refraining from giving a smart ass retort to a man holding a gun. If I had known the answer to my question, I wouldn't have asked it.

"I'll tell you why," he said refusing to look away from my eyes like the act would make me feel some sort of shame.

"Ben," a woman walked up and put a hand on the man's shoulders. His shaking became less violent as he looked at the woman by his side.

The woman didn't look much older than thirty. She was thin but who in the outside world wasn't? Her dark brown hair fell down past her waist. Years of malnourishment stretched the skin across her face into a thin mask.

"Why don't you go help the others and see what's in the transporters these good people brought up?"

"Ok, Margaret," he said completely submissive to the woman as he slowly turned his back to us and walked to the vehicle we had escaped in.

After Ben walked away, Margaret turned to face us.

"You'll have to excuse some of us," she said. "We've been planning this for quite a while and the excitement of everything that's happened is a bit overwhelming."

"So killing thousands of people is what you call exciting?" My father's voice brimmed with anger.

"Of course not," Margaret replied, little atonement in her voice, just tiredness. "Lives on both side of this battle were lost but hopefully not in vain."

"Then why sacrifice your own people? What did you hope to gain from their suicide mission?"

"Salvation," Margaret said. "I knew if we tripped your self-destruct you wouldn't have any other choice but to come out."

"How did you know this is where the tunnels led?" I asked.

A sad smile stretched Margaret's thin lips. "My father helped build the facility down there. When I was a little girl, he showed me everything about it, even the emergency fail safes."

"Why weren't you living down there if your father helped build it?" I asked.

"My parents were among the first to be taken by the Harvesters. I only escaped because they sacrificed themselves to give me a chance at a life." Margaret let out a harsh laugh. "I'm not sure if they would have gone to the trouble if they had known the way my life would turn out."

"But why force us to the surface? Why sacrifice your own people?" My father asked.

Margaret was silent. I wasn't sure she was going to answer.

"You wouldn't have come up any other way. Those who sacrificed their lives were the weakest of us and most likely to die anyway. They gave us the gift of their lives so that we might have a chance to live. There wasn't any other way to find the other underground haven."

"What makes you think there is one?" A man I had only met once asked, as he stepped up to join the conversation.

He was in his sixties with wild grey hair and a mustache. His eyes looked almost black against his pale skin in the dim torch light.

"My father told me there was one, and my father never lied to me. If you don't take us there, we'll kill all of you where you stand," Margaret said without hesitation. "But, we are offering you a chance to begin again if you allow us to join you."

"The stunt your people pulled killed almost half our population," the man accused angrily. "Why would we want murderers living among us?"

"I would be careful who you call a murderer. Your people have been trading us off to the Harvesters for years. There's hardly anyone left here on this side of the barrier because of you!"

"If you had just come to us, we might have been able to work something out," my father said, attempting to be the voice of reason.

Margaret shook her head. "No thanks. I didn't feel like being made into Harvester spare parts."

"We don't deal with Harvesters," the man said, but even I could hear the lie in his words.

"Either you take us to the alternate location or you die," Margaret said like either option was fine with her. "I think the choice is clear enough."

Margaret turned her back to us and joined her people near the transporters.

I looked over at the man who had come to my hospital room and introduced himself to me.

"Mr. President," I heard a woman call.

The man turned toward the woman's voice and walked away from us.

I stared at his back as the man who used to be President of the United States walked away.

CHAPTER SIX

Tears of despair surrounded me. Those who were able to escape the destruction of the Southern Kingdom seemed inconsolable in their loss of paradise. Many of them had never been forced to face the reality of the real world because they were able to make a home in the Southern Kingdom before eternal grey consumed the outside. Being cruelly thrust out of their cushy lives to live in what was left above ground seemed to be more than some of them were capable of handling. I felt lucky in a strange way. At least I knew what it took to survive on the surface. It was the only home I knew. It was where I was most comfortable.

The only difference between my past and present was the fact I was fortunate enough to have more than one friend with me this time. Kirk and Teegan made it out on the last transport to emerge from the lake. I had to admit the circumstances we found ourselves in weren't ideal, but at least we were all alive and together, for however long.

"Man, I just don't think I can stand to see my mom cry anymore," Kale said, coming to sit in the circle we had made around one of the campfires the outsiders let us build to keep warm by.

Teegan put a comforting arm around Kale's shoulders bringing a small smile to his face.

"So does anyone know what's going on?" Kirk asked. "It's almost morning. Why haven't we left for this other underground Shangri-La the outsiders want us to take them to?"

"Because, sweet boy," Doc Riley said, leaning towards the fire to warm her hands, "the council hasn't made up its mind."

"Made up its mind about what? Taking them with us?" Ash questioned. "It doesn't seem like they have much of a choice."

I looked over at the circle of huddled leaders standing less than twenty yards away from us. The group of five, including my father, had been talking with one another for hours, which made me question who my father had been talking to in his secret room. Did he have a direct line to the President in there? Was that who he was arguing with when I discovered his secret lair? It made sense since my father hadn't stopped arguing with the President since they started their little pow-wow over our future with the outsiders.

A loud bang came from one of the transporters. When I looked up, I saw Margaret emerge from the one we used to escape in holding the small black briefcase my father brought with him. Her face contorted by rage, Margaret headed straight for the gathered members of the council. I looked over at my father and saw him warily watch Margaret's progress towards them. His shoulders seemed to pull back involuntarily as he stood straighter.

Margaret breeched the torch barrier holding the briefcase up.

"Who does this belong to?" She demanded. The anger in her voice was on the verge of being manic. "Whose is this?" She screamed.

"It's mine," my father said.

Margaret threw the case at my father making him catch it quickly.

"Open it," she ordered, pulling out a pistol from a pocket of her coat and aiming it straight at my father's head.

I made a move to stand up intent on going to my father, but Ash grabbed the back of my coat forcing me to stay seated on the ground.

"Let me go," I said.

"Your father can handle things," Ash whispered. "If you go over there, you might make things worse. She's not right in the head, Skye. Let your Dad deal with her."

I looked back at my father. He was kneeling with the briefcase lying on the ground in front of him. He unsnapped the clips at the front of the case and slowly opened it.

"Take it out," Margaret demanded, her gun hand shaking but still pointed directly at my father.

My dad reached inside the briefcase and pulled out a small shiny black laptop computer. I felt my breath catch in my throat when I saw what was engraved in silver on top of it. It was the infinity symbol, Lucena's crest.

"Are you the one in charge of making deals with that bitch?"

My father stood with the laptop still in his hands.

"Tell me!" Margaret's men came to stand behind her with their guns drawn on my father like they were daring him to not answer.

"Yes," my father said, his gaze reluctantly looking in my direction. "I'm responsible."

Even though I heard the words come out of his mouth, my mind refused to believe what he was admitting to. He had to be covering up for someone else's sins. The man I knew and loved could never knowingly hand over innocent lives to be butchered by the Harvesters. Or had the war truly changed him that much? With the loss of his family, had my father lost his humanity too?

Before I knew what was happening, Margaret shot my father point blank in the chest. He fell backwards onto the ground dropping the laptop, causing it to shatter like glass.

Everything after that felt like it happened in slow motion. I felt more than heard myself scream for him. I leapt to my feet before Ash could stop me and ran to my father not caring that the men standing behind Margaret might shoot me for trying to help him.

Tears of hot anguish trailed down my face as I knelt down beside him tearing at his coat to find the damage Margaret's bullet had inflicted. A circular stain of blood was rapidly spreading through the blue pullover he was wearing. I put my hand over the wound calling on every bit of power I had inside me to heal him before he died. The people around me became a blur of motion and frantic voices. My mind blocked them out somehow allowing me to concentrate on healing my father. The mingled scent of gun powder with my father's blood hung in the air around me like a fog enveloping my senses. I felt someone give a sharp tug on my jacket only to hear a guttural grunt as that person was tackled to the ground behind me. Gunshots were fired, but I didn't have time to ponder who else might be injured. All my thoughts were centered on my father's wound.

The rise and fall of his chest beneath my hands helped me focus on what needed to be done. I felt my own blood rush through my body and hoped my healing power was working. I still didn't understand how my power worked, but it was always there when I needed it. I prayed it wouldn't abandon me now, not after just being reunited with my dad again. I didn't care what he had done to survive, even if that meant trading the outsiders to Lucena. I could forgive him his faults. I just needed him to live.

"Skye…"

Ash's voice sounded like it was a mile away even though I felt his presence right next to me.

"Skye. You healed him. You can stop."

I forced myself to open my eyes. My father's blood covered my hands like a pair of red gloves. I looked up at his face and saw him looking at me with a mixture of pride and fear.

"How the hell did she do that?" Margaret asked. She stood on the other side of my father staring at me with wide eyes.

I didn't know what to say, but telling the truth seemed the best option.

"I can heal people," I told her.

"What are you?" Margaret lifted her gun until it was level with my head. Her men did the same.

"I'm human, but I have nanites inside me that allow me to heal."

"Then you're a Harvester." Margaret pulled back the hammer on her pistol preparing to shoot.

"No. I'm human." I repeated, unable to think of anything better to say.

My father sat up.

"She's Lucena Day's daughter," he told Margaret. A collective gasp came from both outsiders and people from the Southern Kingdom. "And if I were you, I would put that gun down before you do something stupid like shoot her head off."

"If she's the Queen's daughter, she deserves to die."

"Are you a complete idiot?" My father asked. "What do you think the Queen will do to you if she learns you killed her one and only child?"

"She won't do anything to me," Margaret said defiantly. "She can't cross the barrier."

My father let out a harsh, pitying laugh. "There is no barrier you fool."

Everyone went silent.

"Yes there is," Margaret said. "I see it every night."

"What you see is an illusion."

"Jon...don't..." the President started to walk closer to us but was stopped by Margaret's men.

"Explain," Margaret said to my father.

"The barrier was never sustainable. It took too much energy to charge a field that long and wide. Why do you think we were trading with the Queen? We were buying time to figure out a way to bring the radiation field back up. Lucena could have come through at any time, but she made a bargain with us instead. As long as we rounded up the people she needed on this side of the barrier and brought them to her, we could continue living peacefully down below. The people we traded would have ended up in her hands one way or another."

Margaret lowered her pistol, but her men kept theirs trained on us.

"You're lying," she said.

"What do I have to gain by lying to you?"

"Put your guns down," Margaret said to her men.

Her gaze was caught by the shattered laptop still on the ground at my father's feet.

"Did you use that thing to communicate with her?"

"Yes. She would contact me when she needed a new shipment."

"What will happen if she tries to contact you and she can't reach you?"

"She'll send her people through the barrier to find out what's wrong. The only place we will be safe is the secondary facility."

"Why will we be safe there?"

"There's an identical laptop there. If we can get to it before she tries to contact me again, then we don't have anything to worry about."

"But she'll expect you to still trade with her."

"Yes," my father said, looking up at Margaret. "Can you live with that?"

Margaret let out a deep sigh. The weight of so many lives was now on her shoulders too. She looked around at her people, half starved, standing around in threadbare clothes. I knew what it took to live out here and knew that more than anything they just wanted a warm, safe place to lay their heads. They needed to feel safe even it was just temporary.

"All right," Margaret said, her voice sounding defeated. "We better get going before she figures out what's happened."

Margaret held her hand down to my father to help him to his feet, but I knew the gesture meant more than just helping somebody up. It meant she had made her peace with her decision and couldn't hold a grudge against us anymore. She was just as guilty as the rest of us now.

CHAPTER SEVEN

My family was allowed to stay together in our original transport. I guess I didn't realize it until then, but I did consider my friends to be my family. They were the people I was closest to, and I knew they would have my back in any situation. The surprising part was that even Ian made the cut. He couldn't change the fact he was a Harvester, but he had proven himself to be more human than machine when he helped Jace and me find a way to escape Alliance.

Margaret and three of her men rode with us to the second Southern Kingdom, making the interior of the transporter a bit cramped. No one talked. Zoe held onto one of my hands while we rode in the strained silence, strangely finding strength in a person who felt anything but. Ash sat on the other side of me. He kept his eyes on the armed men sitting opposite us like he was waiting for one of them to do something stupid.

I started to feel a bit silly just sitting there staring at the men. If we were going to have any hope of merging the survivors of the first Southern Kingdom with the outsiders, we would have to find some common ground with one another. Otherwise, we would remain hostile towards each other and never have any hope in building a working community.

I stretched out my hand to the man sitting in the middle of the other two.

"Hi, my name is Skye."

The man was in his late twenties, old enough to remember the war but not too old to be set in his ways. He had curly brown hair and light gray eyes in a round face. Small brown freckles dappled his pale skin.

From the way he looked at my outstretched hand, I wasn't sure if he was going to shake it or shoot it off. Finally, his hand slid into mine as he gave it a firm shake.

"Collin." He said. "This here is Jack and Flash."

The two men sitting on either side of him gave a small nod as their names were called.

Jack was in his forties with grey speckled black hair. When he smiled you could tell a few of his teeth were rotted. Flash was about my age with red hair and an easy grin. He winked at me when he caught me looking at him. It wasn't a flirtatious wink, just one of greeting.

"So," Collin said, "you really the Queen's daughter?"

"Biological daughter. She wasn't my mother."

Collin's eyebrows furrowed. "What's the difference?"

I explained the difference.

"Wow, that's kinda messed up," Flash said afterwards. "So she's your mom and your aunt at the same time."

"Sounds a bit inbreed doesn't it?"

Collin shrugged. "What do you expect from a woman like her? She's a nut and a half."

"So what's your stories? Did any of your families survive the war?"

"We're our own family," Jack answered. "Collin and Flash are like brothers to me."

I squeezed Zoe's hand and looked over at her. She smiled at me because we understood how the men across from us felt.

"My family is sitting in this transporter," I said, looking at all my friends. No one seemed surprised by my statement except for Ian. His expression was guarded giving him a withdrawn look, instantly separating himself from those he thought I considered part of my family.

"Even you Ian," I said to him, causing his eyes to narrow on me like he wasn't sure he believed me.

Ian finally gave me one of his lopsided grins and shook his head. "Only you would include the black sheep of the group."

I shrugged. "Every family needs one."

The men across from me looked puzzled but didn't comment. I didn't give them a chance to anyway. All I needed was for them find out Ian was a Harvester. Who knew how they would react?

It took us almost the whole day to get to the second Southern Kingdom. My father said we were traveling south of our original location which made me realize I was being taken that much further away from Jace.

No matter how hard I tried to block him out, Jace always found a way to the surface of my thoughts. If I could only know for sure he was still alive, I might be able to gain some sort of comfort. Since it was obvious now my father had a way to communicate with Lucena, I decided to ask him if he thought Lucena would allow me to speak with Jace. The emptiness I felt without him near and completing the circle of people I considered family left a gaping hole in my heart.

But every time I thought about Jace I also had to wonder why he asked me not to leave the Southern Kingdom once I reached it. Why had he been so adamant about it when he knew Lucena would blackmail him into staying in the Eastern Kingdom causing us to be separated? What terrible thing had he seen take place in my future which would make him willingly push away someone he said he loved?

The stupid girly part of me began to doubt he truly loved me like he said. You don't give up the person you love so easily. But then the logical part of my brain reasoned he did what he had to do to get me and everyone else to the Southern Kingdom safely. He sacrificed himself for me which made me feel guilty about doubting his love. Basically, I was trapped in an endless circle of guilt and doubt.

"So, the two of you boyfriend and girlfriend?"

Collin's question brought me back to the present situation.

"Who?" I asked.

"You and him," Collin said, nodding to Ash at my side.

An awkward silence ensued. I had no idea what to say for a space of ten seconds. I could feel Ash's eyes on me waiting for my answer just as much as Collin was. I answered the only way I knew how.

"Why do you ask?"

Collin shrugged. "Most of the girls in our group are hooked up with someone. I just wanted to know if you were free."

"Yeah," Ash said, putting a possessive hand on my thigh. "She's taken."

I looked down at Ash's hand wondering why it felt so odd for him to touch me that way. Then I looked up at his face and saw him staring at Collin like he was challenging the other man to call him a liar. When I looked over at Collin, he didn't look convinced about Ash's claim of possession over me.

"Well, you ever change your mind, Skye, I won't be too far away." Collin winked.

Ash was about to get up to do who knows what to Collin, but I grabbed his arm and pulled him back down.

"He's just teasing, Ash."

But my words didn't seem to deflate my best friend's anger.

"You," Ash said pointing a finger at Collin, "Stay away from her."

Collin laced his fingers behind his head and leaned back in his seat. "And if I don't?"

The conversation was taking a bad turn. The whole point of my starting an oral exchange with the outsiders was to make friends with them not cause more problems.

"If you don't leave her alone, dude, you'll have to deal with me too," Kale said.

"And me," Kirk proclaimed.

"And you don't *even* want to know what I'll do to you," Ian leaned forward resting his elbows on his thighs staring straight at Collin. If looks could actually kill, Ian would be a master assassin.

"Hey, hey," Flash lifted his hands in surrender. "No need to start a ruckus. It's just been a long time since we were around such pretty girls. And like Collin said, most of the girls in our group are spoken for." Flash turned his attention to Zoe. "How about you? You hooked up with anybody?"

Zoe's eyes widened. "I...I don't have a boyfriend if that's what you're asking."

Flash cleared his throat. "Think I could take you out sometime then? You know if you're not busy or anything."

Zoe looked over at me like she wanted me to tell her what to do.

"It's your decision, Zoe," I told her.

Zoe looked back at Flash and rewarded him with a shy smile. "I guess that would be ok."

Flash smiled back. "Cool."

The men of our group didn't seem to like the idea of Zoe having anything to do with an outsider from the expressions on their faces, but they didn't say anything.

"All right, children," Doc Riley called from the front of the transporter. "We seem to be here. The President's transporter has stopped."

When we stepped out of our vehicle, a mountain with three carved figures loomed before us. The three men were on horseback and dressed in old uniforms like soldiers from the War Between the States. I couldn't remember their names but knew where we were because I had seen the carving in a travel magazine once.

"Stone Mountain, Georgia," I said aloud.

"Yeah," Ash agreed. "I remember you showing me the picture of the mountain."

It took a while for everyone to get out of their transporters. There were close to a hundred transporters in all. Nearly a thousand people crowded around the base of the mountain waiting to see what would happen next. Word quickly spread through the crowd the President wanted to personally escort the outsiders into the second Southern Kingdom first. I could only assume it was a political move designed to smooth over any ruffled feathers. I hoped the President succeeded in bringing peace through diplomacy because I had failed miserably in my small attempt.

"See you inside," Flash said to Zoe, giving her a quick smile.

Zoe nodded and smiled back.

"Zoe and Flash sitting in a tree, K-I S-S-I-N-G," Kale said in a sing-song voice.

He was quickly rewarded with a slap on the back of the head from Teegan.

"Hey, I was just picking…" Kale defended, rubbing his head.

Teegan pointed a finger at him and wagged it.

"Yeah, yeah, I get the message loud and clear," Kale said.

"You're such a juvenile," Kirk rolled his eyes at Kale.

Kale shrugged. "I know. Can't help it. It's just who I am, man. Love me or leave me."

Teegan wrapped an arm around one of Kale's. She had obviously made her choice.

Being near the front of the crowd, we were able to watch as the President walked to a point at the base of the mountain and placed his hand flatly against it. When he pulled his hand away, a small, square lighted touch pad appeared in the stone. The President quickly entered a code. The sound of grinding stone filled the air as a large portion of the rock next to the touchpad was pulled inward and slid to the right. The entrance seemed to be a little bit bigger than the size of one of the transporters. From somewhere in the depths of the mountain, a light shined brightly beckoning the newcomers to enter. Once all of the outsiders were inside, those of us at the front of the awaiting crowd began to move forward intent on following them in.

"Wait!" My father called out. Everyone stopped and looked to him.

Gunshots from within the mountain were heard but soon cut off by the closing of the large rock wall door. Panic quickly spread through those of us left behind.

"Did they kill the President?" Someone yelled.

"Are they just going to leave us out here?" Someone else cried.

My father just stood staring at the spot on the mountain where the entrance had been.

"Dad, what's going on?" I asked, pulling on the sleeve of his coat to regain his attention.

He looked down at me. Tears welled in his eye as he shook his head. "I'm so sorry, Skye. I wish I could protect you from the bad things of this world but I can't. I've tried but I can't."

"What are you talking about? What's happening?"

"Their fates were sealed when they took us hostage," my father continued, his eyes becoming vacant. "There wasn't any other way."

"Dad, what are you talking about? What's happening?"

My father turned to the crowd. The look on his face was completely void of emotion like he was hiding behind a mask of indifference.

"Everyone please get back into your transporters. As soon as the President returns, we will be heading to the secondary facility."

People began to yell at my father asking him where we were and what was happening inside the mountain.

"Jon," Doc Riley said, "I thought this was the secondary habitation module. If it's not, what is it?"

The crowd went silent awaiting my father's answer.

"It's a Harvester installation."

It was like my father had set a bomb off in the middle of the crowd. People ran for their transporters not needing to know more. But I needed an explanation. I needed him to face me and tell me the truth.

"Was this your plan all along?" I asked my father. "Is that what the council was arguing about: whether or not to bring the outsiders here?"

When my father looked at me, I didn't know who he was. His face was a mask of soullessness.

"We have to do what's best for everyone," he answered, like he was reciting a piece of preplanned propaganda.

"But you didn't," I countered. "You handed the outsiders over without even giving them a chance to fight for their lives. You led them to slaughter like they were a bunch of cattle. What's wrong with you?" I knew I was shouting but couldn't help it.

"How do you know they wouldn't have killed us all once we took them to the second Southern Kingdom?" My father asked. "It was either trust them or get rid of them. After what they did to the original site, the council decided they couldn't be trusted. There wasn't any other choice to be made, Skye."

"So you would rather trust a bunch of Harvesters than other human beings? Is that what it's come down to? We trust the machines more than we do living, breathing humans? People who just wanted a chance to live a better life? What the hell happened to you, Dad? I don't even know who you are anymore. And I'm not sure I want to."

My words broke through my father's manufactured composure. I saw the hurt enter his eyes and twist his face in anguish.

"Skye, you don't understand…" He reached a hand out to me, but I pulled away and turned to walk back to our transporter.

No explanation could make me understand the man he had become.

My friends joined me in the transporter. None of them tried to console me or pretend they understood what I was feeling. I sat staring at the seats Collin, Flash, and Jack had occupied only minutes before. I was sure if I touched their seats they would still be warm. For some reason I felt guilty over their fates even though I had nothing to do with the decision to bring them to the Harvesters. But I was part of the reason they had been traded to the real-life monsters of our world.

I wondered if Margaret regretted her moment of inhumanity when she agreed to go along with the terms of Lucena's truce. Now she was the one being traded for others' safety. Perhaps it was just a perversion of fate. Now she found *herself* in a Harvester breeding camp. My mother always said what you give to the world is what you receive back. I guess she was right.

I'm not sure how much time passed as we waited for the caravan of transporters to start their procession to the second Southern Kingdom. It was probably close to an hour. I had pretty much zoned out by then becoming lost in my own little world remembering happier times with my family trying to recapture the father I once knew, unable to reconcile my memories with the father I had now.

My father's angry voice could be heard outside the transporter just before the door was pulled off its hinges causing us all to jump in our seats. Only one thing could display such an incredible act of strength, a Harvester.

When he stepped through the door, I thought maybe I had fallen asleep and was having a nightmare or at the very least hallucinating.

Freddy, dressed in a black Harvester uniform, stood in the doorway of the transporter. Blue barked at Freddy and made to attack him, but Kirk tugged on his leash preventing him from rushing forward.

"Long time, no see, Skye my love," he said.

Ian made to get up but was quickly forced to sit back down by Freddy's stun baton.

"Don't push me, Ian. Any excuse to kill you will work for me."

"What do you want, Freddy?" I asked, fearing I already knew the answer.

"The Queen said it was time for you to come home, love. She's grown impatient. She told me if you try to fight, I should kill as many people as needed to gain your full cooperation," Freddy looked around at my friends like he was trying to decide which one of them would die first.

I stood up.

"Skye, no," Ash said, grabbing hold of my arm.

I looked down at him. "It's no use, Ash. Don't you see that? I might not agree with the things my father has done, but I can't say for sure I wouldn't have done them to protect you guys. Besides, what Lucena wants she always gets. I refuse to have your blood on my hands."

"Ah, so you're Ash," Freddy said. "The Queen said to bring you and Zoe along too. She has some plans for the two of you from what I gather."

"No!" I surprised even myself with the force I put behind the word. Freddy even jumped slightly. "Leave them alone."

Freddy shrugged. "Like you said, love: what the Queen wants she gets one way or the other. If you want me to start killing people to win your complete cooperation, I will. Kirk first perhaps? Or maybe little mute Teegan? She shouldn't make much noise while I squeeze the life out of her."

Ash and Zoe both stood at my sides, sacrificing themselves to save the others.

"Then you should take me too," Ian said standing to his feet.

Freddy punched him in the gut with his stun baton forcing him to sit back down.

"Now why would I take a git like you to see the Queen? I don't figure you've used sweet Skye's blood to cure yourself yet since you're still with the bleeding heart humans."

"Leave him alone Freddy," the words sounded like an order when I had actually meant them as a plea.

"Or what?"

"You may still think of me as the little girl you tried to auction off," I said. "But I'm the Queen's daughter. Do you honestly think she wouldn't give me your head if I asked for it on a shiny silver stake? If I were you, I would watch what you say and what you do to the people I care about. If you're smart, you won't make me into more of an enemy than I already am."

I wasn't sure where the words were coming from but they had the desired effect on Freddy. He didn't look as sure about himself anymore. If nothing else, the Harvesters feared the Queen more than death. They knew she was the most heartless of them all and nothing could be put past her.

"We need to be leaving," Freddy said. "There's a helicopter waiting to take us to the Queen's residence."

I took a deep breath and felt Zoe grab hold of my hand. I squeezed it reassuringly even though I had no idea what was in store for us.

When we stepped out of the transporter, I saw my father's body lying face down on the ground. I ran to him and turned him over looking for any signs of life. He was breathing but a large red lump was forming on his right temple. I lifted my hand to heal the wound.

"Maybe you should just let it be," Doc Riley said, coming to stand on the other side my father.

I looked up at her. "Why?"

"It'll keep him unconscious until we reach the second facility. It might be easier for him if he doesn't have to see you go, child." Doc Riley pointedly looked around at the other Harvesters standing nearby.

I knew what she was getting at. She knew if my father were awake he would do whatever he could to keep me with him. Such a foolish act would probably lead to his death or the death of others.

I pulled my hand away and leaned down to kiss his forehead.

"Tell him I love him," I said to Doc Riley.

"He knows that, child."

"Tell him anyway"

"Can I tell him you forgive him?"

"You can tell him I understand why he's done the things he's done."

I couldn't say I forgave him of his decisions, but I knew the burden of being responsible for so many innocent lives was the reason he agreed to sacrifice others to keep the ones he cared about safe.

"Let's go."

I turned away just in time to see the President standing with a Harvester near the base of the mountain laughing like they were old friends enjoying an inside joke. I just stared at him trying to control the rage I felt. He was worse than the Harvesters. At least they had a reason for being the way they were. He didn't have the luxury of that excuse. Supposedly, he still had a soul, but I guess that wasn't the only requirement to be classified as a human anymore. Somewhere along the way, the line had been blurred.

"Where's the helicopter?" I asked Freddy.

He started to walk in the opposite direction of the transporters. I grabbed Zoe and Ash's hands leading them towards the next stage of our journey together. I didn't know what awaited us, but I did know one thing.

I had found my way back to Jace.

CHAPTER EIGHT

We rode in a cable car to the top of the mountain where Freddy said a black hawk helicopter was waiting for us.

"Why do you think she wants me and Zoe to come?" Ash asked me as we sat on the bench in the middle of the car.

"Probably to keep me in line," I answered. "She knows I'll take the first opportunity to get away from her. But if she keeps you and Zoe hostage, I can't do anything unless I know we can all go together. It's the same way she blackmailed Jace into staying."

"Do you think she'll let us see Jace again?" Zoe asked hopefully.

"You can bet on it," Ash answered for me. "She'll use whatever leverage she has to make Skye want to stay."

I could hear the jealousy in Ash's voice but chose to ignore it. We had more important things to think about than a silly romantic rivalry.

"I sort of doubt you see Jace anytime soon," Freddy said as he looked out the window watching the ground beneath us slip away. "The Queen's been keeping him busy."

"Doing what?" I asked.

"Finding more freaks like you. He's brought in at least three since you've been gone."

"What's Lucena been doing with them?" I asked.

Freddy shrugged. "Don't know. She keeps them caged in her little laboratory like rats. Guess she's running experiments on them or something. Can't say I care what she's doing as long as it keeps her busy."

"Why do you say that?"

"Because love, when the Queen gets bored she gets nasty. If you think the little games I played in Alliance were bad, you haven't seen what a truly depraved mind can come up with."

I shivered. Not so much from the thought of what Lucena was capable of but of what I might become. Was I seeing a glimpse of my future self? I had half her DNA after all. Her blood coursed through my veins. And my father, well, I knew what he was willing to do even if it was to save lives. How close was I to becoming a monster? Would I be able to turn away from my legacy and forge my own path?

Once we were seated in the helicopter, Freddy instructed the pilot to take us to the castle.

"Castle?" I asked.

"Don't worry your pretty little head about it, princess. We'll be there in a little over an hour. Now shut the hell up so I can have a little peace and quiet before we have to meet her."

The Queen had a castle? This I had to see.

I didn't think it was possible but the world looked even bleaker from the sky. Miles of dead earth surrounded us. Trees looked like white skeletons against a sea of brown and gray. It was like a still life portrait of a wasteland.

A little over an hour later, we arrived at the Queen's castle. I recognized it instantly with its towering turrets decorated with gargoyles and tall water fountain sitting in what once was a large grassy front lawn.

It was the Biltmore Estate. I'd read about it in a book once.

The helicopter landed on the south side of the fountain. Freddy instructed us to follow him. As we walked across the stone gravel towards the front door, it opened but I couldn't see anyone standing in the entry.

"And of course she'll want to make a dramatic entrance," Freddy mumbled.

We followed Freddy into the main foyer of the mansion. As we entered, a circular arboretum directly to our right caught my eyes. It was the only other place besides the Southern Kingdom I had seen healthy growing plants. The bright greens, reds, yellows and blues of the ornamental vegetation seemed obscene for a woman like Lucena Day to be nurturing if you considered how they contrasted with the gray world she helped create.

"Welcome home, Skye."

To the left of us was a grand granite spiral staircase. Lucena walked down it with the erect posture and grace of a true Queen. She wore a short, elegant black sheath dress with horizontal pleats and sheer short sleeves.

I didn't reply to my biological mother, mostly because I was having trouble breathing. Lucena looked so similar to my mom. I wondered why I never realized it before that night by the barrier. It was no wonder I always assumed I resembled my mother. The physical resemblance unnerved me more than realizing I was coming face to face with true evil.

Lucena came to stand in front of us never taking her eyes off of me which compounded the disturbing effect she was having on me. A pleasant smile was plastered on her face like any good hostess, but considering who she was it looked more sinister than welcoming.

"Leave, Freddy," Lucena said dismissively, without even looking in Freddy's direction. Freddy bowed to Lucena and went back out the door behind us with quick strides. I remembered Freddy once looking forward to being in the Queen's favor. Now it seemed like he couldn't wait to get away from her. Perhaps he got more than he bargained for and now regretted ever meeting me.

"Won't you all come join me in the arboretum? I had the cook prepare some snacks for you. After everything you've been through today, I'm sure you're hungry."

"Why are we here?" I asked, finally finding my voice. If she wanted to kill us, she would have done it by now. I needed to know what her real motives for 'rescuing' the three of us were.

Lucena's smile faltered. "Come and have some refreshments first, and we can talk while you eat."

"Thanks," Ash said, cutting me off before I could argue for more information. "I am kinda hungry."

Lucena looked at Ash for the first time, sizing him up in one sweeping glance.

"You've grown quite a bit, Ash. I think you were ten the last time I laid eyes on you." Lucena's gaze slid over to Zoe. "And you seem to have grown overnight, Zoe." Lucena extended her arm out in the direction of the arboretum. "Please, let's sit and talk."

Ash took me by the arm and led me to the arboretum.

"What are you doing? We're not going to pretend things are normal," I hissed at him.

"We're in her home," he replied.

He didn't have to say more than that. I got the hint. This was her turf. If I pissed her off too much, there was no telling what she might do to us or at least to Ash and Zoe. Me she seemed to want to keep safe for whatever reason. So in his own subtle way, Ash was asking me to behave myself and not lose my temper. My life might not be in jeopardy here but his and Zoe's were. One or both of them were disposable pawns in Lucena's game.

I sat down in one of the four wicker chairs around a glass table festooned with small sandwiches, a glass bowl of fruit and a silver ice chest filled with crushed ice decorated with bottled soda pops. I hadn't had an ice cold Coke in a very long time. It was an unexpected treat. Lucena played the doting hostess making sure we all had food on our plates and something to wet our palettes. She sat down and poured herself a cup of tea from a white china tea pot and nibbled on one of the finger sandwiches.

"Now, I know coming here at this time is quite a shock to you," Lucena said to me. "To be honest, I hadn't intended to bring you here for a few more months, but with recent events, it seemed prudent to bring you somewhere safe as quickly as possible."

"How am I safe here?" I asked, unable to keep the disdain I felt for the woman across from me out of my voice.

Lucena smiled but it was strained. "You may not believe it but this is the safest place for you right now. Very few people know I'm here, Harvester or human. And only those I completely trust stay here with me."

"Is Jace one of those people?" I asked.

"Jace is loyal to you which means he's loyal to me since I'm the one responsible for your well-being," Lucena's veiled threat wasn't lost on me. She was still using my safety against Jace. "In fact he's out running a rather important errand for me at the moment. I've made sure he knows you're here to give him an added incentive in completing his mission quickly. I could swear he purposely drags them out sometimes, but it's not really something I can prove since his ability is so unpredictable."

"I still don't understand why I'm here. Why do you want me here with you so badly? What's in it for you?"

"You're my daughter. Why wouldn't I want you with me?"

"So I'm supposed to believe the reason I'm here is motherly love? How stupid do you think I am?"

Lucena smiled but this time it was genuine. "Of course I wouldn't expect you to believe such a simple answer, sweet Skye. If you did, then I would have to second guess your chromosomal composition."

"Tell me why you really want me here."

"In time," Lucena said, shifting her gaze to Ash and Zoe. "Anyone need anything else? I have a wonderful cook. She can prepare anything you want."

When I looked at Ash, I saw him stuffing his face with a sandwich while Zoe was eating with a little more decorum. Of its own accord, my stomach growled. It had been a long time since any of us had eaten or drank anything, almost twenty-four hours. I took a sip of the bottled coke I picked out of the ice chest before sitting down and found its bubbly sweetness like nectar against my tongue. Once I began drinking it, I couldn't stop until the bottle was empty. I ate my fill of sandwiches until I couldn't eat anymore.

After satiating my hunger and thirst, I leaned back in my chair and stared at Lucena.

"Thank you for the food. We needed it."

Lucena grinned and nodded her head in my direction acknowledging my gratitude.

"You can have anything you want, Skye. All you have to do is ask for it."

"Then I want you to have Freddy take Ash and Zoe back to my father. You don't need them."

Lucena rose from her chair. "Oh, I'm afraid I do actually."

"I won't try to escape if you let them go."

"Skye..." Zoe and Ash said at the same time, but I held up a hand to cut off any of their attempts to change my mind.

"I give you my word," I said, staring Lucena straight in the eyes. "I won't try to escape if you let them go. You can do whatever it is you want with me. Just let my friends go back."

"I'm afraid I can't do that. You see I have plans for them."

"What plans?" I asked, realizing my words came out slurred like I was drunk.

"Don't worry, Skye. I don't plan to harm them, just make them better."

I looked at Zoe and Ash. They were both asleep and I knew I was on the verge of it. Somewhere in the back of my mind I remembered being drugged by Julia once upon a time. When would I learn to not drink things people who couldn't be trusted gave me?

"Why am I here?" I heard myself ask again, my eyes feeling like they had blocks of cement on them forcing them closed.

I never heard her answer.

CHAPTER NINE

When I awoke, I found myself completely naked and lying underneath a silky cream colored comforter. I couldn't remember undressing myself. The last memory I had was all of us sitting around the table eating the meal Lucena had prepared. Everything after that was nonexistent. I looked around the room trying to get my bearings and saw a folded note with my name written on it lying on the bedside table underneath a green and white tiffany styled lamp. The heart shaped rock Jace gave me was sitting on top of it like a paper weight.

I sat up pulling the comforter up underneath my arms and reached for Jace's rock, squeezing it firmly in the palm of my hand to find a sense of calm. Then I read the note:

Skye,
There are new clothes for you in the wardrobe by the door.
Please come down
when you are ready.

Your loving Mother

I wadded up the note and threw it on the floor. The smell of flowers seemed to permeate the air around me. It took me a few seconds to realize the scent was on my skin. I held my arm to my nose and took a whiff. It wasn't that the smell was unpleasant but not knowing how it got there was. I ran my fingers through my hair and found it had been washed and dried by unseen hands while I was unconscious. I curled up beneath the comforter feeling completely violated, mentally naked not just physically.

Having been placed in such a compromising position without my consent was unnerving. It made me question what else had been done to me while I was asleep. And where were Ash and Zoe? Waking up to find themselves in a similar situation was my bet. Whatever Lucena had planned for us, I knew I would win money if I betted it was unpleasant.

Eventually, I let my eyes wander around the room. It was what you would expect from something built back in the late 1800's. There was a lot of attention to detail from the decorative crown molding to the exquisitely crafted leafy green wall paper on the walls. I saw a large, ornately carved cherry wood wardrobe standing by the bedroom door and decided to get out of bed to find some clothes to put on. At least that would afford me some sense of protection.

As soon as I stood up, I felt an excruciating soreness beneath my abdomen. It was similar to the cramping sensation I usually felt right before my menstrual cycle only this pain was ten times worse. After standing still for a few minutes, the pain slowly subsided but the ache was still present.

I opened the double doors of the wardrobe and found an array of clothing inside. Everything from party dresses to blue jeans was available. I quickly picked out a pair of jeans and a long sleeved brown cowl neck sweater to wear. From a chest of drawers on the other side of the room, I found some frilly looking underwear and matching bras. They were way fancier than I thought I needed since I was the only person who would ever get to appreciate the delicate lace creations. After I was dressed, I tucked Jace's rock in the front pocket of my jeans. Shoes were the last item on my list and easily found at the bottom of the wardrobe. I chose a pair of brown suede tennis shoes which fit perfectly. And that was the problem. Everything seemed to be tailor made for me. How long had Lucena been planning to have me join her? And now that she had me, what did she plan to do to me?

Just after I put my shoes on, I heard the rumble of a helicopter fly overhead. I walked over to a door which led out onto a balcony at the front of the house. It was a small balcony but seemed sturdy enough since it was made of stone. I peeked through the white gauzy curtains of the glass door and saw a black hawk helicopter swoop down into the courtyard onto the same helipad we landed on the day before. The door to the helicopter slid opened and Jace stepped out.

From that moment on, the only thing I could hear was the hammering of my heart against the walls of my chest. I tightened my grip on the curtain in my hands, almost pulling it from its rod.

Jace turned away from the helicopter and yelled to a Harvester who was walking over to him from the direction of the house. Jace's naturally curly hair was slicked back giving him an almost sinister look if you didn't know the kind heart of the man standing in front of you. He wore a thick black turtle neck shirt underneath a black leather trench coat which hung down to mid-thigh and was cinched in at the waist by a silver buckled belt. Even from a distance I could tell he was tired from the slight slump of his shoulders and the way he hung his head. He seemed to give the Harvester some instructions as he pointed to the helicopter. For some reason, he stopped in what looked like mid-sentence and looked straight up at the balcony as if sensing my presence.

I practically ripped the door from its hinges to get outside. Even before I got to the stone railing of the balcony, Jace was making a mad dash towards the house. I swirled away from the balcony and ran out of the room. I ran down the long hallway only to be met by another long hallway but I had to decide which direction to go. I ran to the left towards the front of the house and prayed to the powers that be I wouldn't get lost in the mansion's maze of corridors. Every time I came to the end of one hallway I was always met by another hallway. I kept going until I heard Jace yell my name from behind me.

When I turned, I saw Jace standing at the other end of the hallway I had just run down. I was breathing so hard my lungs hurt but I didn't care. I ran to him as fast as my tired legs would take me and threw myself into his arms never second guessing he would catch me. I held onto him like he was the only life preserver in ocean with no land in sight. I let go of him enough to look into his eyes and immediately felt my heart lurch unpleasantly in response.

He looked disappointed.

"Why are you here?" He asked me. "I told you not to leave the Southern Kingdom."

I let go of him and took a step back. My whole body felt like it was about to implode in on itself. Why didn't he look as happy as I felt to finally hold him again? Had our separation tempered his feeling for me? Had Jace fallen out of love with me even though he said he would love me forever?

I felt the sting of tears burn my eyes but forced them back. I couldn't think of any words to say to make the moment right again. I tried to hold back my tears but they fell of their own accord. Unable to hide my hurt from him, I turned away and raced back down the hall, too ashamed to let him see the devastating affect his words had on me. Before I made it very far, I felt him grab me around the waist with both of his arms pulling me back against him.

"Skye, please..." He begged tightening his hold, refusing to let me go no matter how hard I fought for release.

My shoulders shook as I cried, but I couldn't stop them from shaking any more than I could prevent the scalding hot drops of disappointment and heartache from falling.

Jace put his hands on my shoulders and gently forced me to turn around and face him.

"Skye, why are you crying? Has she done something to you?"

I shook my head unable to find my voice.

"Then why are you crying and running away from me?"

I looked up into his face and saw his worry over my emotional outburst.

"Because you don't want me here," I blubbered feeling completely stupid for not being able to control the physical display of my heartbreak.

Jace pulled me against him resting his forehead against mine closing his eyes and sighing deeply.

"No, I don't want you here in her house. You don't understand how dangerous this place is for you. I thought you understood that when I asked you to stay in the Southern Kingdom. You're all I've thought about since I've been here. You're all I want."

I closed my eyes and breathed him in. He smelled like leather and Jace. I lifted my hands and caressed the sides of his face. He opened his eyes and lifted his head from mine to look into my eyes. It was then I finally saw what I had hoped to see the first time: want. He did want me. He did still love me. But he was letting his worry for me override everything else.

"Show me," I said.

"Show you what?" He asked, not quite sure what I was asking for.

"If you still love me, prove it," I dared.

"Are you mine to love?" He asked.

I knew what the question implied. He was asking me if being reunited with Ash had rekindled my adolescent longings for my best friend.

"Kiss me," I begged, unable to give him an answer to his question.

Jace hesitated but I knew it wasn't because he didn't want to kiss me. I saw the same desire I felt mirrored in his eyes. I knew he wanted me to tell him whether or not I had chosen between him and Ash yet. I couldn't give him a truthful answer because my heart was still torn by the two men if my life. But I needed him to kiss me like I needed water to survive. My body ached from wanting him to the point where if he didn't kiss me soon I might wither away like a flower left in the sun too long.

"Kiss...," I began but wasn't allowed to finish.

Jace quickly pulled me against his torso. He looked into my eyes like he was searching for the answer to his question there.

"I love you," he breathed against my lips. "I've missed you," he said, continuing to plant light kisses.

They felt like sweet teases. I needed more.

I put my arms around his neck and leaned up forcing him to deepen the kiss. I didn't have to persuade him any further.

The first contact of our tongues lit my body on fire. I put my hands on the back of his head to find balance and to make sure he didn't stop the kiss before I wanted him to. The sound of our heavy breathing echoed in the empty hallway. I couldn't think about anything else except that I wanted Jace, and I knew without a shadow of a doubt he wanted me too.

I began to tug at the belt of his coat wanting to feel his warmth against my body. Our fingers fumbled together undoing the buttons until the leather fell away. I pulled the ends of his shirt out of the black jeans he wore until I could run my hands up his rippled abdomen around to the well-defined muscles of his back. With a groan, Jace quickly pulled the shirt off giving me more room to explore his well-toned torso. But it still wasn't enough for me. I needed to feel his skin against mine. I needed to feel his hands on me.

I pulled back from Jace to take off my shirt in one sweeping motion. He stood staring at me as I let the shirt fall to the carpeted floor. His chest rose and fell like he was having trouble getting enough air into his lungs. His eyes asked me an unvoiced question.

"Kiss me," I answered, not even having to think about it just knowing it was what I wanted.

Jace didn't need any more persuasion than that. He came at me lifting me up, forcing me to put arms around his neck and my legs around his waist.

It was then I screamed out in pain.

The pain was so intense I completely let go of Jace. On reflex he caught me, cradling me in his arms.

"What's wrong?" He asked. "What happened? Did I hurt you?"

I couldn't speak until the pain ebbed away into a dull throb in my pelvic area.

"I hurt here," I said, placing a hand over the affected area.

Our clothes forgotten on the floor, Jace took long, quick strides with me in his arms down the hallway. I kept my eyes closed for most of the trip, only opening them again when he gently laid me down on a bed.

When I opened my eyes, I realized we weren't in the room I had started the morning out in. This room was similar but the walls were of a raised redwood. Velvety forest green curtains hung beside the three windows of the room.

Jace pulled a quilt off of a nearby wing backed caramel colored chair sitting in front of a small marble fireplace. He came back to the bed and covered me with it before sitting down beside me.

"Do you know why you're hurting there?" He asked me. "Have you ever felt pain there before?"

"I've felt something similar but only during my... you know...monthly cycle," I said, feeling shy talking about such things with a man, especially a man I was half naked with. "But the pain was never this bad before."

"Has Lucena done anything to you in the past few days that would cause you to hurt there?"

"I haven't been here that long," I replied. "Right after we got here yesterday she fed us something that made us all go to sleep."

"Right after you got here?" Jace asked in confusion. "How long do you think you've been here?"

"Not even 24 hours yet. Why?"

All of the color drained from Jace's face. "Skye, I got the news you were here four days ago."

I stared at Jace in stunned silence. Four days. I'd been unconscious for four days.

I started to sit up but the pain came back.

"What do you think you're doing?" Jace said, admonishing me for my stupidity. "You need to rest."

I shook my head furiously. "I have to find Zoe and Ash. I have to know what she's done to them. In four days…" I let the implications hang in the air. What could she have done to my friends in four days' time?

"You're not going anywhere," Jace said standing up. "I'll go find out where they are. You just lay on my bed until I come back for you." He went to a wardrobe similar to the one I had in the room I woke up in and pulled out a white button down shirt. "I'll be back as soon as I can." He said slipping his arms into the shirt and heading out the door.

"Jace!"

He ran back into the room.

"What's wrong?"

I held my hand out to him not having to tell him with words how scared I felt.

He took it and leaned down. "Don't worry," he said. "Everything will be all right. Just stay put until I get back. Ok?"

I nodded my head.

He kissed me on the lips and each cheek before squeezing my hand and heading back out the door.

I huddled underneath the quilt in a fetal position, trying my best to ignore the pain which seemed to stubbornly not want to go away.

The words 'four days' still echoed in my mind. What had Lucena done to me in the last four days? Had she harmed Ash and Zoe? Were they even still alive?

The longer I laid there the worse the scenarios playing inside my head got. I had to know they were all right. I had to find them.

I waited for what felt like forever. The intense pain faded back to a dull throb before I decided to try to stand up. I went to Jace's wardrobe and found a black t-shirt to slip on. It was big so I had to pull the bottom of it up together at the side of my hip and tie it into a ball. I walked out the door but had absolutely no idea where in the house I was now. I decided to follow any stairs I came to which went down. By the time I decided I might have gone too far down, I came to a set of opaque glass doors on what I thought to be the basement level of the house.

I peeked behind them and found a laboratory. I walked in and looked around at the various equipment sitting on the countertops having no idea what any of it was for. The only thing I could put a name to was the Bunsen burner. In the middle of the room, stood a large cylindrical tube made of iron. I walked towards it running my hands along the cool metal until I came to a hand shaped indention in the column. I placed my right hand inside it. Steel bars slid out from either side of the opening trapping my hand. The indention illuminated blue and a white light scanned my palm.

"Welcome, Skye," a soft disembodied female voice said to me.

The bars caging my hand disengaged, imbedding themselves back into the column.

I took my hand out of the indention just as clicks, like something unlocking, echoed in the room. The column, which I thought had been a structural feature of the mansion, slowly slid up revealing a glass tube filled with a light blue liquid and a naked woman. Her back was to me. The long brown strands of her hair floated in the liquid around her body giving her an ethereal beauty. Cautiously, I walked around the tube to see the woman's face. I felt the earth beneath my feet give way and was only faintly aware of falling to my knees.

The woman inside the glass tube was my mother.

CHAPTER TEN

I'm not sure how long I knelt by the figure of my mother floating like a ghostly apparition inside the liquid filled tube. She looked like Sleeping Beauty with her closed eyes shutting out the turmoil around her, completely protected within her cocoon from the evils of the outside world. I envied the imagined peace she seemed to have. Her angelic presence comforted and frightened me all at the same time. Was she alive? Was she dead? The only clue I had she was indeed still alive was the gentle rise and fall of her chest. Through partly opened lips she seemed to be drawing in the liquid around her down into her lungs like it was air. My hand shook as I reached out and touched the warm glass shell protecting her. I'm not sure what I expected to happen. If she was really alive, could she sense my presence? Would she open her eyes and look at me?

"Still beautiful after all these years isn't she?"

I looked over at the entrance to the laboratory and watched Lucena walk into the room. She was wearing a white lab coat and high heels which clicked every time she took a step.

"Is she alive?" I asked, my voice hoarse from trying not to cry.

"Her body is alive."

"You say that like there's a difference."

Lucena walked over beside me and touched the glass tube, gliding her hand down its smooth surface like my mother was her most prized possession.

"She's in a vegetative state," Lucena said with a note of regret. "I tried to save her the night you escaped the camp and she was shot, but by the time they brought her to me she was already in a coma. There was no way to bring her out of it."

"But she's alive."

Lucena looked at me like she pitied me. "She has no brain wave activity. If these were the old days your mother would have been put in a grave a long time ago. The woman who you knew as your mother doesn't exist in this body anymore."

"Then why keep her like this?"

"Because I need her."

"For what?"

"For her organs, of course."

I looked back at my mother noting the small incisions across her chest and abdomen.

"You're keeping her body alive for spare parts for yourself," I whispered but Lucena heard me well enough.

"Organ transplants from a sibling or a child are the best matches and they last longer in us for some reason."

I looked up at Lucena. "Is that why I'm here? You've used up my mother now you need to use me too?"

Lucena looked down at me like I was crazy. She shook her head. "No, Skye. I would never do such a barbaric thing to my own child."

"Then what did you do to me?" I asked, placing my hands across my abdomen. "Why am I in so much pain?"

Lucena cocked her head and crossed her arms over her chest. "When I designed the nanites to make humans immortal, I didn't quite expect there to be so many side effects. The degeneration of organs was certainly one of the most severe, but I should have known the nanites would need to gather resources from somewhere in order to preserve everything else. Another was the sterilization of the female Harvesters."

"So that's why Harvesters can't have babies of their own?"

"Yes. For whatever reason, the nanites destroy the eggs as soon as they enter the bloodstream. I've tried to change their programming to prevent it from happening but nothing seems to work. So, naturally since I was the first woman to undergo the conversion, all of my eggs were immediately destroyed the moment I became a Harvester."

"So you can't have any more children," I said, trying to understand why what she was telling me was an answer to my question.

"Exactly."

"But what does that have to do with me?"

"You provided me with what I needed to ensure we live forever."

I tried to piece together the information she was giving me with what I already knew but nothing added up.

"I still don't understand."

"I took your eggs. Now I have the genetic material I need to produce bodies when we need new organs."

I wrapped my arms around my abdomen as if I could protect what had already been lost.

"You took...my eggs?"

"Every woman is born with a set number of eggs in her body," Lucena said like I was her pupil and she the teacher. "There are somewhere in the neighborhood of 1.5 million of them. So, yes I harvested your eggs. We'll need them eventually, especially now that your mother has so little left to give."

"You keep saying we. Who is we?"

"You and I, of course. Didn't I make that clear?"

I stood to my feet.

"No, you didn't. Why would I need organs unless..." I faltered, unable to finish my train of thought out loud because the answer was too horrible to acknowledge.

"Unless?" Lucena prodded, urging me to voice my own conclusion.

"Unless you intend to make me a Harvester too."

Lucena smiled. "I've waited so long for you to join me, Skye. You can't imagine how desolate an eternity alone can be when you're faced with it."

"But you're not alone," I argued, trying to find a loophole which would free me of my fate. "You have thousands of Harvesters at your beck and call."

"There's nothing like having your own flesh and blood by your side though," Lucena sounded almost wistful. "If I had known about the sterilization side effect, I would have had my own eggs frozen. But, now we have your eggs so we don't have to worry about organs anymore."

She sounded so happy, so pleased with herself like she was doing me a favor.

"I will not become like you," I said, clearly enunciating each word to make sure she heard me. "I will not become a monster."

"You will become what I say you become," her head lifted a notch higher. "I am your mother and your Queen. You will do whatever I want and thank me for it later."

I didn't realize until that very moment just how crazy Lucena Day was. To actually hear her call herself Queen of a wasted world sounded ridiculous. She was completely delusional and completely insane if she thought I would ever thank her for making me a Harvester. I knew then there would be no reasoning with her. You can't have a rational conversation with a crazy person.

"Where are Ash and Zoe?" I asked, deciding to change the linear progression of our conversation with a tangent. Plus, it was something I desperately needed to know in order to formulate an escape plan. Leaving them behind was not an option.

"They're both being taken care of," Lucena said, her eyes shifting away from me suspiciously.

"What does that mean exactly?" With Lucena I knew her definition of 'care' clashed with mine.

Lucena looked back at me and tilted her head towards the doors. "Come with me to my other lab. You can see them for yourself."

Just as we were about to leave, Jace rushed into the room, flushed and out of breath like he had been running for a while. His eyes were drawn to me first and then to my mother still floating inside the glass tube. I knew from the look of regret in his eyes he had hoped to spare me from seeing this particular horror.

"Are you all right?" He asked coming to stand in front of me.

"The pain isn't as bad now," I answered.

"That's not all I meant," he said, his eyes glancing behind me.

"I'll be ok," I reached for one of his hands, finely finding my balance with him by my side.

"I was just about to show Skye our little project," Lucena said to Jace.

"Can't she have some time to rest first?" He implored. "She isn't feeling well."

"No," I said quickly. "I need to know what's going on."

Lucena held her hand out in my direction. "See," she said to Jace. "I told you she was resilient, just like her mother."

Jace tightened his hold on my hand and looked down at me.

"Everything will be all right," his words said even if his eyes said the complete opposite.

I nodded hoping he still had the power to see into my future because I needed to believe in something good at that moment.

Lucena led us down a corridor to a set of steps which led to another level below the basement.

"We built this laboratory when Jace was a toddler," she explained to me. "He was always finding a way out of the other lab."

"I'm sorry I was such a rebellious child, my Queen," Jace said, sounding truly humble and apologetic.

I looked at him silently asking him what he was doing. Why did he sound like an obedient Harvester?

He looked at me with a warning in his eyes and an almost imperceptible shake of his head before returning his attention back to Lucena.

"It's all right, Jace. You came around in the end thanks to my daughter."

"What's that supposed to mean?" I blurted out.

Lucena stopped and turned around to face me. "His love for you has made him quite the loyal soldier for me. He wants to keep you safe, and he knows I'm the best person to make sure you are."

"But that's a lie," I said, placing a hand on my abdomen. "You took away my chance of ever having children. How can you say you've kept me safe?"

"She did *what*?" Jace asked.

"Oh please," Lucena said, rolling her eyes at Jace. "You knew I planned to make Skye a Harvester when I brought her here.

I took her eggs to protect them. If it wasn't for me, the two of you might not ever have children."

Jace's whole body became rigid like he might explode with anger.

"How can I have a child?" I asked, hoping to give Jace enough time to calm down. We needed to stay calm in order to find a way out of Lucena's house of horrors. "You took that choice away from me."

"We'll find you a suitable surrogate," Lucena said off handedly like it was the most obvious solution in the world. "A human can carry ever how many babies you want. Did you honestly think I would deprive my own daughter from the joy of having children of her own?"

I stared at Lucena trying to make sense of the woman in front of me. In her own twisted way, she seemed to think everything she had done was completely logical when it was completely insane.

"But I thought the children were going to be used for their organs?"

Lucena let out a harsh laugh. "Not the ones you want to have with Jace! I'm not that barbaric, Skye. The ones we use solely for their organs will be put into a vegetative state as soon as they're born and grown inside a growth tube like the one your mother is in."

Lucena shook her head like she couldn't believe I thought so little of her. "Come along. We can discuss the details after your conversion. Everyone comes out of it... differently. You might not even want children afterwards."

I looked up at Jace and saw the murderous look on his face. I tightened my hold on his hand forcing him to look down at me. I saw the deadly promise in his eyes and slowly shook my head.

"Someday," I whispered.

"Yes, yes, someday the two of you can have all the babies your little heart's desire," Lucena said, continuing to walk down the corridor without turning around. "It's really not that big of a deal."

I was thankful for Lucena's narcissism. She would never think to believe Jace wanted to kill her for what she had done to me. In her mind, she had bestowed me with a great gift.

The hatred on Jace's face didn't ebb away. I wasn't sure I could hold him back from trying to kill Lucena, and I wasn't completely convinced I wanted to stop him. But, I didn't know what the consequences of her death would be. If I knew Lucena at all, her death would cause unknown repercussions. There had to be a reason she was still alive and able to control the Harvesters so completely. As far as I knew, none of them ever questioned an order she gave. Yet, they all had similar powers. They were her equals in a sense. What hold did she have over them? And if we broke that hold, what would happen?

I needed more information and the only way to do that was to play along with what she wanted.

But right now I needed to get Jace's anger under control before he did something we would later regret.

I stood on the tips of my toes and kissed him. I felt him resist it at first, but he soon melted under my touch. His anger seemed to diffuse as my lips played against his.

"I need you," I whispered against his lips hoping he understood I would need his help to escape Lucena's control. A rash mistake on his part could kill us all.

"My, my, I suppose I really should give the two of you some time to yourselves after such a long separation," Lucena said from the other end of the hallway, watching us.

I knew she would be able to hear us even from that distance with her enhanced hearing. It was one reason I had tried to be cryptic with what I said to Jace.

I took hold of Jace's hand again as we continued to walk down the corridor together to see what other horrors Lucena had waiting for us.

CHAPTER ELEVEN

The corridor of the sub-basement was sterile in appearance and smell. The stench of freshly bleached floors filled the air around us. The walls and ceiling were painted white and a white tiled floor lay beneath our feet. Recessed lights made the hallway blinding with their brightness reflected against all the white.

A series of steel doors with touchpad locks at their center ran along the length of each wall.

"This is where we keep the test subjects," Lucena said indicating the doors as she walked down the hallway in front of us. "We have to keep them locked up until their conversion into Harvesters is complete."

"What are you testing them for?" I asked.

Lucena stopped and turned towards us. "They're the ones Jace has been rounding up for me. They're just like you. They each have certain special abilities."

"That night by the barrier you said you gave Jace the ability to use my DNA coding to give him precognition to find me. Is that how you found the others? Did you use their genetic code?"

Lucena smiled, pleased by my own deduction. "Yes."

"But how could you have the gene sequence of complete strangers?"

"They aren't strangers to me," Lucena cocked her head like she thought I should have figured this part out on my own by now. "I helped bring them into this world. If it wasn't for me, they wouldn't exist anyway. So, if you think about it, their lives have always belonged to me."

Then I understood. "They're all from your fertility clinic?"

"Yes, their parents came to me for help."

"What did you do to us?" I asked. "How did you give us our abilities?"

"I didn't *give* you anything," Lucena replied. "I simply helped you all unlock your potential."

"But how? And why?"

"A long time ago I found a set of inactive genes in the human genome which were unique in each person I tested. I designed a set of nanites which were supposed to activate those genes, but I ended up having to place them inside the egg before fertilization so they could be incorporated directly into the chromosomal DNA during replication. Unfortunately, the nanites didn't activate the genes like I had hoped. At least I didn't think so until I realized the nanites had simply gone dormant for some reason. When I engineered Jace, I was able to design his biorhythms to basically wake the nanites up and do what they were designed to do."

"Is that why my mother told you to stay out of our lives? She found out you used me as one of your test subjects."

"You're mother simply didn't share the same vision for the human race as I did. She couldn't understand I was simply trying to give you every advantage your genetic code allowed for."

"That's why they're all the same age as Skye?" Jace asked Lucena.

"Yes," Lucena answered.

"Did you ever try to use the nanites in adults?"

"The ones I put into you and the others were the first nanites I ever developed. The second batch of nanites, which I hoped would activate the genes in adults, were placed in the immunity shot everyone received a few years later."

"The one that killed all the babies?"

Lucena sighed. "Yes, an unfortunate side effect I hadn't counted on. I'm still not sure what went wrong, but it soon became a moot design flaw after I designed the first Harvester nanites. I still wasn't able to tap into the unique gene coding sequence, but I didn't have to. I gave my Harvesters the powers they needed to survive and become the dominant species."

She walked up to one of the doors and pushed the red button on the touchpad. The door became as transparent as glass, and we were able to see a boy with dark colored skin sitting on the lower level of a bunk bed against the far wall. When he saw us his eyes traveled from Lucena to Jace. He stood from the bed and walked towards the door.

"When are you letting me out of here?" He asked Lucena.

"In time, Jackson. Once you're converted I won't have to worry about you trying to escape."

Jackson looked at Jace. "I trusted you, man," Jackson shook his head. "How can you let her do this to me?"

"I'm sorry," Jace said. "I didn't want to deceive you, but I didn't have any choice." Jace looked down at me.

"You sold me out for some woman?" Jackson asked in disgust.

"It was the only way to make sure she was protected," Jace said.

"Whatever, man," Jackson turned his back to us and went to lie down on the bottom bunk bed. "Could I have my privacy back?"

Lucena pushed the red button and the door looked like steel once again.

"What can he do?" I asked.

"Jackson is able to harness power from any source and use that energy as a weapon. We've only seen him burn a hole in the wall of the lab, but that was enough," Lucena laughed.

"How do you keep him from burning his way through that door?"

"Jackson was the first one Jace brought back to me. Luckily we were able to sedate him to keep him from using his powers, but obviously we couldn't keep him in a medicated coma forever. So, for each person Jace has brought back to me, we've had to modify their cells to meet their particular needs. For instance, Jackson's cell is completely insulated from any type of electrical power. The only power source he could pull from would be himself and that would kill him instantly."

Lucena walked over to the cell across the hall from Jackson's and pushed the red button on the touchpad. This time the transparent door revealed a girl with brown hair pulled back in a ponytail wearing the same white scrubs. She was doing pushups against the bunk bed in her room seeming to not have any difficulty at all with the exercise. When she noticed us looking in at her like a bug in a jar, she stopped and walked over to the door. She was rather homely in the face, but her body seemed to be a mass of muscles.

"What do you want?" She asked gruffly.

"Ava here can make plants grow so we've made sure no plants are within the vicinity of her cell. She actually had the roots of a tree invade her first cell as a means of escape before we caught her," Lucena said, completely ignoring Ava's question.

Lucena pushed the red button and blocked Ava from our sight. She then showed us the person in the cell next to Ava's.

"This is Lawrence."

Lawrence was walking back and forth in his cell only stopping when he noticed us on the other side of the door. He was tall and thin with dirty blonde hair grown out to his shoulders. His nails were bitten down to the quick making some of them bleed onto his white scrubs.

"Is it time?" He asked excitedly.

"Not yet Lawrence." Lucena turned to us. "Lawrence has the ability to walk through objects so his power was probably the hardest to control. But we found having an electrical field surround him keeps him in place."

"I only wish to serve you, my Queen," Lawrence said in a rush before kneeling in front of the door with his head bowed in complete supplication.

"You'll soon be a Harvester, my dear Lawrence. I have what I need now to convert all of you," Lucena said before pushing the red button. "Sweet boy but he can be a little annoying in his undying love for me," Lucena shook her head. "At first I let him roam around the mansion, but he kept interrupting my work so I had to put him into a cell."

"Where are Ash and Zoe?" I asked.

"They're in my lab." Lucena continued to walk down the hallway to another set of opaque glass doors like in the first lab.

When we walked into the laboratory, I saw Ash and Zoe sitting on a bed in a glassed in room to the right. Zoe was softly crying while Ash held her. They were both dressed in only a pair of white scrubs.

"Ash! Zoe!" I yelled running to the glass, pressing the palms of my hands against its cold hardness.

They looked up.

"Skye!" Ash yelled.

They both ran to the glass and placed one of their hands over one of mine.

"Are you all right?" I asked, quickly scanning them for any injuries.

"We're ok," Zoe said, drying the last of her tears with her free hand but the puffiness around her eyes told me she had been crying for quite some time.

I turned to Lucena. "Can you let them out?"

"Ash can come out but Zoe must remain in the room," Lucena said.

"Why?"

"Because I know what she can do. She would shield you all and take you away from me before I could stop her."

"It's ok, Skye," Zoe said. "Let Ash come out. We've been cooped up in this room for a while. I think he's getting tired of me leaving a permanent wet spot on his shirt."

Ash put a comforting arm around Zoe's shoulders.

"You know I don't mind," he told her, before kissing the top of her head.

Zoe laid her cheek against his chest. "I know."

The tender way Ash comforted Zoe seemed almost too intimate for the casual relationship they shared. Apparently they had become closer within the last four days. For some reason, I didn't like it.

Lucena instructed Ash to step into the glass ante-chamber separate from the room Zoe remained in. Once the interior door closed and locked, the outside door opened and Ash was allowed to walk out.

He walked straight to me like we were tethered to one another by an invisible pull string and put his arms around me, resting his cheek against the top of my head. My arms went around his waist automatically. We'd hugged each other a hundred times like this over the years. It came as naturally as breathing.

I heard him inhale deeply.

"God you smell good," he said. "Like flowers in sunshine."

"I just smell better than all the bleach in here," I said, trying to play off the compliment.

"No, you've always smelled like that to me."

"Did she hurt you?" I asked.

"It could have been worse," he shrugged.

Ash hugged me closer.

"We'll get out of this," I promised.

I felt more than heard Jace walk up behind me. Ash reluctantly let me go to meet the man he shared my heart with.

I turned so I could face them both equally.

"Ash, I'd like you to meet Jace. Jace, this is Ash."

Jace held his hand out to Ash.

"Nice to finally meet you," Jace said, sounding genuine in his greeting. "Skye's told me a lot about you."

Ash looked at Jace's hand like he was trying to decide whether or not to shake it.

I almost jabbed Ash in the side to make him accept Jace's offer of friendship, but Ash didn't need my prodding, he did the right thing and shook Jace's hand.

Ash fell to his knees screaming.

"What did you do to him?" I yelled at Jace.

"How is that possible?" Jace asked Lucena, his eyes wide in shock. "He shouldn't be one."

Ash crumpled to the floor bringing his knees up to his chest. Sweat broke out across his brow and his breathing became labored.

"Be one what?" I demanded, kneeling down by Ash not sure if I should try to touch him or not.

"What's happening?" Zoe screamed inside her cell, banging on the glass with her fists.

"Oh for God's sake, you people need to calm down," Lucena said coming to stand over Ash with her arms crossed looking down at my best friend with a sense of expectation surrounding her. "We should all have our answers soon enough."

"What answers?" I asked her. "What did you do to him?"

"Let's watch and see," was her only reply.

Ash finally stopped screaming. He looked at me with wild eyes.

"Skye…"

And then he vanished.

"Hmm," Lucena said in the ensuing silence. "Well, I certainly didn't expect that to happen."

I scrambled to my feet looking around the room. "Where did he go? What happened to him?"

"Your guess is as good as mine," Lucena said completely nonplussed by the situation. She walked over to a tray holding six syringes filled with some sort of clear liquid and picked one up with her thumb ready on the plunger. Then she walked over to me and simply stood like she was waiting for something else to happen.

A few seconds later Ash reappeared. His eyes were filled with more fear than I had ever seen before. Lucena took her opportunity and jabbed the needle of the syringe into his neck plunging the unknown solution into his body. Ash instantly went limp but Jace caught him before he could fall face first to the floor.

"What did you do to him?" I asked, touching Ash's face.

"Just a little experiment," Lucena said with a small shrug. "After all these years, I think I might finally be close to a solution to my problem. If he survives, I might be able to give my Harvesters nanites to activate their unique gene sequences. Can you imagine that: a whole army with advanced super powers?"

"What do you mean 'if he survives'?" I demanded.

Lucena shrugged. "He might or he might not. If he does, he would be the first human to survive the treatment. I haven't had much luck with it though so don't get your hopes up."

"You used me to activate him," Jace said bitterly.

"You're the one who shook hands with him," Lucena countered. "Plus, it was something new I was trying. Instead of placing active nanites into his system, I put in dormant ones to see if it made a difference. If he survives…"

"Quit saying that!" I yelled. "He won't die. I won't let him."

Lucena's eyes narrowed on me. "Oh yes, your healing power. I almost forgot about that."

It was like I could see the gears of Lucena's mind triple in speed. "That might just work. Bring Ash over here," Lucena said to Jace motioning for him to lay Ash on a bed inside a room where it looked like surgeries might be performed considering all the various equipment.

"With the other subjects, their hearts gave out soon after being injected with the nanites. It was like their bodies just couldn't take the added pressure of their new abilities. If you can heal Ash until his body is able to compensate for the added strain, he might have a better chance at survival. But, we'll have to wake him up so his power can fully activate."

"But what if he vanishes again?" I asked.

"Let's hope he comes back before his heart gives out. Otherwise he might just die wherever he goes."

Lucena filled a syringe with a large needle from a small bottle of clear liquid.

"Ready?" She asked me.

I nodded taking hold of one of Ash's arms.

Lucena jabbed the needle into Ash's chest which almost made me lose my hold on him from the brutality of the act.

Ash sat straight up struggling for air.

He looked over at me before the world seemed to peel away from us like paper from a wall revealing a new world underneath. A blinding light flashed before my eyes forcing me to close them. I felt my feet land like I had hopped in the air. When I opened my eyes, I tightened my hold on Ash's arm.

We were standing on the side of a road in the middle of a desert with the sun beating down on us. The blue sky was clear except for a few stray white puffy clouds.

"Where are we?" I asked.

But before Ash could answer he fell to the ground onto his knees.

I put my hands over his heart feeling its frantic beating. I concentrated on him letting my body work its magic to heal whatever the nanites in his system were doing to his heart. Slowly, his heart began to beat at a regular, steady pace.

"I'm all right," Ash said, trying to get to his feet.

"Just sit for a minute," I told him, crossing my legs and sitting down beside him.

"Where are we?" I asked again.

"I'm not sure," he answered.

From up the road we heard the sound of a car coming. For a second I thought it was one of Lucena's vehicles as the sun glinted off the silver symbol on the front grill but then I realized it was a symbol used by an old car company named Toyota. Before we knew it, the car zipped passed us like we weren't even there. The sound of music could be heard coming from the opened windows. Just after it passed us, the brake lights came on. Whoever was driving seemed to realize we were sitting on the side of the road because it backed up until it came to a stop right in front of us.

An auburn haired woman leaned her head out the window to look down at us.

"You two need a ride?"

I gasped. Ash remained completely silent as he stared at the woman.

We both knew who she was.

She was Ash's mother, Grace.

"Cat got your tongues?" She teased us with a nervous smile.

We got to our feet. Ash's father was in the driver's seat and a small boy of two years stared at us with wide blue eyes from the backseat.

"You kids need a ride?" Ash's father asked. He was wearing a blue dress army uniform with a matching hat sitting on the dashboard.

"No sir," Ash finally said. "We're fine."

"You sure, sweetie?" Ash's mother asked. "We don't mind giving the two of you a lift somewhere. It can get pretty hot out here," she said looking pointedly at Ash's bare feet.

"No, ma'am. We have friends coming to pick us up but thank you."

Ash's mother sat back in her seat. "Well, I'll be coming back this way after we drop my husband off at work. If you're still here when I come back I'm gonna have to insist you ride back into town with me."

"Yes, ma'am," Ash replied.

Ash's parents waved goodbye to us. We watched the back of their car travel down the road until it was out of sight.

"Was that real?" I asked. "Or are we in a dream?"

Ash shook his head. "I don't know."

He looked up at the sun shielding his eyes with a hand. "It feels real."

Ash quickly grabbed my hand and I felt the earth slip away again. This time we found ourselves back in the glass room with Zoe.

She scrambled off of the bed when she saw us. "Where have you guys been?"

"How long were we gone?"

"Like an hour."

"Ahh good," I heard Lucena say through the intercom system in the room, but I couldn't see her in the lab through the glass. "You're back. And in one piece I see."

"What happened? Where did you guys go?" Zoe asked.

"We were in a desert," Ash said sounding as confused as I felt. "We saw my parents."

"But I thought they were dead," Zoe said.

"They are," I answered. "But it was like we were seeing them in a dream about the past. They were a lot younger than I remember."

There was a banging on the other side of the glass. I turned to see Jace yelling something, but I couldn't hear what he was saying. Finally, he stopped hitting the glass and yelling to look directly at Ash. His mouth moved and the message was clear, 'get them out'.

Ash grabbed my and Zoe's hands but it was already too late. A shockwave of electricity like that from one of the Harvester stun batons dropped us all to our knees. White gas poured from vents in the ceiling. The last thing I saw was Jace banging his fist against the glass screaming my name.

CHAPTER TWELVE

I heard my father's voice. He sounded angrier than I had ever heard him sound before.

When I opened my eyes, I saw Lucena at her desk staring at the screen of the laptop in front of her. It was exactly like the one my father had with him when we evacuated the Southern Kingdom. I let my eyes wander around the room I found myself in. It was a grand bi-level library with bookshelves built into the walls of the room. Each shelf was packed with leather bound books. Even if I read all day every day, it would take me at least ten years to read all of the books in the room.

"You can't do that to her!" my father yelled.

"Jon, you knew this day was coming. Don't pretend you're a naïve twit like my sister. Why wouldn't I give my daughter the gift of immortality?"

"She's not your daughter, Lucena," my father sounded disgusted. "And you know Emma wouldn't want this for Skye."

"Skye's a child. She's been brain washed by you humans into thinking becoming a Harvester is some sort of punishment when it's the complete opposite! That's why I have to do it. To show her we aren't the monsters you make us out to be. We're simply the next step in evolution. She deserves to be the best, and I intend to make sure she has all of the advantages I can give her."

"Then give her a choice like you gave Emma and me. Let her decide her own fate."

"The best choice has already been made for her," Lucena said dismissively. "I just contacted you in case she wanted to speak with you before the operation."

Lucena looked directly at me like she had known I was awake the entire time.

"Would you like to speak with your father, Skye?"

"Yes," my voice sounded dry. I had to swallow a few times before it felt like I could speak again.

"How long was I unconscious for this time?" I asked.

"A day and a half."

I stood from the leather chair I was sitting in and walked to the backside of the desk. Lucena stood and motioned for me to sit down in her chair.

I stared at the face of my father on the computer screen. His hair was an uncombed mess on top of his head and a short beard hid half of his face. It didn't look like he was taking very good care of himself. His eyes held so many emotions: guilt, worry, love. Looking at how quickly he had deteriorated in such a short amount of time worried me.

"Skye…" he began but became choked with emotion and had to stop to compose himself. He cleared his throat and began again. "Skye, you don't know how sorry I am. I never thought she would take you back so soon."

"You knew she planned to do this to me?" I asked, not able to believe what I was hearing him say.

"I thought I had more time. I was trying to figure out a way to hide you before she had a chance to come and get you."

"But you knew she wanted to make me into a Harvester?"

"Yes."

"And you didn't think that was important enough to warn me about?" My voice got higher the angrier I became.

"Skye, please. I didn't want to worry you unnecessarily. I thought I had time…"

I looked away from my father not wanting my last words with him as a human to be in anger. Even if he had been able to take me somewhere and hide me, it wouldn't have mattered. Lucena would have just forced Jace to find me again. There was nowhere in the world I could hide. She controlled everything.

"Did you know about my mother?" I asked, needing to know if he had played a part in what Lucena was doing to my mother's body. "Did you know she has her here?"

The shock in my father's eyes gave me my answer. "Emma's alive?"

"Her body is," I said. "Lucena's been using her organs when she needs them."

My father's shock was soon replaced with an anger of his own.

"No, I didn't know that. I swear to you if I had known I would have done something to stop it or at least died trying."

"Say your goodbyes," Lucena told me sharply. "We have work to do."

I looked at my father hoping it wouldn't be the last time I saw him and felt an emotional connection to him. Once I was converted into a Harvester, I would probably care about him as much as I would a fly on the wall.

"I love you, Dad," I said, meaning every word. "Don't forget that. No matter what happens after this."

"I love you too, Skye," tears clouded my father's eyes. He held his hand out and I knew he was touching my face on the computer screen in front of him.

The top of the laptop in front of me snapped close. Lucena leaned down to look me in the eyes.

"Now let's go make you who you were always meant to be."

I stood from the chair and followed Lucena out of the library. Before I knew it, we were walking down to the sub-basement floor.

"Can I see my friends first?" I asked. "I would like to say good-bye."

Lucena stopped walking down the hallway and turned to me. "Zoe and Ash aren't here anymore, but I suppose you could speak with Jace."

"What do you mean Zoe and Ash aren't here? Where are they?"

"I sent them somewhere else. After the operation I'll tell you what I have planned for them. It just seems cruel to tell you now. I don't want you upset before the conversion."

"Well too late. I'm already upset!"

"You're too human to think about my experiment with them logically. I'll tell you afterwards. If you still want to, I'll even take you to them personally."

I knew there wasn't any way to force the information out of her. She held all the cards and was playing them like an expert.

"Where's Jace?" I asked.

Lucena walked down the corridor a little further and pressed a red button on one of the steel doors.

"Jace," Lucena said looking inside the cell. "Skye wants to speak with you before her surgery."

I walked up to the cell door and saw Jace walking towards me from the set of bunk beds in the room.

"Why are you in a cell?" I asked.

"Because he was being a complete idiot," Lucena answered for him. "He lost his mind when I told him I planned to convert you the moment you came back with Ash from wherever it was the two of you went."

"I tried to warn you," Jace said pressing the palms of his hands against the glass.

I pressed my hands over his wishing I could feel the warmth of his touch one last time. Would my love for him survive the conversion? Would love even be an emotion I would still be able to feel?

The helplessness I felt was mirrored in Jace's eyes, that more than anything else frightened me. He was the only one in the world who knew the person I would eventually become. If he held no hope for me, how was I supposed to?

"What happens to me? Will you still love me after I become a monster?" I asked, desperately wanting to know this wasn't the end of who I was. I needed to know good would conquer evil and that by some miracle I would remain the same person.

"You're too good of a person to become a monster."

"But what if I do?" I asked, feeling scared and uncertain.

"I will always love you. There is nothing you could ever do to change that. Do you remember when we were at Freddy's house?"

The question caught me off guard. Why would Jace waste the last moments we might have together talking about that night?

"The party?"

"Remember what I told you then," he said to me.

My mind raced back to that night. What was Jace trying to tell me without actually telling me in front of Lucena? I honestly didn't know but hoped I would have time to figure it out.

Before I knew it, Lucena pushed the red button on the touchpad.

"What's so important about what Jace said to you at Freddy's?" Lucena demanded.

I thought back to the night Freddy hosted a party in my honor at his house. It was meant as an opportunity to give the people who had bought spots in the tournament to meet their virgin prize.

"He told me…" I tried to remember but that night was so chaotic I had to really think about what had been said. "He told me we had a lot of good times to look forward to in the future."

Lucena's eyes narrowed on me like she was a walking lie detector. "And that's all? That's all he said?"

I sifted through what I could remember trying to find something in what Jace said to me that night which would help me figure out a way to prevent Lucena from making me a Harvester but nothing else seemed important.

"That's all I can remember," I said truthfully.

Lucena studied me closely for a few seconds more before relaxing.

"Then come on. The surgical team is waiting for you."

When we walked into the laboratory, my eyes were immediately drawn to the surgical room. There were six people in the room dressed in white robes, white masks covered their mouths and white rubber gloves were stretched over their hands.

Only then did true fear creep inside my chest chasing my heart until it raced. This was it. This was the end of who I was. There was no hope for me if I let this happen. I would be doomed to live a half-life for all of eternity by Lucena's side. That picture more than anything else made me swiftly turn on my heels and run back down the corridor. I knew what I was doing was a hopeless act but a small voice inside my head ordered me to try, to not give up so easily.

I didn't even make it half way down the hall before I felt Lucena's hand grab one of my wrists and yank me back to her side.

I knew she had been gentle because my arm was still attached, just throbbing with the suddenness of the action.

"You know there's no point to this," Lucena hissed.

When I looked into her face, I was prepared to see anger but instead I saw disappointment.

"Please don't do this to me," I begged. I wasn't above begging for my life. If there was even a glimmer of humanity left inside Lucena, I needed to find it quickly.

"Please," I begged her. "Please let me stay who I am, and I won't try to run away from you. I'll stay with you until I die but don't make me a Harvester."

"We're not monsters, Skye. You don't realize what you would be giving up."

"I don't care! I just want to stay the way I am."

"But I can't let you. I won't stand by and watch you grow old and die," Lucena's eyes looked haunted with pain. "Not when I have the technology to cheat death and keep you alive forever."

Lucena easily drug me back to the laboratory even though I was kicking and screaming for all I was worth. A woman in white scrubs met us at the door with a syringe in one hand. She plunged the needle in my arm causing me to go limp almost instantly. I was still awake and able to move but it was like I had no motivation to do anything but what I was told. The woman had me lie down on the bed in the room and covered me with a blood red sheet. The back of the bed was lifted at an angle. The woman gave me a series of shots down both my arms.

"What are those for?" I asked, drowsily.

The woman looked over at Lucena who was watching the proceedings through the glass in the main part of the laboratory.

"They're the Harvester nanites," Lucena told me through the intercom system.

I felt someone brush out my hair and thought it odd until I felt her cut a large section of it away. Then there was a buzzing noise like my Dad's old shaver. I felt the metal glide across my scalp as it shaved down the remaining stubble of hair. The prick of needles on the now exposed area was next. Then they placed my head in some sort of restrictive metal vise to immobilize it.

"Now try not to move," a man behind me said. "We'll need to use a small saw to cut a hole in your skull to access the center of the brain. You shouldn't feel any pain but you will feel the vibration of the saw and a little pressure. Do you understand?"

I almost nodded and then remembered I wasn't supposed to move.

"Yes," I said.

The whir of the saw startled me as the surgeon began his work cutting away a section of my skull. I didn't understand why I was still awake. Didn't they usually put you to sleep during a surgery? I tried to think about the people I loved hoping to imprint my feelings for them so permanently I would never be able to forget.

Jace was the first person who made it to the surface of my muddled thoughts. I wanted one more moment with him. Did he know how much I truly cared for him? Would he ever know? I wished he had spent more time talking about his feelings for me than bringing up Freddy, a person I wanted to erase from my mind. But why did Jace bring up that night when he knew we would have so little time together?

I tried again to remember the events of that night when I was shot in the chest and first learned I could heal myself.

Heal myself…

"We're almost through, Skye," the surgeon said to me. "The chip is in place. All we have to do is activate it. I just need you to wiggle your toes for me first."

"No," I whispered through the drugs, my one last act of defiance.

"Nurse," the surgeon said.

With that one word of instruction, one of the nurses went to the end of the table and ran something against the length of my foot. On reflex, my foot arched.

"Good," the surgeon said. "Now it'll just take a few minutes to activate it."

I knew what I had to do before that happened. I had to heal myself. Jace had given me silent instructions of his own. He must have known I could heal the damage somehow. There had to be a way to reverse what was being done to me.

I tried to force my mind to concentrate but the drugs were making it hard to do the simplest of tasks. Only fear of what I would become seemed to be enough to clear away some of the cobwebs slowing my thoughts. I felt a jolt of adrenaline and used that to awaken my power. I didn't want to become a monster. I wanted to stay human.

"My Queen," the surgeon said. "Would you like the honor of activating your daughter's chip?"

"Yes," Lucena said. "I think I would."

No time…. No time… were the only words I could think. But I had to try. I had to save myself.

I concentrated on the damage I knew had been done to my brain and skull. Slowly, my blood began to course through my veins like it always did when my power was activated.

"That's odd," I heard the surgeon say. "Why is the hole in her skull reforming before we've even activated the chip?"

"It's nothing to worry about," Lucena said, coming to stand by me. She looked so proud of me. "Healing is Skye's power. It may make her into the perfect Harvester."

I closed my eyes and kept my mind focused. The chip. That was the next thing which needed to be taken care of. I had to get rid of it. Would my power destroy it like it might a virus or a cancer cell? Could my body recognize it as something foreign which didn't belong? I did everything I could to visualize the chip buried deep inside my brain, trying to instruct my power to destroy it.

"Just press enter," the nurse told Lucena.

Lucena walked away from me. I only had seconds now; seconds to remember who I was; seconds to save myself from becoming a monster; seconds...

"And that's it," the surgeon said triumphantly. "A new Harvester is born."

CHAPTER THIRTEEN

Just as the surgeon said those words, the walls of the room reverberated with the sounds of a large explosion somewhere in the depths of the mansion. I put my hands over my face to shield it as the glass from the inner wall of the surgery exploded inward. The high pitched screech of a siren gave a dire warning. The overhead lights in the room flickered off and on before plunging us into absolute darkness. A series of dim emergency flood lights slowly took their place.

"Get out there and find out what's happened!" The Queen ordered.

The doctor and nurses rushed from the room to do as the Queen asked, instantly transforming them from medical personnel into her own personal strike force team.

Guttural cries of pain and the staccato drum of gun fire could be heard coming from the direction of the corridor outside the laboratory.

I tried to move my legs but they felt as limp as noodles.

The Queen put her arms underneath my back and knees, easily picking me up. I felt too light headed to ask where we were going and to be honest I simply lacked the will to care.

The Queen walked out of the surgery room towards the main glass double doors except there wasn't any glass in the doors now, only empty steel casings. Somewhere in the back of my mind I wondered why the Queen wasn't trying to find an alternate route of escape instead of diving head first into the mayhem. The only logical explanation was there *was* no other way out.

The sounds of fighting and the strong stench of blood mixed with gun powder enticed my curiosity enough to force me to lift my head off the Queen's shoulder and discover for myself what was happening in the hallway.

Smoke and dust floated in the air around us visually blocking off what was happening further down the hallway. Shots were still being fired and a ringing sound like metal hitting stone echoed against the walls. Suddenly, through the chaos of the battle, the figure of a man emerged.

His silhouette was tall, almost six feet. He was slim but his upper torso seemed well built from the swagger of his gait. As he came closer, I saw a sword in one of his hands and a pistol in the other one, both glistened with blood which didn't seem to be his.

He stopped ten feet away from us staring straight at the Queen with a gaze only someone who truly knows you and hates what you are can give.

"Michael," the Queen said knowingly. "I guess I should have expected this treachery from you but quite frankly I didn't think you had the balls."

"Put the girl down," the man ordered.

"Or what? You'll kill me?" the Queen taunted. "We both know you won't do that."

"Put the girl down and I'll let you go unscathed."

"Get out of my way, Michael."

Michael stood his ground, daring the Queen to try and walk past him.

Another figure raced out of the smoke. This one I recognized, Jace. I knew I should feel happy, even relieved to see him, but I felt nothing but mild curiosity on what part he had played in the chaos surrounding us.

Blood splattered the white shirt he wore, but I had a feeling none of it belonged to him.

"Grab the girl," Michael told Jace.

Without any other warning, Michael held out his pistol and shot straight at us three times. The Queen whirled around shielding me from the spray of bullets with her own body. Her grip on me loosened as she slowly crumpled to the ground onto her knees. I felt a pair of strong arms lift me out of the Queen's protective hold.

"I've got you," Jace said to me like the words should be a relief to me.

I looked down at my Queen and saw her kneeling on the cold white tiled floor trying to catch her breath as though she had merely had the wind knocked out of her not been shot three times in the back.

"Take the girl and do what my men tell you to do. They'll lead you out of here safely. You have my word," Michael said to Jace as he grabbed a handful of the Queen's hair, yanking her head back forcing her to look at him.

"Why should I trust you?" Jace asked.

Michael looked from the Queen to Jace. "Because I owe your mother a debt. Now go!"

The Queen began to laugh. "Aren't you going to tell him the whole truth Michael?"

"Shut your mouth." Michael shoved the barrel of his gun between the Queen's lips which only seemed to amuse her.

"What is she talking about? What truth?"

"Get the girl out first and then we can talk," Michael said to Jace. "Her safety is your first priority."

Jace tightened his arms around me and ran back down the hallway. I strained to look over Jace's shoulder to see what Michael was doing to the Queen but the smoke and dust in the hallway soon enveloped us making it impossible to see anything but what lay immediately around us. I wanted to scream and tell Jace to take me back to my Queen but knew it would be useless and a waste of energy. I would have to bide my time until I was stronger. Then I would make Michael pay for the humiliation the Queen was suffering through by his hands. If he killed her, I would make sure his death wasn't an easy one.

As we walked down the hallway, I saw headless corpses of my surgical team lying haphazardly across the floor. The only reason I knew who they were was because of the white surgical robes their bodies still wore. Other corpses were scattered at our feet forcing Jace to walk over them, some were dressed in Harvester uniforms and some wore regular human clothes. We passed a couple of people in the hallway who seemed to be planted there in order to instruct Jace how to escape the sub-basement. Each one told him to keep going. Finally, we reached a short burly man standing by a large hole in the wall of the hallway.

"Go through the tunnel, boy," the man said gruffly, handing me a flashlight with one pudgy hand.

"Where is this going to take us?" Jace asked as I lit the interior of the tunnel to find a hole large enough for us to walk through.

"Does it matter?"

Jace seemed to consider the question for a second before answering, "No, I guess it doesn't."

The floor of the tunnel was uneven and the loose dirt made it hard for Jace to walk down it smoothly. I tried to keep the beam of the flashlight pointed straight ahead a few paces in front of us.

"Were you able to heal yourself before the chip was activated?"

"I tried."

Jace stopped walking. "Skye, look at me."

I did what he asked and saw the worry on his face, but I just didn't see how it was my problem.

"We'll find a way to fix you," Jace promised.

Even in the dim light given off by the flashlight, I could see unshed tears in his eyes and knew he was upset by my transformation. The old me would have wrapped my arms around him and tried to comfort him, but now I felt no need to do such a thing. He was simply showing weakness caused by his human emotions.

I looked away, pointing the flashlight further down the tunnel.

"We should go," I said, not wanting to have to deal with his over exaggerated sense of loss.

I heard Jace sniff and knew the tears he shed for me were born from love, but I honestly just wanted him to get over it and find the end of the tunnel so I could prepare for what lay ahead.

After Jace began to walk again I asked, "Who were those people?

"I don't know. I've never seen them before."

"The man said he knew your mother. I didn't realize she was still alive."

"She isn't. Lucena said she died giving birth to me."

I looked at Jace. "Do you believe that? Do you think she's really dead? I thought Emma Blackwell was dead too but I was wrong."

"I suppose she could still be alive but something in my heart tells me Lucena didn't lie about that. I can't explain it, but I'm certain she's dead."

A faint, natural light marked the end of the tunnel ahead of us. When we stepped into the outside world, a handful of people were waiting for us with their guns drawn and swords hanging by their sides.

A woman with short raven black hair stepped forward holstering her weapon.

"Put your guns away boys. These are the people we were sent to fetch."

The woman turned to us and said, "Follow me."

We walked through a thick thatch of woods until we came to a clearing. The woman signaled us with a clinched fist indicating we should come to a halt.

"Why are we stopping?" Jace asked.

The woman held up her index finger like she was telling Jace to wait for something. In the distance, I could hear the distinctive sound of a helicopter's blades chopping the air. In a matter of seconds, a black hawk helicopter landed in the clearing.

The door in the middle of the helicopter slid open and Michael stepped out frantically waving us forward.

The raven haired woman silently disappeared back into the woods without a word of parting.

Before I knew it, Jace and I were sitting side by side in the helicopter with Michael sitting directly across from us.

After we lifted off the ground, Jace asked, "Where are you taking us?"

"To our base of operations," Michael said.

"Which is where exactly?"

Michael shook his head. "The less you know about where it is the better."

"You don't trust me?"

"No, I don't trust Lucena. If she ever got her hands on you, she would know where we are hiding out and after what I've just done, her finding me isn't something I want to happen just yet."

"Why did you come for us?" Jace asked.

Michael looked at Jace as he contemplated the question.

"Like I said before, I knew your mother. She wouldn't have wanted you working for Lucena. It would have broken her heart."

"So was it me you came for?" Jace asked.

"Mostly," Michael turned his attention to me. "You, little lady, were just icing on the cake. We didn't know you would be there when we first started digging the tunnel." Michael looked back at Jace. "Plus, I knew you wouldn't leave without the girl. I've heard the rumors about the two of you."

"And what do the rumors say?" I asked out of curiosity.

Michael grinned. "Just a little something about shirts being left behind in a hallway."

The old me would have blushed at the reminder of my reunion with Jace but the new me didn't feel anything but a want to finish what Jace and I had started in that hallway. I looked over at Jace and noticed the heightened color of his cheeks. I let my eyes travel down the length of him wondering what it would feel like to have sex with him. A burning need suddenly ignited in the pit of my stomach.

"After we get to the base, I'll tell you anything you want to know but right now I'm so tired I'm not sure how coherent I would be. Rest might not be a bad idea for the two or you either,"

Michael said, leaning back in his seat and crossing his legs at the ankles before closing his eyes. "It'll be a while before we land."

With Michael giving himself an excuse to not provide any more information, Jace turned his attention to me.

"Are you feeling any better?" He asked me.

"I have feeling in my legs now."

"Are you feeling anything else?"

"Yes," I said looking at him without trying to disguise the fact I physically wanted him.

Jace looked confused.

"Maybe we should take Michael's advice and get some rest before we get to where we're going," he said. "You just had your brain cut into. You're body needs some time to recover."

"Sleep isn't what I want," I said, laying a possessive hand against the top of his thigh and slowly inching my way down between his legs.

Jace looked at my hand and back up to me. "What are you doing?"

"What do you think I'm doing?" I asked leaning towards him. "I know you want me too."

Jace shook his head. "Not like this. After we figure out how to deactivate the chip, we can talk about what we both want but having you while you're still a Harvester isn't really having you, not the real you."

"A bit prudish of you isn't it? Considering what almost happened back at the Queen's castle. Or have you forgotten how close we came to having sex then?"

"No," Jace said patiently. "I haven't. But you were you then, not a Harvester. As a Harvester, all you're capable of feeling is lust and anger because they're the most primal human emotions. That's the only reason you're acting this way."

"I bet Ash wouldn't be so holier than though about it. He'd take me to bed without asking any questions."

"I think you're wrong," Jace said confidently. "If he truly does love you, he wouldn't let you give yourself to him the way you are now either."

I sat back in my seat feeling angry at Jace. "You're not the only two men I have to choose from. I'm sure I can find a real man to do the job if I have to."

"No, you won't." Jace's statement was absolute. "I'll kill anyone who tries to lay a hand on you."

"You can't kill every man I invite into my bed. Just because you've taken the moral high ground doesn't mean everyone will. I'm offering myself to you first. It's not my fault you won't accept."

Jace leaned forward. "I won't do it because I love you, Skye. And this," he said raking his eyes over me, "is not you. I told you I won't share your heart with Ash, but I also won't share your body with that chip in your head."

"What if this is all I'll ever be? If you love me so much, why not bed me?"

"Because I want the real you and trust me this isn't it."

"Because you've seen my future?" I scoffed. "Just how do you plan to undo what the Queen has made me into?"

"I'm not sure yet," Jace admitted. "But I know you'll be human again and that person is worth waiting for."

Jace leaned back in his seat and closed his eyes. I watched him and knew he wasn't sleeping. I suppose it was easier for him to shut me out by not having to look at me.

One thing he said was right: lust and anger were primal emotions. Ones I didn't want to stop feeling because not feeling anything was worse. I knew what I wanted now. It was just a matter of finding the right time and using a little persuasion to get it.

CHAPTER FOURTEEN

Eventually, Jace actually did fall asleep. I marveled at how men could simply shut down their thoughts and instantly find succor in the world of dreams. I didn't feel the need for sleep and had to endure an almost two hour flight before the helicopter finally made its descent and landed. Michael woke wiping the sleep from his eyes before sitting up straighter and looking at us.

"We should probably take you over to our doctor first," Michael said to me.

"Why?" I asked, suspicious of his motives.

"We know your blood can cure the Cain virus. He wants to study it."

"Why would you be interested in the cure?" Jace asked, not quite fully trusting our new found benefactor either.

"Because if we can figure out what it is about her blood that acts as a cure, maybe we can design the virus to be immune to it."

"What do you mean 'design the virus'?"

"The group I'm with is responsible for making the Cain virus," Michael revealed. "We just haven't found a good way to mass distribute it yet. But if Lucena can use your blood as a cure, what's the point? We need to find a way to make the virus immune to whatever special properties your blood contains."

"How much about me do you know?" I asked.

"Enough."

"That's not an answer."

"I know it's not *princess*, but we've got things to do first. I'll answer all of your questions in good time." Michael slid the door of the helicopter open effectively cutting off any more of my questions.

When I stepped out of the helicopter, I saw we had landed in what looked like an old military base. Michael walked to an old green Humvee and got into the driver's side waiting for us to follow him.

"We'll go see Wilford first so he can take some samples of your blood, and then I'll show you where you can rest."

"What are you planning to do with us?" Jace asked.

"We can talk about that once you're settled," Michael said before starting the engine and driving away from the tarmac.

A few minutes later we stopped in front of a large five story building. Michael instructed us to follow him inside. Once inside we had to go through two checkpoints before being allowed to enter the elevator. In the elevator, Michael pressed the basement button. When the doors opened, we were instantly inside a laboratory.

It looked nothing like the one the Queen had. Where her walls were white and pristine, this lab was old with cracked, tan painted walls and a grungy looking tiled floor which obviously hadn't seen the head of a mop in ages. There was some scientific equipment on the counters, but it looked old. I was surprised any of it still worked.

"Wilford, she's here," Michael called out.

I heard movement from behind some cardboard boxes in the far corner. A man dressed in a blue and white plaid shirt and baggy blue jeans with red suspenders came out from behind the boxes. He looked to be in his early seventies with balding white hair and a white upside down U-shaped mustache hanging from his upper lip. His wire-rimmed glasses were perched on a bulbous nose and from the brown age spots on his face you could tell he had spent a lot of time out under the sun before the war. His face seemed to be puckered into a permanent scowl.

"Well about damn time," he grumbled. "What took you so long?"

"Stop complaining," Michael told him good naturedly. "It's not like you had to risk your life to bring her here."

Wilford grunted, tucking his thumbs under his red suspenders as he continued to shuffle towards us.

"Well," he said stopping a hairs breadth away from me. "I certainly see a lot of that woman in you, girl."

"Thank you," I said. "The Queen is very beautiful."

Wilford's bushy eyebrows shot up as he turned to Michael. "I thought you said you were getting to her before she got converted."

"We tried," Michael said, "but we were a few minutes too late."

Wilford grunted again and looked back at me. "Not sure your blood's gonna be worth a shit now with all those Harvester nanites running around in it. Guess we'll just have to see."

"So you think my blood is no longer valuable to the Queen?" I asked troubled by the thought, knowing how disappointed she would be in me.

"Don't know yet. Didn't I just say that?" Wilford grumbled.

"Take it easy, Wilford," Michael said. "You know what it's like for Harvesters, especially right after the conversion."

"What do you mean?" Jace asked.

"Newbie Harvesters are all about pleasing the Queen," Wilford said, like it was a bad thing. "It's programmed into that damn awful chip in their heads."

"Can you get the chip out?" Jace asked hopefully.

"Sure," Wilford said, "If you want to kill the girl, I can get it out."

"Wilford…" Michael warned.

"Well it's the truth. What do you want me to do, lie to the boy?"

"No but you're making it sound like there's no hope."

"Well, I doubt she can be turned with the Cain virus especially if her blood still contains the cure."

"Then what can be done?" Jace asked. "There has to be another way."

"I … might have a way," Michael said hesitantly.

"What is it?" Jace and I asked at the same time.

Michael shook his head. "If I told you, it would never work. You'll just have to trust me."

"You throw that word around a lot," Jace said. "But you still haven't given us a good reason why we *should* trust you."

Michael looked at Jace. "You can trust me because I'm your father."

Jace slowly shook his head. "That can't be true. My father was a Harvester."

"I was a Harvester once," Michael said. "The first male one in fact."

"So you're infected with the Cain virus?" I asked.

"No."

"Then how did you regain your humanity?" Jace asked.

"I can't tell you that just yet. There were other factors involved," Michael looked directly at me. "But, I'm hoping we can use the same strategy on Skye. It's the only other way I know to fix her."

"I don't need to be fixed because I'm not broken," I said, feeling an irrational anger build inside me. "There's nothing wrong with me. I'm perfect."

Wilford grunted. "Yeah and you'll be perfectly insane just like that woman if we don't change you back soon."

Jace turned his attention back to Michael. "Is my mother really dead? Or did Lucena lie about that too?"

"No, she told you the truth. Lucena had her harvested right after you were born."

"Why?"

"Because I loved her."

"Why would Lucena care?"

"Because I used to be married to Lucena." Michael crossed his arms as if he were fortifying himself to tell us the rest of the story. "As you might imagine, Lucena wasn't the easiest person to be married to. She was demanding in her work and her personal life. When I met your mother, it was like I could actually breathe again when we were together."

"So you and my mother were having an affair?"

"Honestly, I felt like I was more married to your mother than to Lucena. When Lucena found out about the affair, she converted me into a Harvester before she was able to perfect the chip. I think she thought it would make me into someone who adored only her, but she was wrong. I was still able to feel the love I shared with your mother. I think that's how she became pregnant with you. That's why you're the only child of a Harvester and human. After Lucena found out you existed, she altered the chip to make sure Harvesters could only feel love for her. I don't think she liked the idea of divided loyalties."

"Why did you let her take me?" Jace asked.

"I was told you died in childbirth. I didn't even know you existed until a couple of years ago. I've been trying to get you back ever since."

"Wait a minute," I said. "Jace looks like he's at least twenty-five but Lucena didn't start making Harvesters until two years before the war. How is that possible?"

"Jace is actually only fifteen years old. Lucena used growth stimulants to accelerate his aging."

I looked at Jace realizing I was older than him. The thought seemed odd to say the least.

Wilford gasped. His eyes were opened so wide I thought they would pop out of his skull. Michael drew his gun from the holster at his hip and pointed it at something directly behind me.

"Where the hell did the two of you come from?" Wilford demanded, his face was as white as a sheet.

I turned to find out what had spooked them both and saw Simon and Ian standing directly behind me. Simon was smiling as if pleased with himself and Ian just looked shell shocked.

"Where have you been?" I asked Simon. Rose had visited me once already since our first encounter, but I hadn't seen Simon since he released Zoe from his protective shield.

"I wasn't allowed to come until now," Simon replied, knowing full well I knew my future self was the one controlling when and where Simon and Rose traveled to in the past.

"How the hell did I get here?" Ian asked, taking in his new surroundings.

"I'm sorry," Simon said to Ian. "I couldn't take the risk of anyone seeing me when I took you, or I would have explained myself before bringing you here."

"Can someone tell me what the hell is going on?" Michael said, his gun still pointed in Simon and Ian's direction.

"It's ok," Jace told Michael. "They're friends."

Michael reluctantly holstered his weapon but didn't close the catch on the side in order to keep it easily accessible.

"How the hell did the two of you get here?" Wilford asked.

"I think the more important question is why are we here?" Simon said, deflecting Wilford's question.

"Are you here to help Skye?" The hope in Jace's voice irritated me. Why did everyone think I needed help? Why was Jace so insistent on making me human again?

"No," Simon replied. "I've brought Ian here to help you rescue Ash and Zoe."

"Rescue?" Ian asked. "Rescue them from what?"

"Lucena has them," Jace told Ian. "We don't know where they are."

"Ian can help," Simon said.

"I can?" Ian asked. "How the hell do I know where they are?"

"You have the knowledge to find them," Simon said. "That's all I'm allowed to say."

Simon turned to me and placed a comforting hand on my shoulder. "Have faith in your friends to help you. I'll be back when you need me again." He leaned down to kiss my cheek, but I turned my face so that our lips met instead.

I instantly pulled away. The meeting of our lips wasn't the physical release I had expected. Instead of quenching the lust I felt, it made me feel strangely revolted.

Apparently, Simon felt the same from the way he used the back of his hand to wipe any trace of the kiss from his lips.

"I wish you had warned me about that before I came here," he said before vanishing.

"Ok," Ian said staring at the empty spot where Simon had just been a second ago. "Who the hell was that guy and how did he just disappear?"

"He's from the future," I told Ian. "It's how they travel."

"They? You mean there's more of them?"

"Don't over think it, Ian. It would probably just give you a headache."

"Where were you before he brought you here?" Jace asked.

It was a question I should have thought to ask but simply didn't think about. If I had been my old self, I suppose I would have wanted to know how my father and friends back south were doing. But, the thought didn't even occur to the new me.

"I was in the back-up Southern Kingdom helping Doc Riley set up the new orchard unit there."

"How is everyone? Kirk? Teegan?" Jace asked.

"Not the same since Skye left. People down there are divided into two groups now that the cat's been let out of the proverbial bag about trading humans to Lucena. Some of them want to come over here and kick her ass and others just want to keep handing them over to her to save their own asses."

"And what does my father say?" I asked.

"He's leading the people who think we should fight."

"Hypocritical of him isn't it? He was all for it when it served his purpose."

Ian eyed me up and down. "Since when did you turn into such a hard ass?"

"Lucena converted Skye," Jace said.

Ian's face darkened.

"How the *hell* did you let that happen?" Ian said through clinched teeth. "I thought you would protect her while she was with that monster."

"Do you honestly think I willing let it happen?" Jace's voice rose with each word in anger.

Ian's scowl slowly faded. "No," he answered taking a deep breath. "I don't."

Ian looked at me with new found interest.

"So how are you feeling?" He asked me.

"I don't feel much," I answered.

"Riiigghhtt," Ian scoffed, "that's why you just tried to have a battle of the tongues with future boy before he left."

"Well if you think you're such an expert on how I'm feeling why ask the question?"

"People come out of the conversion process differently. I guess I was hoping you had retained some of who you were."

"I'm better than I was," I said.

Ian shook his head. "Just physically stronger, not better. You're weaker in a lot of ways."

"How so?"

"Being able to care about the people around you makes you stronger than any nanites can. It's why the human race will eventually win this war."

"Didn't take you for such a hypocrite. You chose to be a Harvester once."

"Now I'm a reformed Harvester," Ian reminded me. "Do you remember asking me what it was I missed about being human after I became a Harvester?"

"Yes. You said you didn't know me well enough to answer the question at the time."

"I missed being able to feel what it was like to love people. When I was a Harvester, I didn't give a rat's ass about my family or friends. They could have been strangers to me, and I couldn't have cared about them any less than I did. And because of that, do you know what I have inside of me?" Ian pointed to his chest but didn't wait for my response. "I have my brother's heart beating inside my chest. I stood there and watched them butcher him and harvest his organs for me to use. And you know what I did? Nothing. I didn't care enough to stop them. All I cared about was myself. If anything like that happens to you while you're still a Harvester, I don't know if you'll ever be able to recover from it once we figure out how to make you human again."

"Well the solution to that is simple. Don't make me into a weak human again."

Ian looked at the others in the room. "So any of you know how to help her? I'm assuming we can't use the Cain virus since she's the cure to it."

"I may have a way," Michael said. His relaxed stance seemed to indicate Ian's heartfelt confession made him trust Ian a touch more.

"Good," Ian looked at me. "The sooner we get you back to normal the less regrets you'll have later on."

While Wilford was taking a sample of my blood, Michael, Jace, and Ian went upstairs to speak privately. Even with my advanced hearing, I couldn't hear them which seemed to be the point of their departure.

"You know, ever since Michael found out about that boy he hasn't been able to think about anything but finding him," Wilford told me.

"Why did it take him so long to find out about Jace?"

"Lucena kept him a secret from Michael. It took him a while to figure out where Lucena was keeping the boy. But when he did, he didn't let his people rest until they got him out. Guess God was smiling on us when he sent you there too."

"So you could use me as your own personal lab rat?"

"Were you this ornery before the conversion?" Wilford asked.

"Sometimes. Every little thing seems to be aggravating me now," I admitted reluctantly.

"Hope I like you better when you become human again," Wilford grumbled.

"Ditto."

Wilford chuckled.

"Got what you need?" Michael asked as the trio walked off the elevator.

"Yeah, should be enough to work with. If it's not, I know where to find her while you're gone."

"What's that supposed to mean?" I asked.

"You'll have to stay here while we go get your friends," Michael told me. "Wilford will keep an eye on you."

"It's safer this way Skye," Jace said.

"So you're just going to leave me with Mr. Poke and Prod over here? I thought you were supposed to love me? What if he tries to dissect me while you're gone?"

"Now wait just a damn minute little lady…"

"Wilford, she doesn't know what she's saying," Michael said. "It's just the chip making her this way."

"Well, the sooner we get her human again the better," Wilford grumbled, looking even grumpier than usual.

"You people act like I want to be human again," I said. "Well I have news for you. I don't."

"You do," Jace countered. "You're just not thinking straight right now."

The more they insisted they knew what was best for me the angrier I felt. How dare they tell me what I should want. They couldn't read my mind. I was thinking clearer now than I had ever in my whole entire life! Unburdened by emotions like guilt and love made me realize exactly what a great gift the Queen had bestowed upon me. I no longer had to abide by the rules of right and wrong. I could live by my own set of standards and take what I wanted. I wasn't about to let them change me. I was perfect.

CHAPTER FIFTEEN

The men decided it would be in everyone's best interest to lock me up in a specially designed prison cell while they went off to play hero. They didn't talk about the details of the mission to rescue Ash and Zoe in front of me, but I didn't care. Whether they found them or not wasn't my concern. All I wanted to do was find my way back to the Queen and take my rightful place by her side.

The prison was housed in the basement of a building adjacent to Wilford's lab. It was the proverbial dark and dank dungeon with four prison cells, no windows and a singular thick metal door being the only way in or out of the room.

"The bars and door are made of titanium," Michael told me as he opened my cell. "So don't waste your time trying to escape."

I looked around the room and then at Jace. "Are you really going to let them cage me like an animal?"

"It's for your own safety," he replied, though I could read the guilt on his face like the lines of a book. "Wilford will watch over you while we're away."

"And you trust that quack to protect me?"

"Unlike most of the other men on this compound," Michael said, "Wilford is immune to your charms, such as they are."

Before I could protest further, Michael grabbed my arm and threw me into the cell, shutting the door before I had time to react.

"You'll regret doing this to me," I warned them.

"And you'll regret it if we don't," Ian said. "Just chill your heels in there until we get back. Maybe seeing Zoe and Ash again will help you."

"I don't need any help! Why can't you people get that through your thick human skulls! I want to be sent back to my Queen! I want you people to leave me the hell alone!"

"I love you."

Jace's simple declaration brought me up short, unexpectedly diffusing my wrath. I closed my eyes and turned my back to him. I couldn't look at his face, filled with so much love for a person who didn't exist anymore.

"Skye, I love you."

"Shut up," I said through clenched teeth. "You're wasting your breath and your time. I don't want your love."

"You need it now more than ever," he insisted. "And I know deep down you still love me. That's why you can't look at me right now."

I forced myself to turn around and face him to prove his theory wrong. His eyes were filled with so much hope it made me want to rip his face off.

"I never really loved you," I said with false conviction, knowing the old me had loved him very much. "I just let you believe I did because I felt sorry for you. I always loved Ash not you."

The muscles of Jace's jaw clenched.

I smiled.

"Don't listen to her. She's lying her ass off," Ian said to Jace before looking at me. "Or don't you remember crying like a little baby over Jace in the orchard the other day?"

I felt the muscles of my own jaw tighten.

Ian grinned. "Yeah, don't try to play like you don't know what I'm talking about. I know what it's like to be a Harvester, remember that. And right now you're using everything you can to build a wall against Jace so he doesn't reach the real you. I know the tricks, used them myself a few times."

"I'm sorry," I said to Ian. "Do I look like someone who really wants to hear your woe is me stories? You don't know me. So stop pretending you do."

"I know you, sister. Probably better than you do at the moment."

I crossed my arms over my chest. "Don't you people have somewhere better to be right now? I'd much rather be alone than have to deal with all these heart to heart conversations you insist on having."

"She's right," Michael said. "We need to get going. The sooner we rescue your friends the better. I don't know what Lucena's plans are for them, but I'm sure they won't be pleasant."

Jace looked at me. "No matter what you say or how hard you try to push me away, I won't stop loving you. And just remember, I know your future. You won't always be like this. I know you'll find a way to come back to me."

I turned my back to them and heard them leave, finally granting me some peace and quiet.

The cell was sparse with only a small cot tucked away in the corner with a thin dark blue wool blanket and a small pillow. I lay down on the bed and stared at the ceiling trying to think of ways to escape my solitary confinement.

A few hours later I heard the door to the room open and stood to see who it was. Unfortunately, it was Wilford.

"Come to gloat?" I asked him sitting up on the cot.

Wilford shuffled towards the door to my cell and drew out a key from his pant pocket.

"No, I came to help you escape."

Before I knew it, the door to my cell stood wide open with only Wilford standing in the way of my freedom and the Queen.

"Why are you helping me? Is this some sort of trick?" I asked, sure Wilford was trying to get me to stick my head in a trap.

"I'm helping you because that godforsaken mother of yours will kill my granddaughter if I don't."

"You're granddaughter?"

"Couple of years ago, Lucena grabbed my daughter. She was pregnant at the time and Lucena still has the baby."

"What about your daughter?

"The first time Lucena tried to blackmail me by using them I called her bluff. She killed my daughter and sent me her head in a box. She told me if I ever tried to do it again she'd kill my granddaughter."

"So she knows about this place?"

"Of course she does. What doesn't that woman know about?"

"Then why hasn't she destroyed it?"

"Cause she's got me by the balls, doing what she wants. Didn't I just say that?"

"What does she have you doing for her?"

"She gave me the Cain virus to pass off as something I invented. The damn fools here actually thought I was smart enough to make it."

"Why would she do that?"

"Hell, if I know. Why don't you ask her yourself? She's waiting for you out past the guard post."

I stepped out of the cell filled with a new sense of purpose. "Which way?"

"You're gonna have to do something for me first. I can't keep my cover here if it looks like I let you out without a fight. I already destroyed your blood samples, but you need to hit me a couple of times in the face to make it look good to the others when they get back. Just don't get too carried away. You still need me to show you how to get out of this joint."

My first hit clipped Wilford's jaw. For a moment, I thought I might have broken it, but Wilford was sturdier than he looked. The second hit was square on his nose causing blood to gush out, but it was more for effect than destruction.

Wilford turned out to be extremely helpful guiding me through to the back of the compound where a solitary guard post was stationed. He wobbled up to the two guards and told of my escape ordering them to search for me in the opposite direction I needed to go.

"Make sure your mother knows how much I helped you," Wilford said to me.

"I shouldn't have been captured in the first place if you had been doing your job," I replied tersely. "Why didn't you warn the Queen about Michael's attack?"

"He knows someone has been tipping Lucena off about his missions. He only tells the people he takes with him what's going on and only after they get to where they're going. I didn't find out about it in time to warn her. Now," Wilford pointed to the north through a patch of woods, "head that way. There's a clearing a couple of miles out. She'll be waiting for you there."

I turned and ran towards the woods without a second look back. My heart raced when I realized I would soon be with the Queen again. I could physically feel her presence drawing me closer to her like a piece of metal to a magnet. Within a matter of minutes, I found the clearing and my Queen. She was standing with two guards by a small black helicopter emblazoned on the side with her sliver infinity symbol. The Queen was dressed in a white cashmere coat and seemed to glow like an angel amongst the dingy world around her. She smiled when she saw me, making me feel as though the sun itself was wrapping its warm rays of light against my skin. I ran to her and knelt down on one knee with my head bowed in complete reverence.

With a gentle caress, she cupped my chin in the palm of one hand and raised my head until our eyes met.

"You never have to kneel before me, Skye. You are my daughter. You kneel to no one," she said gently.

I stood and felt humbled by her kind words.

"As you wish, my Queen."

"Call me mother," she said as she caressed the side of my face. "You don't know how long I've waited to have you at my side, Skye. I almost thought I had lost you."

"I will always be by your side, mother. I will never leave you."

My mother held her hand out to me, and I joyfully accepted it.

"Now, first things first," she told me. "I need to get back to one of my experiments. Are you still interested in knowing what I'm doing with Ash and Zoe?"

"Yes, but Michael and Jace are on their way there," I told her.

"Ahh, yes. Wilford mentioned they were trying to rescue them with Ian's help, but I have no idea why they think I would keep them in the old breeding camp Ian used to run for me. Either way it doesn't really matter. They won't find anything there. That camp was destroyed by one of the South's bombs months ago."

"You're sure about that?"

My mother nodded. "Oh yes, quite sure."

"Is there any way Ian could guess where you have them?"

"I don't see how. He wasn't important enough to know about all of my installations. Don't worry they won't be taking you away from me again. They'll have to kill me first, and that's something Michael would never let happen."

As I entered the helicopter and sat by my mother, I tried to find reassurance in her words but was left wondering why Simon would go through all the trouble of bringing Ian to help if what he knew actually wasn't any help at all. It didn't make sense. What was my future self's purpose in sending them on a wild goose chase? What was she up to?

CHAPTER SIXTEEN

As we flew to our destination, something the Queen said made me ask, "Why did you say Michael would never let them kill you?"

My mother cocked her head to the side. "No one's told you? I thought Michael or Jace or even your father would have explained things to you by now."

"No," I said, suddenly realizing the people who supposedly loved me were keeping secrets from me. "Explained what?"

My mother shook her head in disbelief. "I find it interesting you don't know, but it's something you absolutely must know now that you are one of us. No one will kill me because if I die what's left of the world dies with me."

"What do you mean?"

"During the war there was so much radiation in the atmosphere it eventually destroyed what was left of the ozone layer. If it wasn't for me, the world would have died years ago."

"If the ozone layer is gone, what's protecting us?"

"I built a shield which acts as an artificial ozone layer. That's why there are so many clouds in the sky. They're part of the design."

"You built one to cover the whole world?"

"No, there wasn't enough energy to sustain a shield that enormous. I was only able to save the eastern part of what's left of the United States."

For years I wondered what was happening in the rest of the world. It was mildly disconcerting to learn the rest of the world was dead, drifting in ash.

"So we're all that's left?"

"Yes, but don't let it bother you. It was a necessary sacrifice."

"So are you the only one who knows how to operate the shield? Is that why Michael didn't kill you?"

"The shield is on an automated program. It can run itself until the end of time. No one will kill me because if I die, the shield will shut itself down. It's programmed to monitor my brainwave activity through my Harvester chip. Once it detects I'm dead, it will power down and allow nature to take its course, incinerating what's left alive on the surface of this planet."

It was then I knew Jace was a liar. The night before we reached the barrier I asked him to tell me something good about my future. He proceeded to weave a fanciful tale describing a scene where I was chasing two children in a field of wheat with the sun shining down on us. We would never be able to see the sun again unless the Queen was dead. And if she somehow died, we would all perish instantly not be growing wheat under a clear blue sky.

I let what the Queen told me sink in before mild curiosity got the better of me.

"Would you mind telling me now what type of experiment you're performing on Ash and Zoe?"

"It's something I've always wanted to try but just never had the right subjects for until now. I'd rather wait until we get there so you can see for yourself, but I have to say Zoe's accelerated growth has helped tremendously."

"She's still aging?"

"Yes. Didn't Doc Riley tell you that?"

"No, she didn't. I was under the impression once she reached her true age her aging would slow down."

"Thankfully it didn't work out that way. Her aging is still accelerated."

"Then she'll die soon?"

"Not before my experiment is complete, thank goodness. She'll probably live another year, though the added stress I've placed on her system may tip the balance. I have people watching her closely just in case."

I felt a knot of dread form in the pit of my stomach with the thought of Zoe's short life expectancy. Doc Riley was added to the list of liars I'd recently discovered in my life. And why didn't Rose or Simon mention it to me? Why hide such an important piece of information? And most importantly, why did it seem to be upsetting me so much? She wasn't even related to me by blood. We may have pretended to be sisters while we were together but that's all it was, pretend. Still, the thought of the child I helped rescue being doomed to a truncated life unsettled me more than I wanted to admit. I tried to shake off the feeling but it seemed embedded in my psyche.

In less than an hour, I felt the helicopter descend to our final destination. We landed behind a large red brick mansion.

"Where are we?" I asked.

"This is the house Emma and I grew up in."

"She never talked about her family much," I said of the woman who pretended to be my mother. "Why is that?"

"I assume she never mention me to you because she didn't want competition for your loyalty. She probably didn't mention our parents because it was too painful to remember them, much less explain what happened."

"Why would it be painful?"

A shadow passed over my mother's face like she was hiding behind it to mask her true feelings from me.

"They died when we were young. Our father wasted away from cancer and my mother died shortly after him."

"Of what?"

"A broken heart I presume." My mother leaned towards me and gripped my arm tightly making sure I listened to her next words. "That's why emotions are dangerous, Skye. They can drown you in self-pity, making you forget everything else which should be important. They make you weak and pathetic. My mother's weakness orphaned Emma and me. After our mother died we came here to live with our grandmother. She raised us until she died, but by that time I was already well on my way to becoming who I am today. I'm only sorry she didn't live long enough to see the woman I became. She taught me everything there is to know about discipline and respect. If it wasn't for her giving me order in my life, I would have never become Queen."

Before I had a chance to ask any more questions, my mother opened the door of the helicopter and stepped out. I followed her wondering how her life and the world would have been different if my grandmother had been a stronger person.

We walked up the steps of a limestone veranda and entered the house through a set of French doors. A line of ten Harvesters stood at attention on either side of the doors as we entered. One man broke the line and came to stand in front of us.

"We have prepared the visitors for your arrival, my Queen."

"Have you had any more trouble with Ash?"

"No, my Queen. He has not transported since the experiment started. Neither of them seems to be able to access their abilities at the moment."

"How odd," my mother said, like she was making a mental note of the abnormality. "It's just as well. It allows me to observe the experiment without having to worry about keeping their powers inert. Where are they now?"

"They are presently in the sitting room, my Queen."

"And how is Zoe handling the extra strain?"

"Eating an extraordinary amount, even for someone in her condition."

"It's to be expected. Just make sure she gets whatever she needs."

The man bowed and walked back to his spot in line.

My mother turned to me. "Follow me. It's time you understand the importance of what I'm doing."

I trailed behind my mother as she walked me through the home absently noticing the tasteful Victorian design of the furnishings and architecture. It wasn't long before we arrived in a glass sitting room in the west wing of the house. Ash's back was to us as he squatted beside Zoe who seemed to be lying on a chaise lounge chair. When he heard us enter the room, Ash immediately stood and turned toward us unblocking my view of Zoe. My mother continued to walk to the pair while I came to a complete stand still, the sight of Zoe temporarily made me forget how to walk.

Zoe tried to swing her feet to the floor but her protruding stomach seemed to deter her movement. Ash quickly placed one of her arms across his shoulders to help her stand.

"I see you are progressing quite nicely," my mother said, coming to stand in front the people I once naively considered to be part of my family.

"Skye," Zoe said beseeching me with her large blue eyes, "help us."

I stood silently staring at the two before asking, "How is she pregnant?"

My mother turned to me and smiled. "I wanted to see if two people with abilities would in turn produce progeny with abilities."

My eyes were immediately drawn to Ash. "Are you the father?"

"It's not what you think, Skye," Ash said, mistaking my question for some form of jealousy instead of what it really was: curiosity. "Zoe and I never…," he let the words fade knowing I would understand his meaning without him embarrassing us all with the words and mental picture they would form.

"Sex is not the only way to conceive children," my mother said. "Artificial insemination is far more reliable and controllable."

"Skye," Zoe held her hand out to me, desperately needing her best friend's comfort.

I looked from Zoe's forlorn face to Ash's confused one.

"You didn't tell them about me?" I asked my mother.

"No, I didn't want to upset Zoe during the first part of her pregnancy. Would you like to tell them, daughter?"

With the use of the term daughter, I could already tell Ash and Zoe suspected the truth. Zoe's eyes pooled with tears and Ash's stance seemed stiffer.

"I'm a Harvester now," I told them. "I've finally become what I was meant to be."

Zoe let out an anguished cry. My announcement seemed to weaken her knees because she immediately sat back down on the chaise lounge. Ash stood stoically by her side holding her hand as she sobbed uncontrollably. I couldn't draw my eyes away from Zoe for some reason. The sight of her anguish caused a faint tinge of pain inside my chest.

"There's no reason for you to be so upset," I told her. "It's not horrible like everyone says."

"No reason?" she wailed. "She's turned you into what you hate the most!"

"I was wrong," I said. "Harvesters aren't the enemy. They're the next step in evolution. I just didn't see it until I became one."

"How did Jace let this happen?" Ash asked tersely. "I thought he was supposed to protect you!"

"Why are you men so egotistical?" I countered. "You always think a man is supposed to save the day. And don't even start promising me you'll find a way to make me human again. I've had about as much of that type of talk as I can stand. I don't want to be human again."

"You can't mean that, Skye," Zoe whined.

I looked to my mother. "Are we done here? I'd rather not have to deal with this unnecessary drama."

The sooner I got away from Zoe the surer I felt the growing pain in my chest would fade.

"We're almost done." My mother walked to a Bombay chest against the right wall and opened the top drawer. From there she pulled out a pair of white gloves with some sort of silver wires attached to the palms.

"Do we have to do this now?" Ash asked. "Can't you see how upset she is?"

"Do you think I care how upset she is?" My mother countered. "Just lift her shirt so I can see how the children are doing. Or do you want them to die?"

"Let her look, Ash," Zoe said, lying back on the chair and lifting her own shirt to reveal a stretch mark streaked belly.

My mother put the gloves on and placed one hand on Zoe's belly while holding the other hand out in front of her. A holographic image of three babies materialized in the air above her outstretched hand and the distinct rhythmic sounds of a hearts beating filled the room.

After a few minutes of examining the hologram, my mother said, "They seem to be doing quite well considering how quickly they've developed."

"What will you do with them after they're born?" I asked my mother.

"It all depends on whether or not they develop abilities of their own. If they do, I intend to convert them into Harvesters when they come of age."

This news made Zoe begin to cry again.

"Can we leave now?" I asked, trying unsuccessfully to ignore the effect Zoe's anguish was having on me.

My mother stood and placed the ultrasound machine back where she got it. Ash knelt down beside Zoe and pulled her shirt back over her belly while gently rubbing her stomach in a comforting manner.

"I'll be back tomorrow to see how things are progressing," my mother told them as she walked to me.

As I turned to follow my mother out of the room, I unconsciously glanced in Zoe's direction and met her tear filled gaze. She silently mouthed the words 'help us' to me. I stared at her for a moment wondering why her pain was affecting me so much. I didn't allow myself to dwell on it before turning away from her to follow my mother out of the room.

CHAPTER EIGHTEEN

Zoe's soft whimpers seemed determined to haunt me even after I left her. I felt like turning around and slamming my fist in her face to make her shut up. Why I once considered humans stronger than Harvesters was beyond me. Humans were constantly making decisions based solely on overwrought emotions. They weren't able to think clearly enough to separate themselves from a situation and grasp the bigger picture. If Zoe had the clarity of a Harvester, she would understand what a great privilege my mother had bestowed upon her. She would be the first woman to give birth to the next generation of gifted children paving the way for the enhancement of the Harvester race. How could she not see the importance in that?

"When will she have the babies?" I asked my mother.

"Within the next two days is my guess."

"Queen Lucena!"

The older Harvester who greeted us when we first entered my mother's home walked briskly towards us.

"Yes, Walsh? What is it?"

"We have your daughter's residence ready for her inspection."

"Good, fetch the car so you can drive her over there."

"I thought I would be staying with you," I said to my mother, not understanding why she would send me away so soon after our reunion.

"We'll be together for all of eternity," she replied. "I thought you might like to have your own place while we are at this camp since I need to keep an eye on Zoe's progress. Was I wrong in thinking you would rather not be here while Zoe and Ash are?"

"No, you're right. I don't want to be around them," I admitted. "You always seem to know what's best for me before I do."

My mother smiled and cupped the side of my face tenderly. "I'm glad you see that now. All I've ever wanted to do is protect you. Jon and Emma just couldn't understand that."

My mother walked me outside to the front of the house where Walsh pulled up in a little silver sports car.

"Walsh will escort you to your home. Feel free to go wherever you want while you're here. Everyone has been given strict instructions to do anything you ask them to do. If anyone doesn't do what you instruct, tell me. I'll deal with them personally."

The drive between my mother's home and my new residence was rather boring since it was so late at night. There were no people on the streets except for guard patrols. A camp's curfew was strictly upheld. Anyone caught out past seven in the evening and before seven in the morning were immediately harvested, no questions asked, no reprieves given. At least that's what I remembered.

The neighborhoods looked almost normal except there weren't any cars parked in the driveways and all the windows of the houses were barred. That was the beauty, or nightmare if you were a human, of the breeding camps. You were able to act out an almost normal life. The torture came when you realized you were only a puppet doing exactly what your masters wanted. Normality was within your reach but always unobtainable.

"We were only told a few hours ago that you would be coming," Walsh said, the fear in his voice palpable. It made me wonder what the Harvesters had been told about me.

"Are you about to try to make an excuse for something?" I asked dryly.

Walsh cleared his throat. "No ma'am. I just wanted you to know that we would have done more to welcome you if we'd had more time. If you find there's something that you need, all you have to do is ask for it, anything at all."

"How many humans are in this camp?"

"Currently we have ten thousand humans. This is one of the Queen's largest camps. We also have a harvesting and growth facility on site."

"Growth facility?"

"They used to be called the Nursery before the Queen upgraded how we store the humans while they grow."

"Show me."

"Now?"

"Do you have something better to do?"

"No," Walsh stammered. "I'll take you there immediately."

Walsh turned the car around in a vacant driveway and started to drive back the way we came.

"The growth facility is near the river," he said without giving a reason why that fact seemed important enough to say.

Walsh pulled up to a chain link fence surrounding a large compound with several large metal warehouses and smaller buildings within. Guard towers surrounded the structure every twenty feet. Walsh pulled up to the guard house nodding his head to the Harvester standing within. When the guard saw Walsh was the one driving the car, he immediately did something to make the gate open remotely and allow us entry.

Walsh pulled up to the nearest warehouse and parked in front of its double doors. When I stepped out of the car, I heard the distinctive notes of classical music being played. It appeared to be emanating from the warehouse.

"Why is there music playing?" I asked Walsh.

"It's used as a stimulant for the subjects."

"But it's nighttime. Shouldn't they be asleep?"

"It would probably be simpler if you just saw for yourself what the Queen has devised," Walsh said, opening one of the heavy metal doors to allow me entry into the warehouse.

When I walked in, the music was now joined by the rhythmic hum of machinery. A series of oversized metal drums lined either wall of the structure. Each stood twenty feet tall and easily had a diameter just as wide. A few Harvesters in lab coats could be seen with clip boards in their hands studying illuminated panels on each metal cylinder.

In the camp my family stayed in, the Nursery was a form of torture for those who had children taken to it. The children were raised by the Harvesters and given growth hormones to accelerate their maturation. Ash's mother would sometimes sneak close to the one in our camp to catch a glimpse of the children taken from her at birth. When she came back, her eyes would be puffy from crying. Ash never spoke about what his mother did, and I never understood why she would purposely torture herself over something she had no control over. It was just another example of human sentimentality which did nothing but cause them pain.

Although I felt sure I already knew the answer, I had to ask, "Where are the humans?"

Walsh motioned with his hand for me to follow him towards one of the black drums.

"We try to keep from talking too much in the warehouses," he said to me in a low voice, just loud enough for me to hear him over the mechanical hum and music. "Sometimes they can hear you and become agitated."

Walsh led me up a steep ladder on the side of one of the drums to a platform at the top. There was a control panel with various buttons situated in the middle of the platform. After Walsh pushed the keys in a specific sequence, I heard the gentle lap of water as half of the cover on the drum lifted back to a ninety degree angle. Lights flickered within the depths of the cylinder, illuminating for me what the human race had been brought down to.

Within the watery confines were a multitude of bodies hung on racks like pieces of clothing. They were all wrapped in a white latex material with various black tubes attached to different parts of their torsos. Some of the bodies looked like full size adults and some looked only as long as both my hands put together. But all the bodies were missing something.

"Where are their limbs?" I asked.

"To optimize room in the drums we cut the legs and arms off. Then we wrap them in a water- proof latex which stretches as they grow. We use the river water to keep them at just the right incubation temperature."

"What do you do with all the arms and legs you collect?"

"We recycle them like we do the meat that's left over from a harvested body."

I drug my eyes away from the hypnotic sway of the living corpses in the water and looked at Walsh. "Recycle them as what?"

"Food for the humans. They can't seem to tell the difference. As long as they get fresh meat, they don't question where it comes from. Humans tend to see what they want to see."

"Are they conscious in there?" I asked.

"Only in the barest sense of the word. They're aware of things to a very small degree. That's why we keep the music playing day and night. It seems to keep them calm."

I turned my attention back to the bodies wondering if any of them could hear me. For some reason the sight of their mutilated bodies disturbed me, especially the smaller ones. The solution my mother had come up with seemed flawless, but trapping humans in a semi-self-aware state between life and death struck a dissonant cord within me. A small voice in the corner of my mind began to scream that I should do something to help the poor souls trapped in limbo. I turned away from the sight in front of me hoping to quiet the small part of my humanity which seemed determined to reawaken.

"You can take me to my house now," I told Walsh as I made my way back down the stairs.

As we exited the warehouse, a white van was passing through the gate to enter the compound and headed for a building directly across the way from us. Once parked in front of the structure, the driver stepped out and went to the back of the van to open the double doors. The muffled cries of countless babies could be heard coming from the interior of the van. An orderly line of five Harvesters stepped out of the building, each pushing a dolly to the rear of the vehicle. The driver pulled out a series of plastic boxes with air holes and stacked them onto the dollies. Once a dolly was loaded, it was wheeled back inside the building.

Out of the corner of my eye, I caught a glimpse of someone in white standing by the gate in the fence watching me. When I turned my head to get a better look, they were gone. I knew who it was though: Rose. Shaking off the odd sensation of being watched by her, I got back into the car so Walsh could drive me home.

I stared absently out the window on my side of the car as we passed through the darkened neighborhoods until something caught my attention.

"Stop the car," I told Walsh.

He immediately did as I asked without asking any questions.

Standing in front of one of the homes was Simon. But he disappeared before I could open the car door to go talk with him.

"Is everything all right?" Walsh asked, having not seen what I saw.

"Yeah," I said, not understanding why Simon would appear just to vanish into thin air again. "Keep going."

I continued to look out the window and seemed to be haunted by brief glimpses of Rose and Simon. One after the other they would appear and disappear before I could even blink my eyes. What were they doing? Trying to drive me insane? If that was their agenda, they were sorely mistaken in their judgment of my reaction because it was only making me angry. I felt like they were playing with me, taunting me with their power.

Finally, Walsh pulled up in front of a large two story brick home with a gated fence and semi-circle drive way. Walsh walked me up to the front door and escorted me inside. Waiting for me there were two women, both of which were human. One looked to be in her late sixties while the other looked younger, possibly in her early twenties. The older one smelled like a rotting corpse wrapped in moldy paper. The enhancement to my sense of smell from the Harvester nanites accentuated the natural decay her body was experiencing. If the younger one smelled any fresher, it was masked by the old ones corruptible scent.

"This is Grace and Mary Anne," Walsh told me. "They've served your mother for many years. I believe Grace was your great-grandmother's housekeeper at one time. Is that right, Grace?"

"Yes, sir," the older of the two women said meekly.

"And Mary Anne was lucky enough to be chosen out of hundreds of women to be Grace's apprentice. She will be in charge of taking care of the Queen when Grace passes."

"Why would my mother want a human servant?" I asked.

"I've asked her that myself," Walsh admitted. "She says they provide her a bit of nostalgia. Grace was the Queen's primary care giver when she was a child. She knows what the Queen likes and doesn't like and is able to anticipate what she needs before she has to ask for it. So, she wanted Grace to pass down her talents to someone else, and I'm sure Mary Anne will someday pass down what she has learned from Grace to another human and so forth."

It surprised me to learn my mother could be so sentimental of the servant who took care of her as a child. It didn't seem logical to keep such a frail looking woman around. How could she possibly be of any value in her state of decomposition?

"Has the Queen's daughter's surprise arrived?" Walsh asked.

"Yes," Grace said, her eyes cast down like the mention of my surprise bothered her. "They are waiting in the parlor for her."

"What surprise?" I asked.

Walsh gave a tight lipped smile. "The Queen thought you might like some help unwinding after your conversion. Please, follow me and I'll show you what she sent over."

I followed Walsh to the back side of the house. When we got to the parlor, I was met by a line of ten male Harvesters standing in the middle of the room, all of which were naked leaving nothing hidden.

"The Queen thought you might like some company this evening," Walsh said. "She chose these men for you to pick from. If you would like to choose one, he's yours for however long you want him."

I looked down the line of men and saw they were all slightly different in race, hair color, skin tone, and height. It seemed my mother had thought of everything in choosing a playmate for me.

One of them stood out among the others. He was tall with a muscular build and short dark brown hair. His piercing green eyes watched me carefully. I knew exactly why my mother had chosen him. His facial features favored Jace too much to just be coincidental.

"I'll take him," I said. "Third one down."

"Grant stay, the rest of you can go."

The other men turned from me and left the room without a word. Grant kept his eyes locked on me.

"Have him wait for me in my room," I told Walsh. "I would like to take a bath and have something to eat before I go to bed."

"We prepared you your mother's favorite meal," Grace said behind me. "It's waiting in the dining room for you."

I turned to Grace and followed her back out of the room.

"You can go now Walsh, but come back in the morning. I would like to see more of the camp."

Walsh bowed to me.

"I will be back first thing tomorrow," he said before leaving.

Mary Anne was waiting for me in the dining room as Grace and I entered. She stood at the far end of the table where a platter with a silver dome cover awaited me. After I sat down in the chair at the head of the table, Mary Anne lifted the dome revealing three slices of rack of lamb cooked only until the meat was left slightly pink inside. Sitting beside them were glazed potatoes and baby carrots.

"I hope you enjoy it," Grace said, her face beaming with pride. "Your mother used to have that meal twice a week when she was a child."

"It looks delicious," I said. "Would the two of you mind leaving me while I eat?"

All I needed was an old woman who smelled like death hovering around me while I tried to enjoy my meal.

"Of course," said Grace. "We'll go prepare your bath for you. Simply ring the bell by your plate to call us back if you need anything else."

After Grace left, I felt like I could breathe again. I still couldn't understand why my mother would want human servants, especially an old one who was a constant reminder of death.

I let my head dangle over the plate of food to breathe in the succulent fragrances, washing away the stench of decay which seemed to linger in the room even after Grace's departure. I didn't realize I was so hungry until I began to eat. Five minutes later, I was finished with my meal and wanted more. I rang the bell to which Mary Anne appeared almost immediately. After asking her for more food, she brought in the rest of the rack of lamb and what was left of the vegetables she and Grace had prepared. It didn't take me long to finish the meal before I asked to be taken to my bath.

Marry Anne led me to a bathroom on the second floor of the house. The room was made almost entirely out of a copper veined white marble. A circular sunken in porcelain tub filled with warm water and bubbles awaited me. I let Grace and Mary Anne help me disrobe. As Grace was folding up my pants, I heard the sound of something solid hit the floor. When I looked down, I saw it was the stone Jace had given to me. Grace leaned down to pick it up.

"What a pretty rock," Grace said. "It looks like a heart."

"Throw it away," I told her. "I don't need it anymore." Even as the words left my mouth I felt a need to take them back, but I didn't.

"All right," Grace said hesitantly as she slid the rock into a pocket in her apron, presumably to throw it out later.

After sliding into the bath water, I felt the tension of the day slip away from me. The scent of a flower I had not smelled in years assailed my senses.

"Is there hyacinth in the bath water?" I asked.

"Yes," Grace answered. "Your mother has people make her bath oils and soaps from it. It's her favorite flower."

It had been my favorite flower too as a child. Perhaps my mother and I had more in common than I realized.

After my bath, Mary Anne toweled me off and helped me don a white silk robe.

"If you will follow me, I can show you to your room," Grace said.

Grace led me down the hallway and opened the door to a room for me. She kept her gaze conspicuously averted from its interior. I assumed she either didn't want to see Grant's nakedness for a second time that night or think about what we would be doing in the room once she left.

"Mary Anne and I are just down the hall if you need anything," Grace said.

I walked into the room and found Grant sitting in a chair by one of the windows. His eyes were closed like he had fallen asleep waiting for me.

"Wake up," I said, wondering if he would have the stamina I needed to finally get rid of the sexual hunger I tried to make Jace quench for me after my conversion.

Grant didn't move a muscle. I stepped closer to him and pinched him hard on the cheek but his head simply fell to the side.

"He won't wake up for at least a day," I heard a woman say behind me.

I turned towards the voice, ready to fight the intruder. Her face was hidden in the shadows of the closet she was lurking in.

"Who are you?" I asked.

The woman took two steps forward so the dim light from the nightstand by the bed could illuminate her face. I felt my heart begin to pump harder as I faced the one person I hadn't counted on ever meeting.

"I'm you," my future self said to me. "And I'm here to make sure you don't do something we'll regret."

CHAPTER NINETEEN

I looked at my future self and cringed inwardly. She looked to be somewhere in her late forties. She was dressed in black jeans, ankle high boots and a black fitted pea coat.

"You should leave before I kill you," I growled. "You've made my life hell ever since you sent Rose."

Rose appeared out of the darkness directly behind my future self. She placed a hand on the other me's shoulder.

"Don't worry, Rose," my future self said. "She's bluffing."

Rose let her arm drop back to her side. I saw my chance and took it. I leapt over the bed between us, instantly wrapping my hands around the throat of the older me. Before I could react, I saw Rose and future I grasp each other's hands. My room melted away instantly.

Sunlight filtered through the trees like the light of heaven shining through the fingers of God. The sound of birds chirping filled the air and the scent of pine trees assailed my senses bringing back memories of my past long buried. I let go of my future self's throat stumbling away from her and Rose to take in the scene around me.

"Where are we?" I demanded.

Future me was bent over at the waist trying to catch her breath. She held up a hand indicating she needed me to wait a minute before she could answer my question.

Rose placed a gentle hand on future me's back and asked, "Are you ok?"

Future me nodded and stood back to her full height.

"I'm ok. I just forgot how strong she is. I didn't brace myself enough before she jumped me."

"You say that like you expected me to choke you."

Future me let out a harsh laugh. "Of course I did, you idiot. I've already been through all of this once. I know everything that will happen."

Future me put a hand to her throat and rubbed gently where two red hand outlines still marked her.

"Where are we?" I repeated.

"More like when are we," future me said.

"Then *when* are we?" I asked tersely.

"Turn around and see for yourself."

I did as she said and found myself staring at the home I once shared with my father and mother. It was a small yellow clapboard house surrounded by a white painted front porch with a swing and two rocking chairs. Flower boxes hung from the railing overflowing with colorful pansies. I saw a small girl run out the front door with her arms stretched out on either side of her pretending she could fly.

A woman wiping her hands on a kitchen towel appeared in the doorway.

"Don't go near the road," my mother called. "Stay near the house."

"Ok, Mommy," the child me replied, blowing air between her lips mimicking the sound of an airplane.

My mother crossed her arms in front of her and watched me play, all the while smiling.

"Beautiful isn't she?"

I looked beside me and saw my future self's yearning to be a part of the scene before us.

"She isn't our mother," I said. "She never was."

"Why are you so stupid?"

"I'm not stupid. It's the truth."

"It's the truth Lucena wants you to believe. Can't you see she's brainwashed you into thinking she's your real mother?"

"She is our real mother."

Future me growled in frustration. "No she isn't! Just because she gave us half our genes doesn't make her our mother." Future me pointed stringently towards the house. "That is our mother. She's the one who gave birth to us, fed us, took care of us when we were sick, read us bedtime stories and even did her best to make up fairytales when we asked her to. That's what a real mother does. Our mother is not that egotistical, vile woman who destroyed the world so she could rule what was left of it."

"She lied to us."

"She did what she had to do to protect us," future me said. "She was and will always be our mother."

I heard the child me cry out and looked back to the scene from my past. I remembered that day. I was five years old and tripped over my little red wagon while I pretended to fly because I had my eyes closed. I watched as my mother ran from the front porch and down the steps to the little girl crying and holding her knee.

"Let me see," I heard my mother say, forcing the younger me to move my hands away and examine the scrape on my knee. "It's just a scratch, sweetie."

My mother kissed the tears on my cheeks away and picked me up in her arms to carry me back inside the house. I knew what happened after that. She would wash the cut on my knee, apply some Neosporin and secure a band aid over the wound. Then she would take me to my bed and hold me until I stopped crying

I placed a hand on my chest absently massaging away a phantom pain.

"Can we go now?" I asked.

My future self-took hold of my hand and the scene faded away only to be replaced by the laughter of children.

We were standing in a new stretch of woods where a gentle breeze rustled the colorful leaves on the trees surrounding us, hiding us from view. Far in the distance on top of a hill, I could see a small boy and girl, no older than four years old, with blonde hair chasing one another around in a circle.

"When are we now?" I asked, presuming my future self had instructed Rose to take me to particular points in my life. "I don't remember this."

"That's because it's your future and my past," future me replied.

"So the sun does come back," I said, staring past the tree limbs to the patches of blue in the sky. "How does it happen?"

I continued to stare at the sky waiting for an answer. When I didn't receive one, I looked at future me and noticed her eyes were shimmering with unshed tears.

"Sacrifices were made," she said, turning her attention back to the children on the hill.

I had a feeling she wasn't going to elaborate any further.

"Are you going to try to show me what I'll be missing if I decide I don't want your future?" I asked.

"I'm showing you what you have to fight for," future me replied.

"I fight for my Queen."

"Wow, did I really sound that dumb? 'I fight for my Queen'," future me mimicked like it was the most ludicrous thing she had ever heard. "There are better things and people to fight for. And three of them are standing on that hill right now."

"Three?"

I returned my gaze and saw that the children had indeed been joined by someone else: Jace.

Jace was chasing after them playfully threatening he was going to catch them both. The boy was faster than the girl and easily out ran Jace. The girl was soon scooped up into Jace's arms, but she didn't seem to mind. Her giggles filled the air with an innocent joy I hadn't heard in a very long time.

Not to be left out, the boy ran back to Jace lifting his arms up.

"Daddy, pick me up! Pick me up!"

"Daddy's hands look full," another me said to the little boy coming into view from somewhere on the other side of the hill. "But mine are empty."

The other me stretched her arms out to the little boy who jumped into my arms and hugged me around the neck tightly. The other me wrapped her arms around the boy and kissed him lovingly on the cheek. I saw her look into the woods where we stood and smile.

"Those can't be my children," I said feeling an unbridled anger. "I can't have children."

"They are our children. You need to realize there's more to motherhood than just being genetically related. In fact, that has very little to do with it in the long run."

I watched as Jace held the little girl in one arm and placed his other arm around my shoulders as we returned to some place on the other side of the hill.

"Why are you showing me all this? Is it supposed to change me? Are you trying to awaken whatever humanity you think I have left?"

The future me sighed. "No, I know this isn't going to change you back. You'll have to fight for that on your own."

"Then what's the point? Did you just want my company while you took a trip down memory lane?"

"You need to wake up and realize Lucena Day is not your real mother just because she gave you some DNA. Emma Blackwell was our real mother. Thankfully, you won't stay a Harvester for very much longer, but you'll make mistakes between now and then, things which still haunt me to this day. Just remember when you regain your humanity that you weren't entirely responsible for your actions. Try to not be so hard on yourself this time around."

"Everybody wants me to change," I said in disgust. "But what you people don't realize is that I like the way I am. I don't want to change."

"There will come a time soon when you will have to make a choice. I pray to God you make the right one because I can't afford to lose what I have in my present. I won't lose it."

"Can you take me back home now or are you going to force me to watch some other heart felt moment from your past?"

"We'll take you back now. But remember what you've seen today. Remember our real mother and remember you can have a happy future if you'll just let it happen. And for God's sake open up your eyes and really see what's going on around you. She hasn't completely wiped away who you are. I think you know that especially after what you saw tonight."

"I don't know what you're talking about."

"You know exactly what I'm talking about. I know when you saw those bodies stuffed in that can like sardines you felt something. You tried to ignore it but you won't be able to for much longer."

I looked away from my future self and noticed Rose had a melancholy smile on her face.

"And what's your problem?" I asked.

"I just feel sad for what you have to go through," Rose said. "You don't know how much I wanted to warn you about what was coming."

"But you didn't, did you?" I said, the words sounding like an accusation. "You just remained the loyal little bitch to this one."

I felt the sting of future me's hand across my cheek before my mind even registered what was happening. The force of the blow was so hard it knocked me back a step.

"Don't you ever call her that again," my future self growled. "You owe her more than you know. She has done nothing but what I asked her to do for your benefit."

Future me turned to Rose. "It's just the Harvester in her lashing out at you. Don't take it to heart. You know that's not how I feel about you."

"I know," Rose replied, giving me a pitying look. "I just feel sorry for everything you had to go through."

"Don't," future me touched Rose on her arm. "It was all worth it in the end."

"This is all heartwarming and stuff," I said rubbing the sting away from my cheek. "But I would really like to go home now."

The older version of myself looked back at me.

"Just remember what you saw," future me said. "I have faith you'll do the right thing when the time comes."

"Will you be making more of these heartfelt trips to me? Or can I count on this one being the last," I asked her.

"This will be the last time you see me until you look in a mirror one day in the future."

"Are you going to be sending Rose and Simon to bug me anymore?"

"They'll only come when they need to, like they always have."

"Well, they don't need to come anymore. I don't need their help."

"The world will need their help in the end. It's their destiny."

Future me took hold of one of Rose's hand and squeezed it tight in a reassuring manner. Then she held out her other hand for me to take. I grabbed it and soon found myself standing back in my bedroom.

The door to the room was open but Grant was still sitting unconscious in the chair I left him in. Daylight seeped through the curtains marking the beginning of a new day.

"Don't burden yourself with regret about what happens today," my future self told me. "You won't be able to change her fate."

"Whose fate?"

But before I could get an answer, Walsh walked into the room. When he saw Rose and future me, he automatically drew his gun intent on pulling the trigger.

"Mom!" I heard Rose yell as she grabbed future me's shoulder and vanished.

CHAPTER TWENTY

I stood there stunned into silence.

Why had Rose just called me mom?

I heard Walsh say something to me but his words were having a hard time breaking though my temporary stupor. Rose had called future me mom, but why? I thought back to the future scene of the boy and girl playing together realizing the girl had to have been Rose. If Rose was the girl, then the boy had to be Simon.

I had always assumed Rose and Simon were related in some way. Their resemblance to one another could only be genetic. The day Rose visited me in the Southern Kingdom I asked her point blank if Zoe was Simon's mother and she refused to answer me. When my mother revealed her little experiment with Zoe and Ash, I knew then who at least two of the children within her womb were: Rose and Simon. Only the offspring of my friends union could produce children with Zoe's shielding capabilities and Ash's time travel gift.

But why had Zoe called my future self mom and Simon call Jace daddy? How did Zoe and Ash fit, or in this case vanish from, the equation?

"Skye!"

Walsh's voice finally broke through my self-contemplation.

"What?" I asked slightly perturbed by the interruption of my thoughts.

"Did they hurt you? Are you all right?" He asked with true concern.

I felt sure he was only concerned about his own hide if I was hurt. My mother would have his head mounted on a pike if he allowed any harm to come to me.

"I'm fine," I said, tightening the sash of my robe around my waist.

"Who were those people?"

"They're none of your concern. And don't mention any of this to my mother."

"She'll want to know about this."

"What exactly were my mother's orders to you about me?"

"To do whatever you needed and to keep you safe."

"Then I'm ordering you to keep your big mouth shut about what you just saw," I snapped. "I'll tell my mother when I'm ready for her to know."

I could see the uncertainty in Walsh's eyes.

"I don't like keeping secrets from the Queen," he finally said. "But she did order me to do what you wanted so I'll keep quiet."

"Good. Now get rid of Grant. He's completely useless to me now. They drugged him with something, but he should wake up eventually."

Walsh walked over to Grant and lifted him easily over his shoulder.

"Come back in an hour," I told Walsh. "I'll be ready for my tour of the camp then."

"I'll be back," Walsh promised as he walked out of my room with his burden.

I closed the door behind him and leaned my back up against it. The uncertainty of Zoe and Ash's future bothered me. Why would Jace and I become their children's parents? Why didn't they seem to have a place in the future?

I decided to leave the future alone for a while and concentrate on the present. The first thing I needed was another bath. The bottoms of my feet were completely covered in dirt from my time travelling experience. It didn't take me long to find Mary Anne but Grace was nowhere in sight. Mary Anne told me Grace had gone back to serve my mother. After I instructed Mary Anne to prepare me another bath I told her to bring me up some breakfast. For some reason, I seemed to be in a constant state of hunger.

Walsh was punctual in coming back an hour later. I instructed him to drive through the camp until something of interest caught my eye.

It was almost eight o'clock in the morning and the humans were just creeping out of their dwellings to travel to their assigned jobs. Most of them were men since a large majority of the women were made to stay home while they were pregnant.

"What type of work do people do here?" I asked.

"Well, we have the normal operations of food production and general maintenance but this camp also manufactures new Harvester chips and nanites the Queen designs. It's probably one of the most important camps she has. I think that's why she tends to invest so much time here."

"Does she allow many humans to become Harvesters?"

"No, not many," Walsh admitted. "But she holds a contest once a month to choose new Harvesters."

"What type of contest?"

"Two families are chosen at random by the Queen. One member of each family is allowed to fight for the right of them all to become Harvesters."

"What happens to the losing family?"

"Depends on whether or not we need organs at the time. If we do, we take them to the harvesting facility to be culled. If we don't, we place them in a warehouse."

I knew for a human family either alternative meant death.

"What is the contest exactly? A fight to the death?"

"Not usually. The Queen changes it up sometimes but normally it's an obstacle course or a puzzle. Part of it tests who is the smartest and part of it sees who is the strongest. Most of the time the Queen throws in something the contestants usually don't see coming."

"Do you know Freddy?" I asked, remembering all too well what Freddy considered entertainment for Harvesters.

"Yes, I've heard about the tournaments he used to host in Alliance. Your mother is far more inventive than him. Plus Freddy's games were more to relieve boredom for the Harvesters there. I sure would hate to catch the Cain virus. I couldn't imagine living trapped like an animal in a cage."

"What have you been told about the Cain virus?" I asked, remembering Wilford telling me my mother invented it.

"I know those damn people fighting with Michael use it against us when they attack. Whoever they infect with it becomes very contagious. If you come into contact with someone who has it, you get it. That's about as far as my knowledge goes though."

I made a mental note to ask my mother why she would invent such a sickness to ail her own creations and aid her sworn enemies. It didn't make much sense to me, but I knew she would only do it for a good reason.

"Take me to the harvesting facility. I've never been in one before."

Walsh drove to what looked like a large hospital. I remembered the harvesting facility in the camp I lived in with my parents was housed inside an old hospital also. But, I was never allowed to go inside. Emma Blackwell was part of a group of people known as grief counselors who were allowed to go into the harvesting facilities and provide comfort to those who were scheduled to be harvested. Now that my mother had decided to store the humans in warehouses, I doubted such a position was needed anymore. The humans wouldn't have the ability to feel anything much less grief.

As we pulled into what used to be the emergency room entrance, a violent commotion was ensuing between a group of humans and Harvesters. The humans were being stunned into submission, but they still tried to fight the guards anyway. One female Harvester stood near the sliding glass doors to the hospital holding back a distraught girl no older than seven years old. She had blonde hair put up in pigtails and was carrying a little threadbare teddy bear in her hands. The child was crying hysterically with her arms out stretched screaming something I couldn't quite make out inside the car.

I stepped out of the car and then realized she was calling out to her mother.

"Mommy!" the girl screamed at the top of her lungs.

"Please don't take her," a woman begged from the front of the crowd. "She didn't know it was wrong to go out. She was just trying to get her teddy bear."

"The rules are the rules," the Harvester holding the little girl back said. "We can't just let it slide because of her age."

"But she didn't know what she was doing!" The mother screamed.

"What's going on here?" I asked stepping up to the Harvester holding the child.

"The girl was caught out this morning before curfew was over, ma'am," the guard said, suddenly caught off kilter by my presence. "As you probably know, anyone caught out during curfew hours is sentenced to immediate harvesting."

"Yes, I'm aware of the rule," I said, not needing a lowly guard to feel the need to instruct me about camp regulations.

"I'm sorry, Ms. Day. I wasn't sure," the guard stammered, knowing I could have her life if I wanted it.

I looked down at the sobbing little girl and knelt down beside her.

"Why were you outside when you weren't supposed to be?" I asked her.

She looked up at me with her blue eyes shimmering with tears and held up her little teddy bear.

"I had to get Oscar," she whispered.

I ran my hand over the bears head and tweaked one of its ears.

"And where were your parents when you went outside?"

"Sleeping," the little girl replied.

"We didn't know she had gotten out," the mother yelled past the guards holding her back.

I stood and walked over to the woman. Everyone, human and Harvester, stopped fighting as I came to stand among them.

"Do you know who I am?" I asked the mother.

"Yes," the woman answered, swallowing hard. "We were all told you would be coming and to do whatever you wanted."

I looked the woman up and down. Her hair was as blonde as her daughter's and her belly protruded with the growth of another child.

"Your little girl was chosen to become a breeder right?" I asked, knowing a child of her age wouldn't exist in the camp if she hadn't been one of the few lucky ones picked to carry on the line of her parents and be allowed to grow to adulthood.

"Yes, she was chosen."

"And yet you let her break a law which demands she be put to death?"

"We didn't think she knew how to get out of the house," the woman cried.

I looked back at the little girl and motioned for her to come closer to me. The guard holding her back relinquished her grip on the girl's shoulders. The girl immediately ran to the awaiting arms of her mother.

"Oh, Lucy," the mother said as she hugged her daughter. "What were you thinking?"

Lucy held up her bear, "I forgot Oscar all night long. He needed me."

The mother hugged her daughter close before looking back at me.

"Thank you," she said and turned to leave.

"Wait," I said.

The woman turned back around.

"I didn't say there wouldn't be a punishment."

"Oh," the woman's composure faltered, "I'm sorry. I thought you were letting Lucy go."

"I am."

"Then, I don't understand."

"It seems to me you are the one at fault here. You should have kept a closer eye on your daughter if you love her as much as you profess. I'm giving you a choice. You can either hand your daughter back over or choose to take her place."

The humans around me gasped, but the Harvesters nodded in agreement with my decision.

"There is no choice," the woman said, handing her daughter's hand to a man standing beside. "Take me."

"No! Take me," the man holding Lucy begged, presumably her father.

"Let me go, Gavin," the woman said. "You know it won't be long before they come for me anyway. I'm almost too old to have any more babies. You need to stay and raise Lucy. Prepare her for her life as a breeder."

The man sobbed as he hugged his wife. The tears he shed seemed pointless to me. Only the woman was thinking logically. Her time was up. At least she had the nerve to face it with some sort of dignity.

The guards seized the woman dragging her away from her family and towards the hospital entrance.

Lucy began screaming again for her mother but her father picked her up and walked away as quickly as he could, knowing I could have both their lives in a second if I so chose.

"I hate you!" the little girl yelled at me, tears of anguish streaming down her face. "I hate you!"

I felt Walsh come to stand beside me.

"Seemed like a fair trade to me," he said nonchalantly. "Though I think your mother would have just harvested them all."

"We have to prepare for the future," I told him. "She'll make a good breeder one day. She has the strength to make it."

"Would you still like a tour of the facility?"

"No," I said. "I think I would rather go see my mother now. Do you know where she is?"

"Yes, she's still at her residence. She's been keeping a close eye on Zoe's progress. The babies are almost ready to be birthed."

"Take me there."

CHAPTER TWENTY-ONE

After we pulled up to my mother's mansion, I told Walsh he could leave. He seemed relieved by the order. I got the feeling most Harvesters feared my mother more than they adored her. In the grand scheme of things, it really didn't matter which way they felt as long as obeyed her every command and never asked questions.

When I walked into the house, I heard someone singing. I followed the sound to the same room I first saw Ash and Zoe in the night before. Ash was sitting on the chaise lounge with Zoe's head lying in his lap with her eyes closed. Tenderly, Ash combed his fingers through her long curly locks and sang a lullaby I often heard his mother sing to him, but the words were slightly changed:

Hush, little baby, don't say a word,
Papa's going to buy you a mockingbird.
If that mockingbird won't sing
Papa's going to buy you a diamond ring...

"Do you think she'll let us keep the babies if they don't have powers like ours?" Zoe asked while Ash hummed the rest of the tune.

"I don't know," he said, although I knew him well enough to know he was lying. He just didn't want to upset Zoe. "I'm not sure what she'll do."

"Maybe we can get Skye to help us."

"I don't think Skye will. Not unless we can find a way to make her human again."

"What about the Cain virus? Do you think that would change her back?"

"I don't think that will work on her, Zo. She's the cure, remember?"

"Oh yeah," Zoe sighed. "I seem to be forgetting a lot of things lately."

"Your hormones are all out of whack," Ash said. "But don't worry, you're just temporarily senile."

Zoe's eyes flew open and she hit Ash on the arm. Ash just laughed.

"He's right," I said, purposely interrupting their small, intimate moment by making my presence known as I stepped into the room. "Your elevated hormones are affecting your memory. Read about it in a book once."

"Skye!" Zoe tried to lift herself up but Ash made her stay still.

"You know what Lucena said," Ash scolded her gently. "You need to be still or the babies will come before they're ready."

Zoe held out her hand to me beckoning me to come closer.

I stayed as still as a statue.

"I came to see my mother," I said, directing my question to Ash while I tried to ignore the hurt look on Zoe's face. "Do you know where she is?"

"Haven't seen her," Ash answered, his voice distant as he looked at me.

I turned to leave but heard Zoe say, "Skye, please don't go."

I was just about to step away when Ash said, "Don't bother, Zoe. She's not our Skye anymore. All she cares about is herself."

I made an about face and walked a little further into the room.

Ash smirked seeing that his ploy worked. I ignored him and finally let my eyes take in the full extent of Zoe's condition.

"You're huge," I said, finding myself unable to pull my eyes away from Zoe's distended belly. "You're even larger than you were last night. You look like you're about ready to pop."

"That's about how I feel," Zoe smiled at me uncertainly. "Skye, would you help me sit up. I need to go to the bathroom."

"Again?" Ash said. "You just went thirty minutes ago."

"When you have three babies pushing on your bladder you can complain," Zoe replied irritably. "Until that miracle day happens just help me."

Ash pushed Zoe up while I pulled her arms.

"Oww, Skye!" Zoe said. "Don't pull so hard."

"Harvester strength," I replied, feeling like I needed to apologize for some odd reason. I was the one helping her out, not the other way around. I did, however, make an effort to not pull on her arms quite so hard.

"Ring the bell, Ash," Zoe said as I helped her sit in a wheelchair parked at the end of the lounge.

"I can take you," Ash replied, making to get up.

"I am not about to let you help me go to the bathroom," Zoe said with a roll of her eyes. "Just ring the damn bell and get the maids in here to help me."

"Such language," I admonished. "You know I read babies can hear everything you say while they're inside the womb."

Zoe looked alarmed for a second then rubbed her belly soothingly.

"I'm sorry little ones," she crooned. "But daddy makes mommy very mad when he doesn't do what she wants."

Ash chuckled. "Why do you always believe what Skye tells you?"

"Because she always tells me the truth." Zoe looked at me with complete trust. "Right, Skye?"

I felt the ice encapsulating my heart crack ever so slightly with Zoe's desire to be able to trust me like she always had. I was more than just a friend to her. I was her sister and mother all rolled up into one person. When two maids came to wheel her away to the bathroom, I felt relieved I didn't have to give an answer to her question.

"Wait until I come back before you leave," Zoe called over her shoulder to me as she was wheeled out of the room.

She was out of sight before I could make a reply.

"She loves you," Ash said behind me, bringing my attention back to him.

His tousled hair and rumpled clothing told me Ash hadn't slept much in the past few days. A fine growth of hair covered his lower jaw giving him a wild, manly look awakening the only primal need I hadn't been able to satisfy since becoming a Harvester.

"And what about you?" I asked, slowly unbuttoning my coat while walking towards him. "Do you still love me?"

"I'll always love you," Ash said, looking me up and down warily as I approached him. "You know that," he replied with just enough hoarseness to his voice for me to know I was provoking the right response.

I let my coat slip from my shoulders and fall to the floor behind me. I crouched down between Ash's legs and let my hands slowly glide up his thighs.

"What are you doing, Skye?" Ash asked, his breathing faster than before.

"What you've always wanted me to do," I said, rubbing the inside of his thighs in a slow rhythmic motion.

"Why?"

My hands stopped moving. I looked up at him.

"Why not? I know you want me," I said cupping one hand over the proof of his arousal.

"No," he said, pushing my hands away from him. "I don't want you. Not like this. Not here. The Skye I love would never do this."

"What is it with you and Jace?" I said angrily, standing to my full height. "Neither of you seem to be man enough to take what you want even when it's offered to you."

"That's because we both love you and you're not yourself right now."

"No, I'm better."

"No. You're not. You just think you are."

"Whatever, Ash. Maybe you're just a coward. You had me alone for five years and never in all that time did you tell me how you really felt about me. Even when I asked you to kiss me on my sixteenth birthday, you couldn't find the balls to kiss me like a man."

"It wasn't the right time," Ash said, the excuse sounding lame.

"Just like now isn't the right time? Aren't you tired of using that as a cop-out? Maybe I should just tear your heart out with my bare hands and end your cowardly life."

"Then do it Skye because you're tearing my heart to pieces anyway. It's killing me to see what she's made you into."

"She's made me into a god," I hissed. "I'll live forever while you'll just rot away into nothingness."

Ash shook his head. "You know what's sad, Skye? You were more when you were human than you are now. You had people who truly cared about you then. Who really loved you and would risk their lives to protect you."

"I have an army of Harvesters to protect me now. I don't need you. I don't need any of you anymore!"

"Skye," I heard Zoe's small voice say behind me, "you can't mean that..."

I turned to face Zoe sitting in the wheelchair near the entrance of the room looking like the goddess of innocence. I snatched my coat off the floor and stormed up to her. Bracing my hands on each armrest of her chair, I leaned down until my face was just inches from hers. Tears fell from Zoe's eyes as if on cue.

"Listen to me carefully," I told her. "I'll even say it slow so your little human mind can comprehend what I'm about to tell you. I – do- not – need - you. I – do - not – love - you. The sooner you *die* the happier I'll be."

I shoved Zoe's chair away from me causing it fly into the corner a few feet behind her and stormed out of the room.

I rolled my eyes as I heard Zoe begin to cry like there was no tomorrow. How someone could weep so much I had no idea. Tears were a waste of energy over empty sentiment.

"Skye..."

I looked up to the second floor landing and saw my mother standing there having obviously witnessed the altercation. A hint of a smile played across her lips.

"Could you come up here for a moment?" She asked.

In less than 10 seconds I was by her side.

"Come with me," she said, looping an arm around one of mine. "I have something I would like to show you."

We walked to one end of the hallway and entered what appeared to be my mother's study.

"How was your night?" She asked me, motioning for me to take a seat in a brown leather chair in front of her desk.

"It was fine," I told her, not mentioning the time tripping events with my future self. I wasn't sure why I was holding back such vital information but didn't see how telling her would do anything but upset her.

"How did you like my gift? I heard you picked Grant."

"Thank you for thinking of me. He was fine."

"Did Grace and Mary Anne serve you well?"

"Yes," I said hesitantly, something my mother picked right up on.

"What's wrong? You can tell me if they did something you didn't like."

"It's not that they did anything wrong," I admitted. "It's just that I don't understand why you keep Grace around."

"Oh," my mother smiled in understanding, "you mean the smell?"

"Yes. How can you stand it?"

"Grace has been with me since childhood. She was one of the few people I could fully depend on. I guess I've just gotten used to her company."

"Do you love her?"

My mother seemed caught off guard by the question but quickly reclaimed her composure.

"Of course not. She's just a human."

A silence hung in the air between us. I wasn't sure where to take the conversation from there. Thankfully, I didn't have to.

My mother stood from behind her desk and walked to a wall with a framed painting of a group of ballet dancers.

"Come here. I would like to share something with you."

As I walked over, my mother touched the picture. It was instantly transformed into a map. The painting had simply been a hologram. It was similar to the old map Ash and I used during our travels but this one didn't include the west side of the United States. It only showed a small circular section of what was once called America encompassing the east central part of the country.

"Is this what's left of the world?" I asked.

"Yes. It's all I was able to save with the shield."

"Where is the machine that runs the shield?"

My mother looked at me and smiled. "Good question. Its right here," she said pointing to a town in Kentucky. You and I are the only ones who know its location now."

"What about the people who helped you build it?"

"I killed them. I couldn't risk anyone else knowing its whereabouts."

"Who maintains it?"

"I left the two mechanical engineers who designed it there. They make sure things stay working."

"Do you have a backup plan?" I asked. "Machines usually break beyond repair at some point. It won't last forever."

"It'll last long enough. The natural ozone layer is slowly repairing itself, but it will take a few thousand years for it to be complete. The machine should last until that time."

I let my eyes wander around the map noting the blue and red dots marking specific areas. There were also gold points marked but there were only two of them.

"What do the different colored markers mean?" I asked.

"They're all camps. The red camps manufacture energy of some sort like gas or electricity, the blues ones are the food manufacturing sites and the gold ones mark the camps which make Harvester chips and nanites."

Walsh had told me the camp I was in made Harvester chips and nanites. One camp was in Roanoke, Virginia and the other one was in the middle of Geneva, New York. Considering the time it took to fly to the camp, I had to be in the Roanoke camp.

"So you grew up here in Roanoke?"

"Yes. Emma and I came to live with our grandmother when we were ten years old."

"What was she like? Your grandmother."

"Well she didn't like kids," my mother said matter of factly. "She mostly made Grace take care of us. She subscribed to the school of thought that children should be seen and not heard. Emma and I would usually end up in the attic playing so we didn't disturb her."

"Did she just ignore you?"

My mother let out a harsh laugh. "I wish she had. No, our grandmother made sure we learned the meaning of discipline. Every night before we went to bed she would come in and whip us with a willow branch."

"For what?"

"She said children almost always do something wicked every day and wanted to make sure we were properly chastised for it."

"Even if she didn't see you do anything wrong?"

"I didn't mind the whippings that much," my mother said, a far off look on her face like she was mentally reliving the events from her childhood.

"What did she do to you if she actually caught you doing something bad?"

"Put us in the cage."

"What was that?"

"It was a room in the basement not a real cage. Emma and I just called it that. The only way in or out was through a trapdoor. There aren't any windows down there just a twelve by twelve room. She wouldn't let us have a flashlight saying it would make us weak to depend on something so transient."

"How long would she keep you there?"

"Depended on what we did. If it was just talking out of turn, a few hours. One time I broke an expensive vase because Emma and I were playing chase in the house. She kept me down there for a week, only letting Grace bring me food once a day. I tended to get into trouble a lot when I was younger but her discipline made me better, more focused."

"Didn't anyone try to help you?"

"Grace did," my mother's focus returned to me as she let go of the past. "She would sneak down at night after my grandmother went to sleep and talk to me through the trapdoor to keep me company so I wouldn't be so frightened. It was all she could do because my grandmother kept the key to the door on her bracelet."

I understood better why my mother kept Grace around. Deep down she felt a connection with Grace, whether it was gratitude or some undying loyalty I wasn't sure. I couldn't fault her for keeping someone who had helped her when she was defenseless to help herself.

"That helps explain why you care for her so much," I said.

My mother looked at me like she didn't understand why I would come to such a conclusion.

"You care for her because she cared for you when you needed it the most," I tried to explain.

"Caring for a human isn't logical," my mother said, holding her head high.

As if knowing we were talking about her, Grace walked into the room pushing a silver cart through the door with a tea service, a plate of biscuits, butter and jam.

"I thought the two of you might like a snack," Grace said wheeling the cart to my mother's desk.

"Thank you, Grace," my mother walked over to the other woman.

The stench of death hung in the air around Grace, but I tried not to let it bother me. She was, after all, my mother's first loyal servant in what would become a world of them.

Grace smiled, pleased with her foresight in providing what my mother wanted. I suppose it would be hard to replace Grace in my mother's eyes. The woman knew what she needed without having to ask for it. That was a rare talent in a servant.

My mother breathed in the heady aroma of freshly baked biscuits and picked up the butter knife, studying its dull edge.

With one swift motion, my mother twirled the butter knife in her hand and stabbed Grace directly in the heart. The older woman grabbed at the knife but was unable to summon the strength necessary to pull it out of her chest. She fell to her knees with one word slipping from her old cracked lips.

"Why?"

My mother towered over Grace, her expression filled with disgust.

"To prove a point to my daughter. To show her you should cut the people you once cared about out of your life because they can only be a liability in the long run. I don't need you anymore, Grace. I'm not that child who needed you when she was locked in the basement. That person hasn't existed for a very long time."

The pain on Grace's face didn't seem to only be physical. My mother's words appeared to be stopping her heart just as deftly as the dull blade of the butter knife.

I watched the light of Grace's life fade as she closed her eyes. Her breathing slowed and I could hear the beats of her heart go silent.

A glowing gossamer mist floated above Grace's corpse, hovering there as if it were watching us. Then it quickly shot out of the room.

"What was that light?" I asked.

My mother pulled her gaze away from Grace's body to look at me.

"Her soul," she answered.

"I've watched people die before but I've never seen that."

"You weren't a Harvester before either," my mother said. "We see things normal humans can't."

"What will happen to my soul when I die?"

"You're a Harvester and my daughter, Skye. You'll never die so don't worry about it."

"But what if something happens that even you can't control? What will happen to my soul?"

"I don't know," my mother said looking back down at Grace's corpse. "I'm not completely sure we still have one."

CHAPTER TWENTY-TWO

I went to Grace's body and studied the corpse while my mother went to get some servants to clean up the mess. Grace's face looked younger now for some reason. Had the release of her soul unburdened her body? I was just about to walk away from her when a glint of pink caught my eye. I bent at the waist and picked up the pink heart shaped stone peeking out of the pocket of Grace's apron.

I stared at the rock in the palm of my hand wondering what I should do with it. When I heard the door to the study open, I quickly pushed the stone into the back pocket of the jeans I wore deciding to worry about it later.

My mother and a female Harvester walked into the study. The Harvester quickly picked up Grace's body and took her away. We sat down to eat the tea and biscuits like nothing had just happened. To say this seemed odd to me would be an understatement. The unexpectedness of my mother's action and the realization that humans had souls you could actually see when they departed the host body still had me reeling.

As a child, my parents took me to church on special occasions such as Easter and Christmas. They weren't devout Christians but they did believe in a God and tried to pass on those teachings and values to me. When we were inside the breeding camp, it was forbidden to talk about a higher power because we weren't supposed to believe in a deity. We were supposed to only worship our Queen. Anyone caught trying to keep the practices of the old way alive were immediately harvested. Some welcomed death as a way to show how strong their faith was and bare witness that they would not forsake their God. I once looked up to those people but now realized just how ridiculous it was to have faith in a being you couldn't see when you had one of flesh and blood standing right in front of you. The Queen could in fact grant you immortal life as long as you spent that life worshiping her which brought up a question I needed to ask.

"Wilford told me you designed the Cain virus," I said. "Is that true?"

"Yes," my mother informed me, setting her cup of tea in its saucer on her desk.

"But why? Why would you design something to take away a Harvester's immortality?"

"Simple math really," my mother said with a small shrug of her shoulders. "There are too many Harvesters and too few humans to meet the demand for organs. As long as the Harvesters believe the resistance is the one who developed the Cain virus, they have no reason to suspect me and their hatred of the resistance is strengthened."

"That's why you let Michael and his group live? So suspicion stays directed towards them?"

"Exactly. As long as they exist, anyone who happens to be infected blames them not me. And if a Harvester gets out of line, it's simple enough to have them infected by sending word to Wilford who in turn directs Michael on who he should infect next."

"So the resistance is actually working for you, they just don't know it."

My mother smiled. "Brilliant wouldn't you say?"

"I wouldn't expect anything less from you."

There was a knock on the study door.

"Come in," my mother instructed.

Instead of opening the door and walking in the room like a normal person, the intruder of my private time with my mother simply walked through it while it was still closed.

"Lawrence," my mother said in a slightly annoyed tone. "What is it this time?"

I remembered Lawrence. His ability, of course, was being able to walk through walls and who knew what else. I could only attribute my mother's sudden irritation to his appearance as meaning he was still bugging her. She had said as much when she introduced me to him back at the castle. His undying love and loyalty got on her nerves. I could only imagine that loyalty had increased a hundred fold if he had undergone the conversion into a true Harvester.

I hadn't thought about the other people like me who had powers until now. Apparently Lawrence either wasn't released from his cell or had no desire to escape when Michael and his crew launched their rescue mission. It made me wonder where Jackson, the boy who could harness the power around him, and Ava, the girl who could make plants grow, were now.

"My Queen," Lawrence said, bowing at the waist, "I was asked to inform you of a problem."

Lawrence's beady little eyes shifted in my direction. A half smile played across his lips like he was pleased to see me.

"What problem Lawrence?" My mother said irritably, sitting back in her chair. "I can't read your mind."

"I'm sorry, my Queen," he said humbly. "There is an uprising among the humans in the northern quadrant."

"What are they upset about this time?" My mother asked, seeming bored by the topic already. Apparently this wasn't the first time she had encountered such an occurrence.

"There was an incident at the harvesting facility this morning," Lawrence looked at me briefly before returning his gaze to my mother. "Your daughter could probably give you a more detailed account than I can. I was told she was there."

"What happened Skye?"

I related the story about the little girl caught out during curfew hours and the choice I gave to her mother.

"I don't see anything wrong with what you did," my mother told me. "In fact, you were more lenient than I would have been. Next time, let them both be harvested to teach the other parents a lesson."

"I'm sorry," I said, feeling as though I had let her down in some way.

"As it is, there isn't any reason for the humans to be so ungrateful," my mother stood from her chair. "I'll need to take care of this," she told me. "The humans can spread discontent like wildfire if it isn't put out immediately. You should stay here where it's safe, Skye. This shouldn't take too long."

"I'd rather go with you," I said standing from my chair. "I should learn how to deal with situations like this so you don't have to do it all the time."

My mother seemed to consider my words then nodded.

"All right, you can join me. But if things get out of hand and I tell you to come back here, you do what I say. Understand?"

"Yes. I'll do whatever you tell me."

"Then let's go and remind the humans how fragile their lives are."

As we made our way to the foyer, I could see Walsh waiting for us by the front door.

"So how many humans are misbehaving?" My mother asked him.

"A couple of hundred. They are demanding that the mother of the little girl be released from the Harvester facility."

"They're demanding?" My mother asked almost amused. "Well now, let's go teach them a lesson, shall we?"

Five Harvester SUVs and the Queen's limousine were waiting for us at the front of the house. Walsh rode in the back of the limo with me and my mother. Lawrence was relegated to ride in one of the SUVs with the regular guards.

"So, is Lawrence a Harvester now?" I asked.

My mother sighed. "Honestly, I thought it might shut him up, but it only seemed to make him worse. I love undying loyalty from my subjects, but he takes it to the extreme."

"Then why don't you just kill him?" I asked.

My mother looked surprised by my suggestion then smiled. "I'll take it under consideration. But, I would hate to lose someone with his abilities. I find it interesting."

"How does he do it?" I asked. "How can he walk through things?"

"At a microscopic level, everything has small spaces between their molecules. Lawrence is able to temporarily disassemble his body at a molecular level and squeeze through those spaces in objects."

"What happened to the other two people you had at the castle, Jackson and Ava?"

"They're here with me. Apparently Michael was only concerned about rescuing you and Jace. At least that's what Wilford told me."

"Wilford told me you have his granddaughter," I said. "That's the reason he still helps you."

"Poor deluded fool. I don't know why he trusts what I say."

"So you don't have her?"

"She was placed in the warehouse years ago, but he still thinks I would keep my word to him and protect her as long as he does what I ask."

"Have you spoken to him lately? Has he said anything about what was happening over there?"

"If you're asking whether or not the wild goose chase Jace and the others went on to find Ash and Zoe was over, no they hadn't returned to Michael's camp yet. But, I'm sure they're back by now. Is there anything you want to know? I'm sure I'll be in touch with Wilford again this evening."

"No," I said halfheartedly, even though Jace's face seemed determined to haunt me. "I don't need to know anything."

"Do you want me to bring Jace to you?" My mother asked, knowing full well what, or in this case who, I wanted. "I could have him here by tonight if that would make you happy."

The temptation to accept my mother's offer almost overwhelmed me. I felt a physical need to have Jace by my side again but knew it might not be the best thing for me at the moment. If he found out what my mother was doing with Ash and Zoe, he would feel honor bound to rescue them. His hero complex would kick in, and I might end up having to kill him.

"No. I don't want him here yet," I said. "I'm still getting used to being a Harvester. I think having him here would just upset me more than anything."

"Probably a wise decision," my mother said. "Humans always feel entitled to act on their emotions, most of the time without thinking things through."

As we approached the demonstration, I saw a line of Harvester guards pushing the humans back from the Queen's convoy. Lawrence had said there were only a couple of hundred demonstrators but from what I could see the crowd must have quadrupled in size since that time.

We stepped out of the car and walked up to the steps leading to the entrance of the harvesting facility. Behind me I could her jeers and cries of outrage clearly, but one voice stood out among the others. When my mother and I reached the head of the stairs, I looked out into the crowd and found the owner of that voice.

The little girl whose life I saved that morning was staring straight at me screaming at the top of her lungs about how much she hated me and how she wished I was dead. She kept eye contact with me until I finally broke it off, unable to meet her gaze any longer for some reason. Deep within my subconscious the part of my mind which still held the last shred of my humanity wept over the child's loss. I firmly shut the door on my weakness, choosing to ignore its cries of despair.

As the Queen calmly surveyed the crowd of discontented humans, she slowly lifted her right hand and snapped her fingers. The guards who had escorted us to the facility quickly dispersed into the crowd grabbing people at random and bringing them back through to stand in front of me and my mother at the base of the steps. The Harvesters used their stun batons to force their chosen humans to their knees. The noise of the crowd lessened as they warily watched to see what fate my mother had in store for those in front of her.

"Do any of you honestly think this little demonstration will change anything?" My mother asked.

"We just want Eliza back," a man said from the front of the crowd. I instantly recognized him as Gavin, the woman's husband. "She didn't do anything wrong!"

"Are you her husband?" My mother asked.

The man nodded. "Yes. Please show pity on her, Queen Lucena. She's been a good breeder for you. She doesn't deserve to be harvested yet."

"From what I understand, your wife chose to be harvested in order to save your daughter's life."

"She had no choice," the man said bitterly, pointing straight at me accusingly. "Your daughter knew Eliza would rather die than see her own flesh and blood butchered."

"Then what's the problem?" My mother asked. "Your daughter broke the rules. By all rights, she should be dead now. Yet, my daughter showed leniency in giving your wife a choice which is a lot more than I would have done if I had been there. As it is, your little demonstration has just cost the lives of these people in front of me."

Screams of 'no' and outrage could be heard coming from the crowd while whimpers of hopelessness came from the twenty people on their knees in front of us.

"Take them," my mother instructed in a low voice but loud enough for the Harvesters to hear.

The twenty sacrifices were drug up the stairs and into the hospital within a matter of seconds.

"You'll burn in hell for this!" Gavin screamed. "You're both going to hell!"

My mother smiled.

"Would you like to be next?" she asked the man. "Perhaps we should just make this a family affair and be done with it."

My mother turned to Walsh and seemed to give him a silent command with just her eyes. Walsh walked over to the man and grabbed both him and his daughter, dragging them forward to stand directly in front of us.

"Please," the man begged, "leave my daughter alone. This was all my fault not hers."

"I know it was," my mother said looking him up and down in disgust. "And now you've made your wife's sacrifice for nothing. Take them in."

The crowd grew silent as the man and his daughter were drug into the harvesting facility crying for mercy. My mother's gaze returned to the crowd.

"If any of you would like to join them, please stay where you are and my Harvesters will gladly escort you inside as well."

It was like someone had thrown a bomb into the crowd. Within a matter of seconds the demonstrators scattered, none of them having the conviction to stand up for what they had whole heartedly believed in only moments before.

"And that's how you handle humans," my mother said, satisfaction in her voice. "Threatening their mortality and playing on their fear of death lets you win every single time."

My mother decided to stay at the harvesting facility to make sure there were no more disturbances.

"Skye, I need you to go back to my house and keep an eye on Zoe for me," she said. "She should have her babies at any moment. If she goes into labor before I get back, tell Walsh and he'll get in touch with me immediately. It won't take me long to get back to the house."

"If that's what you want, I'll do it," I said.

"I know it's hard to be around them because they remind you of your old life. And as soon as the babies are born, I'll move them somewhere else so you never have to see them again. But you know how important these babies might be."

"Yes, I know. I'll be fine."

And then my mother did something completely unexpected. She leaned in towards me and kissed my cheek. The look in her eyes as she pulled away confused me. It was almost as if she let the mask she presented to the world fall for a split second, showing me the love she felt for me.

She turned away from me quickly before I had any more time to contemplate her odd behavior. I knew she cared for me. That was obvious the first time I met her. But could the Queen of the Eastern Kingdom truly love someone? How was that even possible after being a Harvester for all these years?

As Walsh and I drove back to my mother's home, I contemplated my own feelings. Was my mother's momentary lapse proof that Harvesters were doomed to retain a portion of their humanity? Would I always be forced to fight against my true nature, that small voice within who yearned to be released and allowed to feel again?

I didn't know any of the answers to my own questions, and I had a feeling even if I asked my mother to provide them for me she wouldn't be able to. Either that or she would lie and say her humanity died the moment she became a Harvester. I felt sure there wouldn't be a simple answer either way.

After we returned to the house, I asked Walsh, "Is there a way I can keep an eye on Ash and Zoe without actually having to be in the same room as them? I don't think I could stand that."

"Yes, your mother has been observing them from her study. I can show you how to activate the holographic surveillance system in there."

Once we were back in my mother's study, Walsh showed me the control panel inlaid in her desk. With a few quick codes, a holographic image of the sitting room Ash and Zoe were still in came to life in front of me. It was remarkably detailed with only a hint of transparency. If I didn't know better I would have thought I had been transported to the room below me as a silent observer.

They were playing a game of checkers which seemed to bore Walsh to tears. He quickly made an excuse about needing to see to something else in the house. I sat in my mother's chair and watched the two play for a while before becoming bored myself. After a while I stood and tried to find something on the book shelf to while away the time.

"Ash," the image of Zoe said behind me as I browsed my mother's selection of classical novels. "Would you do something for me?"

"Sure, squirt. What do you need?"

There was a long pause, and I began to wonder if Zoe was going to answer.

"Would you...kiss me?"

My attention was immediately drawn back to the hologram.

Ash looked shocked and Zoe looked extremely embarrassed. Zoe raised her hands to her eyes covering them in shame.

"I know. I know. It's a stupid thing to ask," she admitted.

"No, it's not stupid," Ash said clearing his throat in an attempt to hide his own discomfort. "But why do you want me to?"

"It's just that..." Zoe let her hands fall back into her lap as she seemed to search for the right words to better explain her request.

"It's just that it seems really weird that I'm having your babies and we've never even kissed. I mean look at me," she said with her arms stretched wide. "I'm as big as a house, about to have three babies, and I haven't even kissed a boy for goodness sake."

Ash grinned. "Do you really want me to be your first kiss? Wouldn't you rather share something like that with a boy you love?"

"That's just it," Zoe said, an earnest yearning transcribed on her face. "I've had a crush on you since we met. I just couldn't tell you because when you met me I looked like a child. But I'm not a little girl, Ash. I'm a woman. A woman who wants to be kissed by someone she loves."

"Oh," Ash's voice faltered, suddenly failing to know what to say.

Zoe looked despondent. "I'm sorry. I shouldn't have said anything. Now I've embarrassed you."

Ash stood from his chair and went to kneel by Zoe. He placed a comforting hand on her back.

"You didn't embarrass me," he told her. "I'm actually flattered, Zoe."

Zoe lifted her head and looked down Ash.

"I know you love Skye," she said. "And I'm not asking you to fall madly, deeply in love with me. I just want to know what it feels like to kiss someone."

"I don't think that's asking too much," Ash said, full of understanding. "Do you think you can stand up?"

Zoe eagerly nodded.

Ash stood back up and helped Zoe to her feet. I walked closer to the holograms watching them carefully; scrutinizing every look exchanged and nervous twitch of their lips. The scene looked vaguely familiar and then I remembered why. Ash was my first kiss. Now he would be Zoe's too.

Ash cupped Zoe's face with both hands and slowly brought his lips into contact with hers. The kiss was slow at first, gentle and tender like Ash was afraid he might break Zoe if he pressed her lips too hard. Zoe wrapped her arms around Ash's neck and deepened the kiss letting him know she was anything but breakable.

I slowly walked around the two virtual figures instantly feeling my blood begin to boil. This was nothing like the first kiss I experienced with Ash; a kiss which haunted me for two long years. That kiss was filled with awkwardness and an unyielding posture on Ash's part. I always thought it was because Ash wasn't attracted to me in a romantic way until he professed to have always been in love with me just recently. And here he was kissing another girl like there was no tomorrow. Meeting each passionate moan from her with one of his own.

I stormed over to my mother's desk determined to shut the hologram off when I felt the floor beneath my feet tremble.

Ash and Zoe pulled away from each with an audible smack as their lips separated.

"Did you just feel the earth move?" Zoe asked out of breath.

Before Ash could answer, the hologram dissolved, the lights went out and the floor beneath my feet heaved before giving way. The last thing I remembered was falling through the air and hitting my head against something hard enough to knock a Harvester unconscious.

CHAPTER TWENTY-THREE

Two angry voices surrounded me. I couldn't make out what they were saying at first because of the ringing in my ears but their words slowly filtered through.

"We should cut her damn head off!" I heard one man say.

"And have the Queen hunting you down like a dog?" Another man's voice replied in agitation. "Do you really think she'll let you live very long if you kill her daughter? No, we get what we came for and leave. That's the smart move."

"Who gives a shit about being smart? I want that bitch to know what it feels like to lose someone she cares about."

I heard the movement of rubble around me but couldn't seem to open my eyes or move my body. The injuries I sustained in the fall seemed to have not healed sufficiently to make me mobile. I felt someone grab me roughly by the hair and bend my neck back at an awkward angle. The sharp, cold edge of a blade was pressed squarely against my throat.

"I hope you rot in hell," I heard the man say just as he made the first slice through my skin.

"Get away from her!"

My head was suddenly released as something or someone slammed against my assailant. I heard the popping sound of flesh meeting bone and the scuffle of feet. Grunts of pain and heavy breathing told me the fighting was ferocious. Finally, I was able to pry my eyes open enough to see what was happening around me.

Ash was slamming his fist into the face of the man I had to presume tried to slit my throat just seconds before. The man finally lifted his hands palm forward in surrender before dragging himself as quickly as he could in the opposite direction of Ash The other man quickly ran after his friend not wanting to attract Ash's wrath upon himself.

Ash spun around to face me. His lower lip was cracked and bleeding but other than that I couldn't see any other injuries. With quick strides over the rubble of brick and wood around me, Ash was by my side in a matter of seconds cradling my head in his hands.

"Skye, are you all right? Can you get up?" He asked worriedly.

"I need a minute to heal," I whispered, willing my body to heal itself with my innate power faster than the Harvester nanites could.

Ash laid my head back down gently and stood to survey what remained of the mansion my mother grew up in.

"What the hell happened?" He said more to himself than me.

When he looked back down at me, he said, "I need to get back to Zoe. She's trapped under a beam over there." He pointed to some point behind me. "I can't move it by myself. I'm going to need your help."

Before I could ask him why he thought I would help, Ash strode off to wherever Zoe was. While my body healed itself, I had time to ponder Ash's question. What the hell *had* happened? As I looked at the devastation around me, I had to assume some sort of bomb had been set off in the house. But who would have the audacity to do such a thing to the Queen's residence?

In only a matter of minutes, I felt completely healed of the wounds I sustained in the explosion. I sat up and looked behind me to find Ash crouched near a large section of the roof. I got to my feet and walked over to him. Even though I was under no obligation to help them, I felt compelled to rescue Zoe. I knew my mother wanted the children Zoe carried and reasoned with myself that was reason enough to help extricate her from the rubble.

"Here comes Skye," I heard Ash say in a reassuring tone to Zoe as I approached them.

Both of Zoe's legs were pinned beneath the beam. Tears born of pain streamed from the corners of her eyes marking telltale trails of her distress through the caked on dust covering her face.

Ash stood to his feet.

"It's too heavy for me to lift," he confessed, not ashamed, just stating a fact.

I couldn't stop staring at Zoe's face for some reason. Her anguish reminded me of the first time I ever saw her cry. Back then, her pain stemmed from the full weight of realizing she had lost her entire family years before. The sorrow filling her eyes now pulled me in, making my heart ache uncomfortably.

"Move," I told Ash, "or you'll just be in my way."

In no time at all, I had the section of roof trapping Zoe moved to the side releasing her from its weighty hold.

I knelt down beside her legs and forced myself to meet her eyes.

"Can you move them?" I asked.

"No." Zoe's voice quavered, fighting against the pain she felt to answer me.

Ash sat down by Zoe gently wiping away her tears.

For a split second, I debated with myself about the pros and cons of healing her legs but there really wasn't any other choice, not if I wanted to make her mobile. I placed my hands on her thighs and felt the heat of my healing power take over. The process of healing was becoming like second nature to me now. I no longer had to struggle to concentrate on what needed to be done. It was like the nanites which helped me tap into my ability were on an accelerated learning curve now that they had been awakened. I only had to think about what needed to be done and they helped me accomplish the task.

In less than a minute, Zoe's legs were healed and her cries stopped.

"Thank you, Skye," she breathed, finding relief from her physical pain.

"There's the bitch!" I heard from a great distance. My eyes were drawn to a crowd down the street. I saw the man Ash had beat up leading a pack of at least twenty humans. "Let's kill her!"

I bent down and lifted Zoe easily into my arms, cradling her like I would a child. Suddenly, I felt the front of my shirt become drenched with water. Zoe's whole body began to tremble.

I looked at her and saw the same worry I felt mirrored in her eyes.

"Did your water just break?" I asked low enough so Ash couldn't hear. All I needed was for him to devolve into an expectant father with a lynch mob on our trail.

Zoe bit her bottom lip and nodded.

"Where are you taking her?" Ash asked warily.

"Honestly, I have no idea," I said crisply, "but unless you want to fight that crowd of humans heading this way, I suggest you follow me."

Not wanting to make us an easy target, I headed for the woods behind what was left of my mother's house. A few Harvesters were nursing their own wounds as we passed, and I ordered them to take care of the approaching humans.

"Should we kill them," one Harvester asked.

"Only if you have to," I answered, "but try to incapacitate them first. I don't think the Queen would want to waste so many breeders unnecessarily."

I was vaguely aware of how much my logic sounded like the Queen's. The thought didn't settle well, especially with Zoe staring at me so intently. Just from her expression, I knew she was hoping to see the old me return to her. Just a glimpse of who I was would be all she needed to feel safe in a place where safety was an illusion.

In no time at all, we were in the shelter of the forest hidden from prying eyes.

"So where are we going?" Ash asked behind me.

"Anywhere that seems safe," I told him.

The irony of the role reversal between Ash and me wasn't lost on me. In the old days, I asked him the exact same question hundreds of times as we traveled through the Eastern Kingdom. Back then he was the decision maker; the one who kept track of where the breeding camps were as well as the hot zones so we didn't run into them. I depended on him to keep me safe in a world where such a word shouldn't even exist anymore. Now, he was depending on me to keep him and Zoe out of harm's way when I wasn't even sure that was my goal.

After twenty minutes of walking, we came to a narrow river. There was a boat house and a medium sized fishing boat tied off at the dock in front of it.

"We need to stop here," I told Ash. "See if you can find something soft for Zoe to lie on."

Without question, Ash did as instructed. There wasn't a lot in the boat house except for some life preservers, sail cloth and rope. Ash laid the preservers down then piled the sail cloth on top of them to construct a make shift bed.

After I lay Zoe down, Ash saw that my shirt was soaked. His eyes grew wide.

"Take that bucket over there in the corner and get some water out of the river," I told him. "See if the boat has a galley so you can boil it first. Search around for any towels or cloth while you're in there too and bring it all back here."

Ash's eyes seemed glued to my shirt. I snapped my finger in front of his eyes forcing him to focus on my face.

"Did you hear what I just told you?" I asked in exasperation.

"No," he admitted. "Sorry."

I repeated my instructions setting him into action.

After he left I looked down at Zoe in the dim light of day filtering through the windows. She had her eyes closed and was slowly breathing in and out. How had the little girl I rescued from Simon's shield come to this? She was a child having children of her own. Was this her destiny? To be the mother of Rose and Simon? Future me said Rose and Simon were destined to save the world. Should I even let them live? Since what was left of the world belonged to the Queen, then that made them her enemies, right?

"Are you in pain?" I asked Zoe, feeling confused about what I should do.

Zoe looked up at me like I had completely lost my mind.

"I'm about to give birth to three babies," she grimaced. "What do you think?"

I found myself almost smiling at Zoe's show of spunk.

"I think you're in a great deal of pain," I answered. "Why aren't you screaming?"

She grimaced as a contraction hit her. When it passed, her face relaxed.

"I'm trying not to scream. I don't want to worry Ash."

"You really do love him, don't you?"

Zoe's eyes widened in shock.

"I saw the two of you kissing before the bomb went off," I explained. "I heard your little confession to him. But, I'm wondering why you never mentioned it to me."

"I know how you feel about him," Zoe said, trying to control her breathing. "I never would have told him if I thought you actually loved him."

"Ash has been a part of my life for eleven years. You've known him for less than a month."

"You only knew Jace for a few days before you told him you loved him," she reminded me. "Or was that a lie?"

"No," I admitted. "It wasn't a lie when I said it."

"Then stop badgering me about Ash and help me have these babies."

Zoe finally let out a blood curdling scream. It was like an alarm went off because Ash came barging through the door of the boathouse just as I knelt down between Zoe's legs to check the progress of the birth.

I could see the head of the first baby crowning as Zoe pushed for all she was worth. Ash sat behind her back helping to prop her torso at an angle and letting her squeeze both his hands as she continued to push. After a few pushes, I had the first baby in my hands. It was a screaming baby boy. I laid him down on the sail cloth quickly because the second baby was following right behind. The second baby was a girl and just as vocal as her brother. Both had tufts of blonde hair crowning their heads. When I looked back expecting to see the third baby's head, I saw the baby's bottom instead.

"Something doesn't feel right," Zoe moaned.

"Keep pushing," I told her. "You're almost done."

She shook her head vehemently. "No! Something's wrong!"

I looked up at Zoe's face and met her eyes. "The baby's in a breech position," I explained. "But it'll come out if you just push."

"No! You're lying to me. You just want the babies to take to the Queen! You don't care about them."

"Either way, you have to push or you might kill the baby," I tried to explain to her. "In this position, it's possible it won't break any bones but the longer you talk about it the most likely outcome is it'll suffocate to death or get choked by the umbilical cord. Now if you want this baby to have a chance at living you need to push now!"

With one final cry, Zoe pushed for all she was worth, spilling out the baby and the afterbirth. The umbilical cord was wrapped around the little girl's neck. I quickly tore it away from her throat to allow her to take her first breath of the world. If that had been the only problem, I would have felt relief. But the true horror of the situation must have been written on my face.

"What's wrong?" I heard Zoe scream at me. "What's wrong with my baby?"

I stared in disbelief finding it hard to find the right words to explain what I was seeing. With a shaky hand, I gently traced the edges of the baby's exposed heart, feeling its life force thump gently against the tips of my fingers. I felt hypnotized by its rhythmic pumping of blood.

Before I knew it, Ash was beside me staring helplessly at his child.

"Can you heal her?" He asked me, the hope for a miracle in his voice.

I looked up at him feeling uncertain but finally answered, "No. I can't heal this. She needs a doctor."

"Heal what?" Zoe asked. "What's wrong with her?"

I explained the deformity to Zoe which made her dissolve into a new set of tears.

Ash's eyes slid from the baby to look at me. "You know Lucena will never fix her. Why should she waste the time when she has two healthy babies to run her experiments on?"

I knew Ash was right. The baby was deformed and expendable. The Queen would have it destroyed before spending time and resources to save its life. She had two perfect babies who would prove her hypothesis about hybrids to be true. Each would inherit their parents' powers. I already knew that for a fact. But, the small frail creature in front of me would never be given a chance at a normal life. She wasn't worth the effort.

I watched as Ash reached out to trace the side of his little girl's cheek, needing to bring the small life some comfort from the world she had been born in. Just as his skin was about to touch hers, he vanished.

I stared at the empty space and found myself shaking my head.

I met Zoe's eyes and saw she was leaned up on her elbows looking at the void Ash had left behind.

With a heavy sigh and a new set of tears, she cried, "Seriously?"

CHAPTER TWENTY-FOUR

I found the river water Ash boiled still sitting on the small gas stove on the boat. A pile of mismatched towels was sitting on the galley table also. I picked it all up and brought it back to the boathouse. After cleaning the babies off and wrapping them in towels, I laid them beside Zoe so she could watch them sleep while I cleaned her up and healed the tear in her flesh caused by the babies' births.

"They're so small," Zoe said, staring at her children. "I'm not sure what to name them."

I looked up at Zoe with a frown.

"You know what to name them," I told her. "Simon and Rose."

I could literally see the light bulb go off above Zoe's head.

"Oh my God," she said, eyes wide. "I should have realized that."

When Zoe looked back at the babies, she seemed wary of them.

"They're still yours," I said to her. "They need you now."

"I know," she said, her voice sounding little. "But what about the other girl?"

I pulled the hem of Zoe's gown down and started to wash the blood from my hands in what was left of the river water.

"I don't think she's going to make it," I said bluntly, seeing no need to pander to Zoe's human emotions. "She doesn't seem to exist in the future."

As if knowing we were talking about them, both Simon and Rose began to cry. Zoe's motherhood gene seemed to kick in as she sat up and picked one of them up. She exposed one of her breast and coaxed the baby to begin suckling at the nipple.

"Oww," Zoe said as the babe began to draw milk from her body.

I sat there and watched them for a minute wondering what it felt like to hold your own child in your arms and feed it with food your body made naturally in order to ensure your progenics survival. I knew I would never get the chance to experience the closeness between a mother and her child and felt a small part of myself fade away.

After a few minutes, Zoe lay one baby down and picked up the other who hadn't stopped crying to be fed while its sibling ate its fill. The third baby remained still. I got up to check to see if it was even still alive. Content in its makeshift white towel wrap, the baby was quietly making quick observations of its surroundings. How much it could actually see probably wasn't much. I remembered reading in a book once that babies could only see 8 or so inches in front of them clearly. I bent down and picked the baby up being careful to not touch its exposed heart. As soon as she was cradled in my arm, the baby's eyes locked on my face. A hint of a smile curved her tiny lips as she continued to watch me.

"I want to name her Hope," Zoe said.

"What do you think about that?" I asked the baby. As if in response it closed its eyes and promptly went to sleep in my arms.

After a while, I laid Hope back down beside her brother and sister.

I heard a splash of water and looked behind me to find Ash. He had reappeared with one foot firmly stuck in the bucket containing the bloody river water.

"Where have you been?" Zoe asked not trying to hide her frustration with him. "We were worried sick. How could you leave when we have three babies to take care of?"

"It wasn't by choice," Ash replied, not seeming to take Zoe's anger to heart.

"Where did you go?" I asked.

"You mean when?" Ash said pulling his now drenched foot out of the bucket. "I went back to my first day of kindergarten. My Mom was dropping me off and trying to give me pointers on how to make friends."

"Did you happen to bring anything back?" I asked.

"No," Ash looked confused. "Should I have?"

"Bringing back some supplies for your kids would have been a smart thing to do," I said crossing my arms.

"Well I'm sorry, your highness," Ash said with a mocking bow. "I don't exactly have this time travelling thing down yet. Next time I'll try to make sure I materialize near a Wal-Mart."

And with those parting words, Ash disappeared again.

"Hope he remembers to go to Wal-Mart," I said dryly.

I heard Zoe bust out laughing. I looked over at her and couldn't prevent myself from smiling a little. Even in the face of everything she had been through that day, she could still find a way to laugh. Human behavior was odd and unexplainable sometimes.

After she stopped laughing, Zoe wiped the tears from her eyes and looked up at me.

"Skye, I'm hungry," she said simply.

"What do you want me to do?" I asked. "Go catch a fish in the river with my bare hands?"

Zoe giggled. "No. But it's probably safer for you to go find food than it is for me to try and find it. You're like a god now right? Nothing can hurt you."

Nothing but having my head chopped off by a bunch of angry humans, I thought to myself.

"All right. You stay put and try to keep the babies quiet while I'm gone. I'm not sure what's going on out there right now, but if the human's blew up the Queen's house, there's no telling what else they've done."

Zoe cocked her head and looked at me like I had suddenly grown horns on the top of my head.

"What's wrong?" I asked.

"You called Lucena the Queen not your mother. It's the first time you've done that since I've seen you."

"Slip of the tongue," I said with a shrug. "She's both."

"No," Zoe said a light a hope in her eyes. "No, you're starting to think about her differently."

"No, I'm not."

263

"Yes, you are."

"No, I'm not."

"Yes…"

"Stop!" I said, becoming frustrated. "We're not five years old, Zoe. I said it was a mistake. Leave it at that."

Zoe shrugged. "You can say what you want, and I'll think what I want."

I growled in annoyance. "Why are you so stubborn?"

"I'm only stubborn if I know I'm right," she said before pointing her index finger at me. "And you know I'm right. You just don't want to admit it to yourself yet."

I held my hands up, fingers splayed to act as a wall against Zoe's righteousness.

"Think what you want," I said turning towards the door. "I'll be back when I can."

I locked and closed the door to the boathouse behind me telling Zoe not to open it for anyone but me.

I started to walk back through the woods the way we came but decided to veer off to the right in hopes of finding a house with some food in it. I was vaguely aware I was avoiding the sensible thing to do which would be to go back to the Queen's home. The Queen was probably there by now, but I wasn't certain yet what I planned to do about Zoe and her babies. This brought a question to mind. Why did I care what happened to them? I should be running to the Queen and proudly handing over her triumph in genetic manipulation, but I wasn't. I was holding them secret from her which didn't seem right, but it didn't seem wrong either. I knew I couldn't keep them hidden forever, and that I would have to make a decision one way or the other soon.

As I reached the edge of the wooded area, I heard the unmistakable sounds of gun fire. The sky was made even cloudier with smoke from what had to be a multitude of burning buildings. Considering the breadth of the human uprising, I could only assume it had been planned for months if not years in advance. The events at the hospital seemed to have spurred the rioters into action. Perhaps they no longer cared about what the Queen might do because they knew she could have them killed and/or harvested at any moment of her choosing. That was the beauty and fault of her power. She could in fact kill anyone she wanted with the tiniest twitch of her finger, but by doing that she instilled in humans a hatred so deep it was able to overcome their natural instinct to survive and simply thirst for revenge.

I walked out into a small, quiet cul-de-sac. Only one of the homes was set on fire leaving the others to fend off the flames of their neighbor or eventually succumb to the blaze over time. I hoped the people living in the homes were either joined in the fighting or had left for their own safety. One small yellow house, which reminded me of the one I once shared with my parents, had its front door wide open. I dashed from my hiding place in the woods and into the house.

The house appeared empty. It was sparsely decorated which made me wonder if anyone lived here at all. I found the small kitchen easily and quickly discovered what remained of the food supply. A few cans of soup and a loaf of bread in the cupboard and a small container of milk in the refrigerator was all that was left. Either the people who lived here had taken most of the food with them or the Queen wasn't giving her subjects much to survive on these days. Considering the fact she was feeding them recycled meat and the bareness of the cupboards in the home, led me to the conclusion that the Queen's food supply might be running out. Could that be one of the reasons for the human riot? Starvation had been the cause of more than one war in history. Perhaps the humans figured they had nothing to lose and everything to gain.

I found a canvas bag in one of the drawers of the kitchen and quickly deposited the food into it. As I walked out onto the front porch of the house, I heard the distinct click of a shotgun being drawn back and loaded.

"Don't move," I heard a man say to the left of me. "Put the bag down and slowly turn to face me."

I did as he said and found myself staring into the eyes of not a man but a frightened teenage boy. His arms were shaking as he pointed the barrel of the shotgun at my head.

"Do you know who I am?" I asked him.

He looked confused for a moment before his eyes widened and his breathing came faster.

I heard more than saw him begin to pull the trigger. Without thinking I lunged forward grabbing the barrel of the shotgun with my right hand and tearing it out of the boy's grip just as he pulled the trigger.

I held the gun at my side and looked back at the boy.

If he had been frightened before, he was terrified now.

"Go ahead," he said with more bravado than I thought he would be able to muster. "Shoot me and get it over with."

"Are you so ready to die?" I asked.

"At least I'll die on my own terms."

"I won't kill you if you answer some questions for me."

Distrust entered his eyes but I also saw a flicker of hope.

"What do you want to know?"

"Do you know what's up the river?"

The boy looked confused by my question but finally answered, "I've only gone up near the fence there. Not sure what's past it."

"No one's tried to escape that way?"

"It's an electrified fence over water," the boy said. "What do you think?"

He had a point.

"Ok, thanks for the info," I said before hitting him in the head with the butt of the shotgun.

He slumped onto the porch without making a peep.

I picked up my bag of provisions and decided to keep the shotgun with me, just in case.

It didn't take me long to make my way back to the boathouse, but when I got there I heard two distinct voices coming from the inside.

One was of course Zoe's, but the other one belong to someone I had almost completely forgotten about, Lawrence.

I ran for the door of the boathouse and slung the door open.

Lawrence was standing over Zoe holding one of the babies in his arms. He looked up at me not at all surprised by my sudden appearance.

"Skye," he said with a pleased smile, "your mother sent me to look for you. She'll be happy to know you're safe."

I trusted Lawrence about as much as I would trust a snake slithering between my legs. His manic devotion to the Queen indicated to me he had a few screws loose.

"Where is she now?" I asked, walking in and laying down the bag and shotgun against the wall by the door.

"The Queen is putting an end to the human rebellion. She should have it in hand soon." Lawrence looked down at the baby he held. "She'll be glad to know you took care of Zoe and the babies. She's been waiting for their birth. Have they shown any signs of having powers yet?"

"No," I said meeting Zoe's frightened eyes, "they haven't but they're less than an hour old."

"I noticed one was defective," Lawrence said looking down at Hope at his feet like she was a bug on the floor who should be stomped out of existence.

"She just needs a doctor," I said.

"Your mother doesn't like imperfection." Lawrence looked over at me. "It would be better to just get rid of it now and not bother her with having to dispose of it herself."

"Skye…" Zoe said, a desperate plea in her voice.

"I'll handle it Lawrence," I said, taking on the tone of superiority I had heard the Queen use with her subordinates. "Why don't you go tell the Queen I'm safe and intend to keep Zoe here for the time being? As soon as she has the human's under control again, ask her to send someone to help me move them all."

"If that's what you want to do," Lawrence said walking towards me still holding the baby in his arms.

"Give me the baby," I told him in no uncertain terms.

"The Queen ordered me to bring at least one of them back to her if Zoe had given birth."

"And I'm telling you to give the baby to me."

"I can't do that," he said, certain in his resolve.

"You're not leaving here until you give me the baby."

Lawrence made to dash out the door past me, but I was faster. I grabbed him by the throat and pinned him against the door frame. Slowly, I began to squeeze his throat while he made choking sounds trying to gasp for even the smallest sliver of air. With my other hand, I easily took the baby he held and saw that it was Rose he had almost left with.

I heard more than saw Zoe come up behind me and take Rose out of my arms.

"Skye, you're killing him," she warned.

"No," I said. "If I were going to kill him, I'd rip his head off."

"What are you going to do with him?" She asked in a small voice. "What are you going to do with us?"

I knew then what my choice would be.

I slammed Lawrence's head against the doorjamb as hard as I could. The distinct sound of cracking bone told me I had crushed the backside of his skull. His eyelids drooped as he fell unconscious.

"Skye!" Zoe said in alarm. "I thought you said you weren't going to kill him."

"He's not dead," I replied, throwing Lawrence's limp body in the corner of the room. "He'll heal. I just hope he doesn't regain consciousness until we're gone."

"Gone?" Zoe said, uncertainty in her voice. "Where are we going Skye?"

"Up the river. We need to find a way to get you and the babies to Jace's people."

"Skye…" Zoe put her hand on my arm.

I shrugged it off.

"Don't," I told her. "Don't touch me. Don't thank me. Don't do anything but help me get the babies to the boat."

"But…" She began.

I never let her finish the thought. I had one hand clamped against her lips and the other behind her head to make sure she was looking at me.

"Just do what I say before I change my mind," I said slowly. "Do you understand? Because if you don't I swear I will take you to the Queen before you can take another breath. Do we have an understanding?"

Zoe nodded.

Zoe carried Rose to the boat while I carried the other two babies. After I got them settled in the cabin of the boat, I went back to get the bag of food and the shotgun from the boathouse.

I bent down over Lawrence to check the wound on the back of his head and found that it was already starting to heal. Not wanting him to run to the Queen too soon, I banged his head against the wooden boards of the floor. Feeling satisfied that he would be out for a while, I stood back up only to hear the sound of the shotgun being drawn again for the second time that night.

"Don't move or I'll blow your damn head off."

CHAPTER TWENTY-FIVE

I recognized the man's voice but couldn't quite place where I knew him from.

"Turn around slowly with your hands in the air," he ordered gruffly.

I raised my hands and turned to see who had the shotgun this time.

To my surprise, it was Jackson, the boy who the Queen had locked up in the basement of the Biltmore Estate. I remembered he had the power to manipulate electricity, a fact which made me smile.

"What are you grinnin' at?" He asked harshly.

"I'm just glad to see you, Jackson. You might find it hard to believe but you're exactly who I need right now."

Jackson raised the butt of the shotgun to his shoulder and wrapped his finger around the trigger like he was preparing to shoot.

"Wait!" I said. "I can get you out of here."

Jackson eased his finger away from the trigger.

"How?" He asked skeptically.

"By taking the boat out there up the river."

"Isn't there a fence around this joint?"

"Yes, an electrified one. But, if you can absorb the electricity running through the fence, I can use my strength to make a hole large enough for us to get through it."

Jackson's eyes narrowed on me. "How do I know this isn't just some trap? Aren't you a Harvester now? At least that's what I was told."

"Yes, I'm a Harvester."

"Then why would you want to help me?"

"It's not you I'm trying to help," I said honestly, "but your power will make it easier to get past the fence."

"Why are you trying to leave? I thought you'd become that bitch's right hand around this joint."

"I have to get a friend out of here before it's too late," I said, only then fully realizing why I was doing what I was doing.

Zoe needed my help. The babies needed my protection. The fact that I was betraying the Queen seemed inconsequential for some reason.

"So where is this friend?"

"She and her children are already on the boat waiting for me." I let my hands fall to my side. "By helping them escape, you get a free ride out of here too."

"Well, I need you to help *me* get a friend out too." Jackson took two steps backwards and looked to his right while still holding the gun on me. "Ava, come on. We might have a way out of this joint after all."

Ava, the girl who could make plants grow, stepped into the doorway.

"You sure we can trust her?" She asked looking me up and down like I might attack her at any moment.

"Hell no," Jackson said. "But I'll keep an eye on her. I've got the gun."

I smiled. They didn't seem to like it.

"What the hell are you smiling at this time?" Jackson said, his finger easing back towards the trigger.

"I find it amusing you think that gun is what's protecting you."

"Let's see how funny you think it is if I have to shoot you."

"You won't," I said. "I need you. And as long as you help me, I won't let anything or anyone harm you."

"And I'm just supposed to take your word on that?" Jackson scoffed. "I'm supposed to believe you and just trust you'll do what you promise?"

"Well, like you said, you have the gun. Keep it aimed in my direction all you want. It doesn't make any difference to me. Just don't get in my way, and I'll stay out of yours. We'll use each other until we get out then we can go our separate ways."

"We don't have anything to lose at this point," Ava pointed out to Jackson.

Jackson lowered the gun but held it close to his side.

"Let's go then," Jackson said.

"Hold on a sec." I turned to Lawrence and kicked him in the head seeing the indention of the tip of my shoe smash his skull inward.

When I looked up at Jackson and Ava they both looked stunned by my unexpected action.

"Just want to make sure he doesn't wake up anytime soon," I explained before grabbing the canvas bag with the food and walking past them out the door.

Before Jackson would even let me on the boat, he asked Ava to search the cabin, presumably to double check my story about Zoe and the babies. The cry of the babies could be heard clearly as she opened the door to the cabin.

"Close the door unless you want every Harvester within a half mile radius coming to investigate," I told her.

Ava closed the door quickly cutting off the cries.

"I'll drive the boat," Jackson said, actually sounding excited about it. "My dad used to have one of these before the war. We'd take it out almost every weekend."

"So, what you were like five or six?" I said, remembering that Jackson had been born around the same time as me. "How can you even remember how do to it now?"

"You don't forget the good stuff," he said. "Why don't you go down and help your friend with the babies? Sounds like she's got her hands full. Ava and I can handle the boat."

I shrugged. "Just make sure you keep an eye out for the fence. I don't want to be roasted alive."

I went down into the cabin and quickly shut the door. Whatever was wrong with the babies, they were being very vocal about it.

Zoe was sitting on the padded V- shaped bench which conformed to the bow of the boat holding a baby in each arm, trying to rock them and sooth their agitation with a hummed tune. I walked over to her and picked up Hope who was quietly sleeping.

"How can she sleep through all this noise?" I asked.

"I don't know, but her brother and sister are about to drive me stark raving mad," Zoe complained.

I stared at Hope's thin pale face and wondered why the Queen hadn't seen her deformity before she was born. Or had she seen it and just not worried about it since Rose and Simon were so healthy? All she needed was for one to survive to prove or disprove her hypothesis.

As if sensing my presence, Hope slowly opened her little eyes and yawned. She stared at me with her bright blue eyes which seemed too large for her small face. A happy smile lit her face as she gurgled at me.

"She likes you," Zoe said.

"She doesn't know me," I replied, completely sure that if the babe I held could understand what I was she wouldn't look at me with so much trust.

"She knows you better than you know yourself right now, Skye."

I sat back and relaxed against the wood paneling.

"I don't know what I'm doing," I confessed to Hope. "But I know if I take you back to the Queen she'd have you killed before she wasted her time fixing you."

Hope gurgled in response.

"You know I'm right, don't you?" I sighed heavily, trying to understand why I felt the need to save the little human cradled in my arms. She trusted me with an innocent openness only someone who's never had to struggle can have. But what was I saving her for? A life in a dark world where you had to hide and run while surviving on whatever scrapes the modern world had left behind? Wouldn't it be kinder to just kill her now, to save her from having to live in a dying world?

I heard the engine of the boat groan to life. I'd had my doubts the engine would even crank. It had apparently been used recently for some purpose. I just hoped whoever used it didn't come looking for it anytime soon.

The boat slowly pulled away from the dock and set us on our way to freedom. Something within me wanted to stop what I was doing and immediately return to the Queen's side. I felt torn between my desire to be with her and my need to see Zoe and the children somewhere safer. I knew they would never be safe with the Queen. She cared about them about as much as a child does bugs trapped in a jar. She would never let them go, and they would probably never survive her tender loving care.

"Where are we going Skye?" Zoe asked me, having finally rocked both Simon and Rose to sleep.

"She needs a doctor," I said, looking down at Hope, "a surgeon who can fix her. If we can find a way to get to where Jace is, she might have a chance."

"Where is Jace?"

I thought back to the map the Queen had in her office. Michael's camp had been marked on it.

"We need to go South," I told Zoe, laying a sleeping Hope on the bench.

I walked over to a small desk near the door of the cabin with a bunch of maps strewn across its surface. I found one showing the river we were on and followed it to where it would take us. I saw that the waterway would lead us straight to a large lake called Smith Mountain. If I were going to bet on a place to find transportation, it would be there. Before the war people always loved to live by water. The majority of those people were usually wealthy. Hopefully one of them had left a large enough vehicle to transport us all.

"Skye."

I turned from the map to look at Zoe.

"Why are you helping us?" She asked. "Why didn't you just let Lawrence take us to the Queen?"

I turned away from her unable to stand the worry I saw in her eyes to continue my study of the map.

"Don't question your good luck," I told her. "I'm still not sure I won't change my mind."

"You won't," Zoe said with more conviction than I felt. "Your love for us won't let you."

I let out a harsh laugh. "Love isn't really an emotion a Harvester is supposed to be able to feel."

"I don't think that's true. The Queen loves you."

I turned back to Zoe. "What makes you say that?"

Zoe shrugged. "It was obvious when I saw you with her. There was a light in her eyes after she brought you back with her that wasn't there before. They may say Harvesters can't feel love, but I think some of them do."

I couldn't deny what Zoe said might be true. Even I had noticed the Queen's love for me. Maybe Harvesters weren't as immune to human feelings as they liked to believe.

CHAPTER TWENTY-SIX

About thirty minutes later, Jackson opened the cabin door.

"Hey, we're at the fence," he yelled down, leaving the door open for me to come out on deck.

"Stay here," I told Zoe. "This shouldn't take very long."

When I got up on deck, Jackson was standing out on the bow an arm length away from the fence. The hum of electricity and an odd metallic odor seemed to fill the air around us.

"Do you think you can absorb this much electricity?" I asked, looking at the fence dubiously. There was so much electricity pulsing though the steel fence that the hair on my arms was standing on end.

"I don't know," Jackson admitted. "But if we want to get out of here I'm going to have to try."

I looked around the deck and saw a large red and white buoy ring with a rope attached around the outside of it.

"Wait a sec," I said, grabbing the buoy and handing it to Jackson. "Put this around your waist. If you start to fry, I'll pull you back."

"Thanks for the mental picture," Jackson said, taking the buoy from my hands.

Jackson positioned the floatation device around his waist.

"You might outta stand back," he told Ava.

"No, I'll stand here with her," Ava said. "If she doesn't pull you back, I will."

"Don't trust me?" I asked her, slightly amused.

"You're a Harvester," she answered, not needing to say anything else.

I just shrugged.

"Ok, well, here goes nothing," Jackson said, turning to the fence and only hesitating for a heartbeat before grabbing the chain link with both hands.

I'm not sure what I expected to happen but the entire thing seemed a bit anticlimactic. After a few minutes the hum of the fence faded into silence indicating Jackson was slowly sucking it dry of power. Eventually Jackson let go of the fence and turned to face us. Sweat was pouring down his face and his clothes were starting to smolder.

"That's it," he said before collapsing onto the bow.

"Jackson!" Ava yelled running to her friend. As soon as she tried to touch his face, she cried out in pain drawing back a hand burnt raw. The metal on the bow began to glow red hot around Jackson's body.

I cursed softly under my breath. Before I could even take a step forward, Jackson's body began to convulse violently. Ava had the good sense to step back just as her friend's body melted a hole through the deck. I knew the hull of the boat wouldn't be far behind.

"Grab your stuff and jump off the boat," I ordered Ava.

"But what about Jackson?" She asked, completely hysterical.

"Get off the damn boat, Ava, unless you want to be sucked down with it!"

I threw the door to the cabin open and rushed in.

"Is everything all right up there?" Zoe asked. "I heard the yelling."

"Jackson's melting a hole in the boat," I said, realizing how silly the truth sounded. "We've got to get off."

I grabbed Hope and the leather bench cushion she was resting on. Zoe carried Simon and Rose in each arm. By the time we reached the deck, the bow was already starting to tilt forward as it filled up with water. I saw Ava swimming off to the woods to the right towing an unconscious Jackson like a life guard would with one arm around his chest under his armpits. I assumed the cold river water must have dissipated the heat his body was emanating enough for her to hold him.

"How are we going to get the babies and ourselves over there?" Zoe asked.

"Follow me," I told her heading to the back of the boat where the ladder leading to the water was.

Once there I tucked the bench cushion under one arm and held Hope close to my chest with the other. After I descended the steps, I placed the cushion on the surface of the water to make sure it would float and not simply sink. Thankfully, it was water tight. With one hand I held the cushion steady while placing Hope, Simon, and Rose on it before completely stepping off the ladder into the water.

It didn't take us long to swim to shore, but by the time we reached it, the fishing boat was already half submerged in the river.

Soaking wet but still alive, Zoe and I pulled the bench pad to shore. The babies were only slightly damp from their first swimming experience.

Zoe was doing her best to cajole Simon and Rose to stop crying. When I leaned down to pick up Hope, her face lit up with a smile at the sight of me. I began to wonder if she thought I was her mother since I was usually the one who held her. Her siblings always seemed to be in more need of attention even though they were perfectly healthy.

"My God, what happened?"

I turned to look behind me and saw Ash standing there with a backpack slung over one shoulder.

"Did you bring back some supplies?" I asked, not feeling like answering his question when he could plainly see what had happened for himself.

"Yeah," he said crouching to the ground to open the pack. "You're lucky my Mom used to work at a Target. I was able to snatch some stuff before I teleported again."

"Hey who's this?" Ava asked coming to stand by us.

"Ava, Ash. Ash, Ava," I said in way of introduction.

"Oh, you the baby daddy?" Ava asked Ash.

"How would you know that?" Zoe asked.

"Guards talk." Ava shrugged. "Heard about what the Queen was doing with the two of you. Jackson and I figured we'd end up being next. Figured that was the reason she hadn't made us into Harvesters yet." Ava shivered at the thought. "I can't imagine having a litter of babies."

"It wasn't a litter," Zoe said defensively. "It was only triplets."

"Ok, half a litter," Ava amended.

"How's Jackson?" I said, feeling a need to change the subject.

"Unconscious but still breathing," Ava reported.

I looked back to Ash. "Did you happen to bring us any clothes?"

"I brought Zoe and the babies something to wear, but didn't know you would be soaking wet. Best I can do for you is a dry towel," he said rummaging through the contents of his bag and handing me a coral colored towel with a decorative border.

"Guess that'll have to do," I said grabbing the towel with my free hand. "Here hold Hope," I said handing her over to Ash.

Just as he was about to take hold of her, he vanished again.

"I really wish he would stop doing that," I growled in irritation.

I tossed the towel to Ava. "Here dry yourself off as much as you can. Maybe when he comes back he'll remember to bring some clothes for us too."

After Ava toweled off, she held Hope for me. Zoe changed into the clothes Ash brought for her. I found a pack of diapers, wipes and clean clothes for the babies in the supplies Ash brought back from the past. While I was changing Simon into a long sleeve onesie, I heard Zoe begin to whimper softly. When I looked up at her, I saw she was crying and pulling down the purple sweatshirt she wore past her hips. Zoe's outfit brought back to mind a childhood show I once watched with a big singing purple dinosaur.

"What's wrong?" I asked. "Are you hurt?

Zoe shook her head. "No," she whined. "But look at how big this shirt is!"

"And your problem with that is?" I asked, not seeing what the size of the shirt had to do with anything.

"Ash must think I'm as big as a house!" She cried. "Why else would he have brought back something so big for me to wear?"

"You've lost me," I said, still not understanding why she was so upset.

"She's having a girl moment," Ava explained with a roll of her eyes.

"You just had three babies," I said to Zoe, continuing to snap the bottom of Simon's outfit. "He probably just wanted you to be comfortable and warm."

Zoe sniffed and seemed to realize how ridiculous her behavior was. "I don't know why I care," she said, coming to help me change Rose into some dry clothes. "It's not like he cares about me in that way. He loves you."

I didn't miss the envious way Zoe made her statement, but I did intentionally ignore it. All I needed was to have an argument with a hormonally imbalanced Zoe. Whether or not Ash still loved me was completely irrelevant. We had bigger problems to contend with at the moment. Namely, where we should head to next.

"Man, what happened?"

Jackson came stumbling towards us holding his head with both hands. His clothes were wet like the rest of us but he had a lot less of them. There were so many holes in his jacket and pants it looked like he had been attacked by a horde of angry giant moths. His shirt was nonexistent.

"You sunk the boat," I informed him, standing to take Hope from Ava to change her clothes while Zoe finished up with Rose.

Jackson looked out onto the water but the boat was already completely submerged.

"Remind me not to ever do that again," he told me. "It was just too much. I've never been around that much power before."

"Don't worry," I told him. "You did what we needed. With or without the boat we stick to the plan and go through the fence. There has to be a house around here. We'll just have to hope they left us some transportation. You got enough juice left to jumpstart a car if we need it?"

Jackson flexed his hand and pointed his index finger at a nearby tree. A stream of what looked like lightening shot from the tip and struck the tree burning a hole straight through its trunk like a pin point laser.

"Good," I said, trying not to show how impressed I actually was by Jackson's display of power. All I needed was for him to think he had the upper hand in our little détente.

Once the babies were dressed and wrapped up in the blankets Ash brought, I made a pseudo baby carrier out of the backpack and placed Simon and Rose inside it. I was adjusting the straps of the backpack on my shoulders when Zoe said, "I can carry Hope."

"No, I can carry her," I told Zoe, taking Hope from Ava myself.

"I can help," Zoe said. "You don't have to do everything yourself, Skye."

"Don't argue with me," I told her. "I could carry a truck on my back and not feel the weight. Harvester strength, remember? Besides, you'll all be able to travel faster without carrying the added weight. The faster we can get away from here the safer you'll be."

Before Zoe could argue further, I walked up to the chain link fence and tore a hole in it with one hand large enough for us all to pass through.

It was late afternoon, and I knew we would need to find shelter soon. I didn't want to announce our presence by building a fire so finding an abandoned house was my top priority. I still had a mental picture of the map from the boat in my memory and knew our best bet would be to travel south until we found a road, then I would have a better idea about where we were exactly.

Only fifteen minutes after we started walking away from the river deeper into the woods, Simon and Rose began to cry again. We stopped so Zoe could breast feed them. While Zoe was busy satiating their hunger, I sat with my back against a tree and checked Hope. As far as I knew, she hadn't cried once to be fed.

"Have you tried to feed Hope?" I asked Zoe.

"I tried to when you were on deck dealing with Jackson and the fence," she replied, holding a suckling Simon to her breast. "But she wouldn't latch onto the nipple."

When I looked back down at Hope, I wasn't sure if it was my imagination or if she really did seem to look paler than before. I had no way of knowing what her condition meant for the rest of her organs. Was her heart pumping enough blood to them to keep them functioning? I hoped Ash would reappear and perhaps take Hope to the past to find medical help, but I didn't know when or if he would come back in time. All I did know was that Michael's rebel base should have a surgeon who could help her. Since Ash's power didn't seem to be under his control, I couldn't solely rely on it to help us.

Once Zoe was through feeding Simon and Rose, we continued our way southward and came upon a forked road with a ranch style home sandwiched in between. A silver Dodge Durango was still parked behind it, but it had one flat tire which would need to be fixed if we were going to be able to use it at all.

Once we searched the interior of the house, we were able to find clothes which fit all of us allowing us to shed our river soaked garments. After setting Zoe and the babies up in the house, Jackson and I went to see what the Durango would need to be made road worthy. Luckily, it still had its spare tire mounted to the underside. I let Jackson deal with that while I went to scout a house up the road which had an array of outer buildings surrounding the main house. I knew we would need to find as much gas as we possibly could. We were still almost three hundred miles away from Michael's camp.

The only gas I was able to find was in the tank of an old tractor the owners had stashed away in a small shed. It was better than nothing. It didn't take long to siphon it out with a garden hose into a small gas can.

When I got back to the house, I noticed Jackson was no longer working on the Durango. The spare tire was still leaned against the side of it with the flat tire sitting on the ground beside it. Assuming Jackson went into the house for some reason, I set the gas can on the ground and turned to walk towards the backdoor of the house to find out what the holdup was. As soon as I faced the house, I was met by an image which stopped me in my tracks.

Behind the screen door leading back into the house, Lawrence stood with his arms crossed over his chest watching me.

CHAPTER TWENTY-SEVEN

Lawrence stepped through the screen door without opening it and walked into the backyard.

"What have you done to them?" I asked.

"Nothing yet," Lawrence said, a sly grin spreading his thin lips. "They're still in the house."

"You shouldn't have followed us, Lawrence." I slowly walked towards him.

"You didn't think I would just let you run away with Zoe and the babies, did you?" He cocked his head. "They're too important to the Queen."

"They're more important to me."

"But you're not the Queen," he said snidely, finding some sort of queer satisfaction in his statement. "She'll be sorely disappointed in what you did to me."

I laughed harshly. "The Queen detests you Lawrence. If you had any sense at all, you would know that."

"I'm smart enough to know you're betraying her."

"Planning to tell her that the next time you see her?" I asked stopping right in front of him.

"Yes, I do."

"I'm sorry to hear that," I told him before hitting him with the flat on my hands on his chest sending him flying into the air. He didn't stop until his back slammed against the brick wall of the house, causing an indentation to form around his body.

He recovered quickly and ran at me like a linebacker, hitting me in the midsection with his lowered shoulder crashing us both against the side of the Durango. The vehicle tilted precariously before rolling over onto its side.

I wrapped an arm around Lawrence's neck, squeezing with enough force to make him relinquish his hold of my waist.

"You really shouldn't have followed me," I told Lawrence, tightening my arm around his throat until he made choking sounds. I knew I had a decision to make. I could simply try to incapacitate Lawrence again like I did at the boathouse, or I could rip his head off and not have to worry about him anymore. I decided he needed to die.

I was just about to tear his neck to shreds when I heard my name called softly. I looked towards the house and saw Zoe holding one of the babies in her arms watching me.

The look of horror on her face made me hesitate. She had to understand what I was about to do. It was the only way to make sure Lawrence didn't follow us again.

"He needs to die. I have to do it," I said to her.

"No, you don't." She stepped out of the house. "You don't have to be a murderer."

"He's just a Harvester, Zoe. It's not like I haven't killed one before."

"But you had to then," she told me. "You don't have to now. Just knock him out long enough to give us time to escape."

I snorted. "I've already tried that once. He found us anyway. No," I said shaking my head, resolute in my decision, "I need to kill him this time to make sure he doesn't tell the Queen where we are."

"Don't, Skye," she begged.

"Why do you care what happens to him?" I asked, not trying to hide my frustration. "He doesn't care about anything but pleasing the Queen."

"I don't care about him. I care about you."

"You're not making any sense, Zoe."

"If you kill him in cold blood, I don't think you'll ever be the same again. You're not a murderer, Skye. That's not the type of person you are."

"I'm a Harvester, Zoe. Murder is what we're built for."

"But you're not a true Harvester anymore," she said, total conviction in her voice. "Or you wouldn't be trying to help us. If all you were is a Harvester, you would be doing what this one is trying to do: take us back to the Queen. Instead you're helping us escape from her. She may have put a chip in your head, but you're not letting it control your choices now. You're in charge of your own life not her."

"He needs to die," I said, tightening my hold around Lawrence's neck. By this time he had already passed out from lack of oxygen, even Harvesters needed to breathe.

"Then don't kill him for me," Zoe pleaded. "I don't want his blood on my hands because I know you would only be doing it to protect us. I wouldn't be able to live with his death on my conscience."

I snapped Lawrence's neck but didn't tear his head off. His body fell limply to the ground. I stood and dusted myself off.

"Satisfied?" I asked Zoe.

"Thank you, Skye."

The relief in Zoe's eyes told me she still thought I had a chance to be saved. That somehow I would magically revert back to my old self. I didn't want to ruin her fantasy, but I knew in that moment how idyllic she was. Miracles were possible in her world, and I didn't have the heart to shatter her hope of my returning to her the way I was. Even if I did regain more of my humanity, I knew in that moment I would never be the same person again. I was forever changed, only time would tell whether or not it was for the better.

When I followed Zoe back into the house, she showed me where Lawrence left Jackson and Ava. They were knocked out cold lying together on one of the beds.

"He only left me alone so I could take care of the babies," Zoe explained.

"You stay here while I take care of Lawrence. Maybe they'll be awake by the time I get back."

"What are you going to do with him?"

"Take him to the river and dump him in it. Hopefully, he'll float down far enough to not be a threat to us for a while."

"You promise you won't kill him?"

"Zoe," I said in irritation, "if I was going to kill him, I would have ripped his head off a few minutes ago instead of just breaking his neck."

"Ok," Zoe said, seeing she was quickly making me angry with her incessant questioning, "I trust you. I know you'll do the right thing. You always do."

I stood there and stared at Zoe wondering how she could have so much faith in me after the things I said to her back at the Queen's house. My words to her then were meant to make her hate me, to forget about trying to save me from what I had become. But she was still trying to remind me of who I once was.

"I'll be back," I said, turning my back on the hope in her eyes.

It didn't take me long to haul Lawrence to the river. I ripped his clothes off and tore them into strips to strap his body to the bench cushion. Just for good measure, I made sure his neck was still broken and proceeded to break his legs and arms to give his nanites more repair work to slow down his healing. Once I sent him on his way down the river, I made my way back to the house.

My original plan of staying at the house overnight was completely shot now. If Lawrence had been able to find us so easily, the Queen wouldn't be far behind. Our best bet was to keep moving. I knew Zoe and the babies desperately needed some down time, but I couldn't afford to give it to them. They would have to take what rest they could while I drove us to Michael's camp. After I got them there, I wasn't sure what I would do. I still felt a pull to go back to the Queen's side and serve her as diligently as I could, but I couldn't deny the other part of me which wanted to save Zoe and see Jace again.

What did he think of me now? Could he possibly still love someone who had, in essence, betrayed him? Someone who had chosen to be with the Queen instead of him. It seemed like Jace and I had been apart more than we had been together, but I couldn't deny I still felt a need to be with him. A part of me yearned to be near him, to feel his breath against my skin and hear him say he loved me. I could feel his phantom touches and longed to feel the real thing.

When I cleared the woods, I saw Zoe standing with Ash at the corner of the house. He was holding her close to him with their foreheads touching and eyes closed. He was whispering something to her, but I could hear him clearly.

"We'll find a way to save her," he promised.

"Save who?" I asked, making my presence known before I approached them.

Ash quickly pulled away from Zoe like he'd been caught doing something he shouldn't.

"Hope," he answered.

"Good." I came to stand with them. "For a minute there, I thought you might have joined Zoe's crusade to save my soul."

"I still have hope for you," Ash said.

"Don't waste your energy," I told him walking towards the Durango. I pushed it back into an upright position intent on finishing to mount the spare tire.

"Why don't you actually do something useful and try to take your daughter to the past to get her help?" I said to Ash.

"I don't think I can," Ash replied, filled with regret.

I stopped walking and looked back at him. "Why not?"

"Every time I get near the babies it makes me teleport."

"Yeah," I said. "Kinda noticed that annoying fact. Why do you think that is?"

"I'm not completely sure." Ash shook his head. "But I think my time traveling is connected to my emotions. I seem to only travel between people I love."

I looked to Zoe and saw the shock on her face. Ash had traveled back to her here at the house not to me in the woods. Now she had a reason to hope he truly could love her.

"Don't you love your children?" I asked harshly, feeling an irrational need to hurt him.

"I think that's the problem," Ash said. "I love them too much. It's like they overload my system when I get too close to them."

"So basically you're useless."

"Skye!" Zoe said in a disapproving tone.

"No," Ash said looking at Zoe, "she's right. I can't help you take care of them. I desperately want to but my power won't let that happen, at least not yet. I just have to find a way to control it better."

"If it *can* be controlled," I said.

Someone had to keep things real. Zoe still wanted to live in the land of unicorns and rainbows, a child's world. The sooner she realized Ash might not be a permanent fixture in our lives the better. We had real problems to deal with. Problems he apparently was useless to help with.

I bent down and started to mount the spare tire.

"You need to get the children ready to leave," I told Zoe. "We don't need to be here when the Queen comes calling. Have Jackson and Ava woken up yet?"

"No," Zoe answered, "not yet."

"Maybe you can go wake them up," I said to Ash. "Since you can't help with the babies, it's the most useful thing you can do right now. I might need Jackson to jump start this thing for us."

Ash looked confused. "Who are Jackson and Ava?"

I briefly told Ash who they were, how I first met them and what powers they possessed. Ash followed Zoe into the house to see what he could do to wake the other two up for us.

I filled the gas tank with the gas I obtained from the house up the road. I seriously debated with myself on whether or not I wanted to go into the house. My worry over Hope's welfare won out over my desire to stay away from Ash and Zoe. Separately, I could handle them but together I felt outnumbered.

When I walked into the house, I saw Ash leaned up against the kitchen counter watching Zoe as she stood at the kitchen table with all three babies lined up for what looked like diaper change time.

"I never knew babies could produce something that smells so bad," she said to me wiping Rose's bottom with a wet wipe. "Do you think something's wrong with them? It's not supposed to smell like this is it?"

I heard Ash clear his throat and knew he was trying to not laugh at Zoe's naiveté.

"They're fine, Zoe," I told her, giving Ash a disapproving glare. "It's normal."

"Ok, if you say so," she said, though I could still hear the doubt in her voice.

I helped Zoe get the babies ready for travel while Ash went to wake Jackson and Ava. Jackson came walking out on his own asking what happened to Lawrence. I told him about sailing him down the river. Jackson agreed we needed to leave as soon as possible and went out to see if he could get the Durango started.

"The girl isn't waking up," Ash came and told us. "She must have been hit harder or something. I think she needs a doctor."

I cursed inwardly wondering what else could possibly go wrong.

CHAPTER TWENTY-EIGHT

The Durango had enough room in the back for Zoe to lie down with the babies and rest. Jackson and Ava sat in the second row of seats and Ash sat up front with me. I didn't turn the headlights on as we drove away from the house. Night was upon us now, and I didn't want to draw any unwanted attention. It seemed to make my passengers nervous.

"I can see just fine," I told them. "Harvesters can see in the dark."

"I keep forgetting you're one of them," Jackson said from the back seat. "You don't act like one."

I ignored him not wanting to start a philosophical discussion on the behavior of a Harvester. Unfortunately, Ash jumped at the chance.

"He's right you know. You don't always act like a Harvester."

"Don't you start too," I said. "I get enough grief from Zoe without you harping on how different I am."

"We love you. We want our old Skye back."

"She's not coming back."

"I think you're wrong. I think you're more like your old self than you want to admit."

"Listen," I said, my frustration growing, "as soon as I get Hope to a doctor, I plan to go back to the Queen. So, forget whatever little fantasy you've built up about me in your mind."

"Why do you care what happens to Hope so much?"

My mind went blank. I didn't have an answer to Ash's question because I had no idea why her life meant so much to me.

"I like to root for the underdog, I guess." Even to me my answer sounded lame.

Ash didn't speak after that. After a while I looked at him and saw that he had fallen asleep. I had no way of knowing what his time jumping was doing to his body. Surely it was having an effect. How could it not? I wondered how long he would be able to continue travelling back and forth from the present to the past without it killing him. It made me wonder if there might be a way to reverse what the Queen had done to him. My limited knowledge of genetic manipulation simply wasn't enough to help me know if it was reversible or not.

My train of thought brought me back to a question I kept asking myself: why did I care? The Queen's ability to awaken Ash's unique power was a triumph. Now she knew how to do it for almost anyone she chose, but in order for it to work, I would need to be by her side ready to heal them before their hearts gave out. Was that the reason I was so important to her? To help further progress her plans in the next evolution of Harvesters? I didn't think so. At least, it wasn't the only reason.

No, in spite of herself, she loved me. I saw it plainly written in her eyes at the hospital after she handled the initial riot. For all of her talk and propaganda, the Queen had failed to eliminate one of humanities most basic emotions even within herself.

We were on the road for over four hours before the Durango died underneath us. I braked to a rolling stop waking everyone instantly.

"What's wrong?" Ash asked, wiping sleep from his eyes.

"I don't know," I replied. "We still have gas. It must be something mechanical."

"Pop the hood," Jackson said. "Maybe I can figure something out."

After spending almost an hour fiddling under the hood, Jackson wasn't able to diagnose the problem with the engine.

"Skye!" Zoe yelled from the back. "Something's wrong with Hope!"

I ran to the back of the Durango. Apparently without thinking, Ash ran back with me and got too close, instantly vanishing. I didn't have time to think about that, all I could focus on was the sound of Hope's ragged breathing.

"How far are we from a doctor?" Skye asked, rocking Hope in the crook of her arm.

"We're at least thirty or forty miles away," I said. So close yet so far away.

"We can walk that," Zoe said, nodding her head to make the task seem more doable than it was. "We can do it. I know we can."

"Listen," I told her. "I can make it there faster than any of you. I'll take Hope on ahead and guys stay here. I'll get Michael to send help back."

Without questioning my decision, Zoe kissed Hope on the lips and handed her over to me. When I looked down at Hope, I could see how quickly she was deteriorating. Her skin now held a bluish tint telling me she wasn't getting enough oxygen. I touched her forehead with my hand and called on my healing power to help prolong her life, but it seemed to have no effect on whatever was wrong with her.

"Save her," was the last thing I heard Zoe say before I took off running down the road.

I held Hope close to my chest to keep her as warm as I could while I ran. With each step I took I became more and more determined to save her. But the same question repeated itself in my mind: what was I saving her for? The world as it was wasn't worth living in. An image of the world as it could be flashed in my mind. My future self had shown me a world where the sun shone and children could laugh. That was a place in which Hope deserved to live in. She had been dealt a bad hand in the game of life, and I was determined to change her luck. All I had to do was get her to Michael's camp.

After two hours of running, I stopped to catch my breath and check on Hope. Her little eyes were open staring up at me. Her lips were parted as she fought to draw in a single breath.

"Hang in there," I told her. "Don't you dare die on me. Not when we're so close to getting you help."

I took off running again knowing there wasn't a second to lose.

Thirty minutes later Hope struggled to lift one of her tiny hands up like she wanted to grab onto something. I stopped running and I placed my index finger against her small palm. Her fingers wrapped around it tightly and she stared at me with such intensity, as if she were telling me it was time to let her go.

"No," I said, filled with determination. "You stay with me. You only need to fight a little longer. Then we'll be together forever."

I rocked her in the crook of my arm and tried to think of something, anything to give her a reason to stay alive. A memory from my own childhood flashed in my mind. Whenever I was sick or frightened, my mother would sing to me. I didn't remember many songs but knew of one I had just heard recently.

Hush, little baby, don't say a word,
Mama's going to buy you a mockingbird.
If that mockingbird won't sing
Mama's going to buy you a diamond ring...
If that diamond ring turns brass,
Mama's going to buy you a looking glass...

She smiled then as if she understood what I was trying to do. Her eyes closed slowly and her fingers lost their grip around my finger. With one last shuddering breath, her body went completely limp in my arms.

Instantly, I saw the light of Hope's soul leave her body and hover in front of me as if she were saying one last goodbye. Her soul crept closer to me and then suddenly passed through my body making me feel the pureness of her love for me and how much she wanted me to finally find peace.

I fell to my knees holding Hope's lifeless body to my chest, tears of loss and new found hope streamed down my face. In that moment, I felt like my heart was outside my body too, exposed to the world as it grieved over the loss of such an innocent and pure soul. Hope's last gift to me broke down the barrier I had been hiding behind. A protective wall meant to separate me, the Harvester, from me, the human. My resolve to keep the two parts of myself separate completely shattered, and I knew it was only because Hope had found a way to share her undying love for me.

I wasn't just a Harvester, and I wasn't just human. I was both. A fact I felt sure the Queen knew all too well. Even though she tried to make Harvesters believe they were superior to humans, she knew the line of distinction was blurry. The power of strength and immortality Harvesters felt blinded them to their human side, at least enough to make them accept her brainwashing mantra that human emotions made you weak. But now, I knew the truth.

I felt a warm hand tentatively touch my shoulder. When I looked beside me, I saw Jace's concerned face.

Without saying anything, I stood, still cradling Hope in my arms and let him wrap us both in his warmth. I let my soul cry out its anguish while he held me close, providing me a safe haven to relinquish my pain. Once my tears were spent, the story of my life as a Harvester spilled out of me. Jace listened to it all without saying a word. I wasn't sure what he would think of me afterwards, but I knew I had to tell him everything. I didn't want there to be any secrets between us, and he needed to know the type of person I was now. I would never be the girl he said he was in love with, and he needed to decide for himself whether or not he could accept the new me.

After I spilled my heart out to him, he remained silent. I pulled away from him to look at his face and wasn't prepared for what I saw in his eyes: utter devastation.

"Do you hate me now?" I asked, needing to know if I had forever changed his feelings for me.

"It would take a lot more than what you just told me to hate you," he replied.

"Can you still love me?"

"It would take a lot more than what you just told me to make me stop loving you too."

My heart felt lighter, free of the burden of my regrets and filled with the promise of love I saw on Jace's face.

I looked down at Hope's peaceful face and silently thanked her for showing me who I truly was. She had given me back my life, and I would never forget her for it. I was filled with an intense determination to make sure her sacrifice hadn't been in vain and knew I would keep the love her soul shared with me in my heart forever.

"How did you find me?" I finally asked Jace.

Jace looked behind me causing me to follow his gaze, and I saw Rose standing a few yards away in the middle of the road. I felt an instant rage and stormed up to her slapping her hard across the face with all my anger.

"Why didn't you do something?" I yelled at her. "You knew where I was. You could have saved her!"

Rose held a trembling hand to her face over where I hit her, tears brimming in her eyes.

"I couldn't save her," she said.

"Why? Because my future self said you couldn't? Can't you think for yourself you god damn coward?"

"Skye…" I heard Jace say behind me, warning me I had gone too far.

Tears spilled from Rose's eyes. "I couldn't save her because she needed to save you."

"Don't do that," I warned her taking a step back from her before I hit her again. "Don't you dare put the blame of her death on me!"

"Her death was no one's fault," Rose said, dropping her hand to her side and taking a step towards me. "Hope's fate was to show you your humanity again. Even if I had taken her to a doctor, it was never her destiny to live out a normal life. She was meant to help you realize who you are so you can save the world."

I felt my anger towards Rose slowly ebb away because I knew she was right. It made perfect sense even though I hated to admit it to myself. It seemed we all had our parts to play if the world was to be saved, even if we didn't like them.

Before I knew it, Simon appeared with Zoe by his side.

As soon as I saw Zoe, I walked over to her.

"I wasn't able to save her," I said, taking the full responsibility of Hope's death on my shoulders.

Zoe held out her arms, and I placed Hope in them for one last time.

As Zoe held her daughter close, she began to cry the tears only a mother can shed over the loss of a child. I hesitated before taking her in my arms much like Jace had and let her use me as her anchor while her world spun out of control. I didn't try to console her with words and convince her Hope's death was meant to be. It would have just been too cruel. Instead, I simply held her and joined in her grief.

Eventually, Rose and Simon helped everyone reach Michael's camp. We held a funeral for Hope on a small hill within the compound. Michael promised to erect a monument to her there when the war was over.

With mention of the war, I knew my work had just begun. We would need to find a way to defeat the Queen and discover a way to bring sunlight back to the world.

CHAPTER TWENTY-NINE

After the funeral, I was surprised to see Simon and Rose stick around for our first strategy meeting on how to defeat the Queen.

"If we could just kill the bitch, things would be so much easier," Michael said as we all sat around a table in his office.

"Why can't you?" Zoe asked.

I explained to her about the artificial ozone layer protecting what was left of the world and the consequences of killing the Queen.

"So we can't just kill her," I finished. "If we do, she'll take the rest of the world with her."

Zoe sat silently, seeming to be lost in her own thoughts, as we discussed what needed to be done next.

"We should hurt her where it counts," I said. "She showed me where all of her important installations are."

"She let you look at the map?" Michael questioned, suddenly becoming excited. "She doesn't show that to anyone."

"I guess she trusted me."

"What did you do to earn that trust?" Michael questioned.

"Things I would rather not talk about right now. They're not important anyway."

"We don't need to dwell on things from the past," Jace said, coming to my defense. "We need to look at what we can do to ensure our future."

"I have an idea." Zoe's words were so soft we almost didn't hear them.

"What's your idea, Zo?" I asked.

"Kill the Queen."

"We just told you why we can't do that," I said patiently.

"You can if I replace her shield with one of my own."

"Can you do that?" Ian questioned. "You think you can make one that big?"

"I won't know until I try."

"She'll be able to make a large enough one," Simon chimed in completely confident.

"And it holds?" I asked, knowing if he and Rose said it would work then it would.

"Yes, it will stay up for many years to come. After you bring down the Queen's shield, sunlight will come back, but my mother won't be able to do it alone. Rose and I will have to help her."

"But won't that be kinda hard for you people to do?" Michael asked. "Standing there for so long?"

"No," a new voice in the room said.

We all turned to find the new addition to our group and found an older man standing by the office door. Jace made to stand up thinking we had been infiltrated, but I grabbed his arm before he could leave the table.

"It's Ash," I said.

Ash came to stand behind his children.

"Once they combine their power," the older Ash said, "the shield they make will grow exponentially and almost cover everything the Queen's shield does now. After they do that I'll place them in stasis like Zoe was when Skye first found her. All we have to do is get them close to where the Queen's shield emanates from now."

"I know where that is," I said, remembering its location from her map. "I can get us there."

I looked at the older Ash and asked, "After we kill the Queen and dismantle her shield, how long will they have to keep their shield in place?"

"A long time," Ash answered. "You will have passed away by the time they're able to come out of stasis."

I heard Zoe's sharp intake of breath.

"No," I said, not willing to have Zoe ripped from my life, "there has to be another way."

"There is no other way," this time it was Rose who answered. "We've known this was our fate since we were children. You helped prepare us for this. We're ready."

"But what if I'm not?" I said, feeling close to tears.

"Skye." Zoe took hold of my hand. It was the first time I noticed the wrinkles and brown spots on her skin, a sure sign of aging. "You know I'm dying. At least my life will have meant something if I do this."

I knew Zoe would be dead within a year's time. Her accelerated aging hadn't stopped. It seemed as though the pregnancy had done what the Queen predicted and worsened it.

"But I don't want to lose you," I said, feeling the warmth of my tears trail down my cheeks.

"You won't lose me completely." Zoe smiled at me with wisdom far beyond her years. "You'll have my children to raise for me. There's no one in the world I trust more than you to take care of them." Zoe looked at Simon and Rose. "And look what a great job you did. They're everything I could ever hope them to be."

"Then I guess it's settled," Michael said, standing from his chair. "Show me where we need to go, Skye, and I'll make the arrangements."

After I showed Michael where the shield was located, I noticed older Ash give Rose and Simon a hug, something the younger Ash was unable to do just yet. I assumed that meant Ash would be able to control his powers better in time. When Rose and Simon left to go back to their own timelines and make their goodbyes, older Ash pulled Zoe off to the side. I heard him tell her he needed to speak with her about something but was unable to hear anything more after they left.

"We should be able to have things ready by the morning," Michael said, folding up the map from his desk. "Why don't the two of you go on and try to take your minds off of things until then?"

I suddenly found Jace grabbing my hand and pulling me after him out of the office with Ian chuckling knowingly behind us.

"Well, I wonder what he has on his mind." I heard Michael say as we made our way out of the room.

"Where are you taking me?" I asked Jace.

"No questions." He smiled mischievously back at me as we raced down the stairs of the building to the outside. "It's a surprise."

If I hadn't been a Harvester, I'm not sure I would have been able to keep up with Jace's quick pace. He acted like the devil himself was nipping at our heels. We traveled to the other side of the compound to a street lined with small houses. I assumed this was where the military families used to live when the station was operational.

Jace stopped at the door of one of the homes and lifted me into his arms.

"What on earth are you doing?" I asked, unable to stop myself from laughing at his outrageous behavior.

"Welcoming you home," he said before opening the door and stepping over the threshold.

We entered a small living room with a brick fireplace on the far wall and a space off to the side which seemed to be the designated dining area. The walls were painted off white and the furnishings were made of a homey brown suede.

We also found an unexpected visitor waiting for us. Standing in the middle of the living room was older Ash.

"I'm sorry," he said. "I know I'm intruding, but I need to speak with you."

Jace set me on my feet and closed the door behind us.

"What do you need to tell me?" I asked.

"I'm actually here to speak with Jace," Ash said.

As we walked over to Ash, Jace said, "What about?"

"I wanted to ask you to be a father to my children."

"But the younger version of you is still around," Jace said. "Won't he get mad about that?"

"He will at first until he realizes it's the best thing for them." Ash looked at me. "Remember me telling you that my time jumps were linked to my emotions?"

"Yes."

"I won't be able to control them until I'm much older. Even though I want to be with Rose and Simon and help raise them, they'll never know me as their father until much later in their lives. If I've learned anything from our time at the breeding camp, it's that having two parents who love you more than anything and who will protect you against everything is important to kids. You and I know that all too well."

I nodded my agreement, too choked up with emotion to say anything.

Ash looked back at Jace. "You are a good man. And I already know what a great father you will be to my kids, but I felt I should ask you in person to do me this favor."

Jace held his hand out to Ash. Ash clasped it in between both of his hands.

"I would be honored to stand in your place until you can," Jace said. "And know that I will do my best to raise them with Skye the way you and Zoe would want."

"You do," Ash said with a sad smile. "You'll both raise them well."

Ash let go of Jace's hand and looked back at me. "My younger counterpart may say some harsh things to you," he warned me. "But just know he doesn't mean them. He's just jealous because he can't have you for himself. He'll come to realize you were never meant to be together. Jace is the man you're supposed to be with."

"How long will it take for him to realize that?" I asked.

"A while," Ash smiled chagrined. "Just be patient with me, Skye. I'll come around to understanding your choice eventually. Remember that when I'm being a complete ass to you though."

"I'll try," I said, now dreading the next time I saw the Ash from my present.

"Anyway, I should be getting back to Zoe. I never got to hold Simon and Rose when they were babies. This'll be my only chance to be with all of them while they're young."

"Will I see you again?" I asked. "This version of you anyway."

"No, you won't see me like this again after I put Zoe and the kids into stasis. I have my own life in the future to get back to.

One I don't want to miss out on." Ash put his hands on my and Jace's shoulders. "Take care of one another. Stay strong and win this war."

Ash disappeared.

Jace and I sat down on the couch together. We were silent for a long time, both thinking about what Ash had said to us.

"So not only do we have to save the world," Jace finally said. "But we just became parents too." He sighed heavily. "I think the parent thing scares me more."

I looked at him and saw the worry on his face. I couldn't stop myself from bursting out in laughter. He soon joined me.

After we settled down, Jace gently lifted one of my hands and brought it to his lips. I turned into him and soon found myself enveloped in his warm embrace. His lips met mine tentatively as we slowly reminded each other of what the others lips tasted like.

Before I knew it, Jace laid me down on the couch with his body pressed in close to mine, deepening our kiss to fully express all of his pent up yearnings. I ran my fingers through his hair to the back of his neck urging him even closer, needing to feel the heat of him against me. I ran my hands up the warm flat planes of his back underneath his shirt and found the material too confining. In one swift movement, I tore the material straight down the middle exposing the muscular expanse of his back for further exploration. Jace moaned against my mouth and quickly shed the rest of the shirt, allowing me free reign to run my hands over his chest and abdomen.

Breathing heavily, Jace pulled his lips away from mine and looked into my eyes.

"If you don't want to go any further," he said. "We should probably stop now. Otherwise, I'm not sure I'll be able to."

"I thought you said you would remember," I said, wrapping my legs around his hips feeling the proof of his desire against me.

"Remember what?" he asked, trembling slightly as I moved my hips against his slowly.

"I told you the next time I offered myself to you not to think so much," I gently scolded, reminding him of my words not so long ago when we were in a similar situation.

Jace grinned and lifted me up in one quick motion, my legs stilled wrapped around him.

I didn't hear any more stupid questions for the rest of the night.

I woke up the next morning with my legs tangled up in the white sheet on the bed. Jace lay next to me still sleeping and snoring softly. I lay there with my head on the pillow staring at his handsome profile and watching the gentle rise and fall of his chest. The night before had been perfect in every way. Jace had been attentive and gentle in his love making, showing me without words how much he treasured me. If anyone had been the aggressor, it had been me. Sometimes his slow advances drove me insane, and I had to take things into my own hands, as it were.

I suppose all girls fantasize about their first time making love, turning it into something reality would be hard pressed to match up with. I always thought Ash would be the person who took my virginity, but now I couldn't imagine anyone living up to the high standard Jace had set.

Unable to stop myself, I let my fingers trail lightly down Jace's chest feeling the warmth of his skin against the tips of my fingers, stopping just below his belly button where the sheet lay across the lower half of his body.

"Don't stop," I heard.

When I looked back up at Jace's face, I found him watching me with half closed eyes, closing them fully as my hand ventured underneath the sheet.

Later, I lay wrapped in his arms spent of energy. What little sleep I had gotten the night before had just been used up in a totally worthwhile way.

"We should definitely start out our mornings like that from now on," I said in complete sincerity.

I heard the rumble of Jace's laughter inside his chest.

"Your wish is my command," he replied, kissing my forehead.

I leaned up and kissed him on the lips not being satisfied with such a simple show of affection.

"Can I ask you something?" He said, his tone turning serious.

"You can ask me anything."

"Was I your first?"

"Yes," I said. "Why would you think you weren't?"

"Before you left to be with the Queen..." he started but couldn't seem to bring himself to finish.

"Oh, that," I said remembering what I had said to Jace about finding someone to satisfy my sexual needs if he wouldn't. "No, I was never with someone while I was with her. I came close," I admitted, not wanting to hide anything from him, "but that's when my future self came to visit me. She told me she was stopping me from doing something I would end up regretting."

"I'm glad she did, or you did I guess. All this time traveling gets me confused sometimes."

"You're not the only one," I confessed.

Jace was silent for a while, and I could tell he wanted to ask me something but didn't seem to know if he should or not.

"You might as well ask me whatever it is your thinking," I told him. "I'm an open book to you. I'll tell you the truth about anything."

"Was I...did I..." he put a hand to his forehead. "Crap how do I ask you this without sounding like a complete idiot?"

"Just ask," I said, kissing him in an attempt to ease his tension.

"You were my first too," he confessed. "Was I good enough? Was there anything that I didn't do that you would want me to do?"

I smiled.

"What?" He asked. "Why are you smiling like that?"

"I was just thinking that for two virgins we did pretty well last night… and this morning… and hopefully right now."

Jace smiled and rolled me over onto my back proving my hope was right.

CHAPTER THIRTY

It was decided we would travel to the Mammoth Cave National Park in Kentucky. The plan was to set up Zoe, Rose, and Simon in one of the larger caverns and dynamite the entrance to the cave so no one would inadvertently discover them, keeping them safe. The Queen would have no way of knowing about the existence of their shield leaving us with the element of surprise. She would still mistakenly think she was safe when she would become the total opposite.

Jace and I rode in the same helicopter with Zoe and the babies to the location. I wanted to spend as much time as I possibly could with her before she was lost to me forever.

"Promise me one thing," she said to me.

"I'll promise you anything. You know that."

"Don't tell Simon and Rose about me and Ash until they're older."

"Why?" I asked, confused why she wouldn't want her children to know what a brave woman their mother was and the sacrifice she was making to save the world.

"I want them to think of you and Jace as their mother and father," she said to me, handing me a white envelope. "When the time is right, give them this note. I don't want them to blame you for honoring my last request."

"I'll do what you ask, but I don't like it. I don't like to lie," I said. "And I will find a way to stop your aging before you're woken up. I promise. You'll be able to live out a normal life with Rose and Simon."

"I know you will," Zoe said with a knowing smile. "Ash told me what my future holds, and I'm ready for it. I only wish you were going to be there when I wake up, like you were the first time."

I squeezed Zoe's hand silently wishing I could be there too.

Rose and Simon met us at the entrance to the cave. They were both dressed in white flowing gowns made of a gauzy fabric and had a third one ready for Zoe to put on.

"Uncle Kirk and Aunt Teegan made them for us," Simon said in explanation. "They said if we were going to be stuck in a cave for God only knows how long, we should at least look fashionable when we're woken up."

"Will I see Kirk and Teegan soon?" I asked them.

"You know we can't answer that," Rose said.

I shrugged. "Had to try."

Once we all walked to the large cavern which would be Zoe and her children's home for a while. Older Ash appeared to play his part in the event.

"So what's the future like?" I asked him.

"Bright," he said with a smile, one of the few I ever saw him give so readily. "Don't give up hope, Skye. My future will be your present soon enough. There's a lot more you have to do to make that happen though, but I know you will. You're strong and you're brave. You always have been. You'll be the one who saves us all in the end."

I hugged Zoe goodbye for one last time determined not to cry but failing miserably as my heart was forced to let her go.

"I love you," she said to me squeezing me tight. "Don't forget me."

"I'll never forget the little pigtailed girl I found," I said.

"It's time," Simon gently reminded.

Zoe reluctantly let me go. She kissed baby Rose and Simon who were cradled in Jace's arms and walked over to their adult counterparts. After she kissed them both on the cheek, she told them how proud she was to be their mother. They formed a circle facing one another and held tightly to each other's hands.

Jace came up to me and handed me baby Rose. I looked down at the child in my arms and instantly felt a connection which hadn't been there before. When I looked up, I saw adult Rose smiling at me like she knew this was the moment when our true relationship started.

The smell of electricity filled the air as their shield suddenly appeared and disappeared, spreading as far as it could to the outside world. As if knowing exactly when to do it, older Ash touched them all on the shoulder one by one to put them into stasis, forever trapping them in time until the day came when they could be awoken.

"The angels are in heaven," I heard Michael say into the walkie-talkie he had in his hand. "Get ready to blow the charge as soon as we've cleared the cave entrance."

As I looked at the three figures dressed in white, I realized how appropriate Michael's code name for them was. They *were* our angels, gifting us with the opportunity to save what was left of humanity.

I knew then without a shadow of a doubt what my next step would have to be.

I had to kill the Queen.

Made in the USA
San Bernardino, CA
19 November 2015